No Frills, Just Thrills !

A Letter From The Archivist.

Dear Readers,

The title you are about to read and enjoy is the first in a series of re-releases from the acknowledged "King Of Thrillers", Edgar Wallace. We are delighted to have the opportunity to publish this sorely neglected author. A release of "The Fourth Plague" is planned for the Autumn and further suggestions for titles from our loyal readers would be welcomed.

The rest of 1999 will include vintage classics from the following authors: William Hope Hodgson, E.C.Tubb, H.Rider Haggard, Guy Boothby (the occult adventures of Dr.Nikola), Jules Verne and Sapper.

An announcement will be made in the next few months of the winner of our search for a pulpster. This competition has drawn a huge response with synopses and manuscripts arriving from all corners of the globe. Our thanks to all of you who have taken part - there will be a follow up competition , ending June 30th 1999.

If you would like to join our regular mailing list to receive news of available and forthcoming titles then simply fill out the coupon in the rear of this book to receive our free catalogue and regular news of new titles from the land of Pulp Fictions. There is a Prize draw twice a year, the lucky winner receiving free copies of Pulp Fictions novels. Could it be you ?

Better Read Than Dead !

GW00707453

The Chief Archivist
Pulp Fictions
c/o Pulp Publications Ltd

Pulp Fictions - The Collection

"Fantastic Fiction, Fantastic Fun . I'm addicted to Pulp Fiction!" - James Herbert

The Lair Of The White Worm by Bram Stoker.
(ISBN: 1-902058-01-1)
Murders In The Rue Morgue and Other Stories by Poe
(ISBN: 1-902058-02-x)
The People Of The Mist by H.Rider Haggard
(ISBN: 1-902058-00-3)
She by H.Rider Haggard
(ISBN: 1-902058-03-8)
Ayesha - Return of She by H.Rider Haggard
(ISBN: 1-902058-04-6)
She & Allan by H.Rider Haggard
(ISBN: 1-902058-05-4)
When The World Shook by H.Rider Haggard
(ISBN: 1-902058-07-0)
Kidnapped By Cannibals by Dr Gordon Stables
(ISBN: 1-902058-06-2)
Journey To The Centre of the Earth by Jules Verne
(ISBN: 1-902058-08-9)
The Mysterious Island Part One: "Dropped From The Clouds" by Jules Verne
(ISBN: 1-902058-13-5)
Allan and the Ice Gods by H.Rider Haggard
(ISBN: 1-902058-11-9)
The Green Rust by Edgar Wallace
(ISBN: 1-902058-10-0)

Coming Soon - May 1999

The Mysterious Island Part Two: "Abandoned" by Jules Verne
(ISBN: 1-902058-14-3)
Dr.Nikola -Occult Adventurer by Guy Boothby
(ISBN: 1-902058-17-8)
The Boats of The Glen Carrig by W.Hope Hodgson
(ISBN: 1-902058-15-1)

THE GREEN RUST

BY
EDGAR WALLACE

"No Frills, Just Thrills"

This edition published 1999 by
Pulp Fictions
A Division of Pulp Publications Ltd

ISBN 1-902058-10-0

Printed and bound by: W.S.O.Y in Finland
Cover Template Design copyright - The Magic Palette
(all rights reserved)

Edgar Wallace
— Introduction by David Pringle

We tend to associate the pulp magazines — garish-covered, rough-papered, all-fiction magazines which flourished during the first half of the 20th century — solely with the United States. To most of us, these now-rare cheaply-produced magazines, with all their thrills and spills, seem to be as American a phenomenon as jazz music or Hollywood western movies. *Argosy*, *All-Story*, *The Blue Book*, *Adventure*, *Black Mask*, *Weird Tales*, *Ranch Romances*, *Amazing Stories*, *Dime Detective*, *Thrilling Wonder Stories* — their very titles seem the quintessence of a bygone American popular culture. But just as there have been French jazz-bands and Spaghetti westerns, among many other European versions of U.S. pop culture, so too, once upon a time, were there British pulp magazines. (I have argued elsewhere that although the first pulp, Frank Munsey's *Argosy*, was undoubtedly American, the pulps in general took their greatest inspiration from the mainly British "gaslight magazines," the turn-of-the-century middle- class monthlies such as *The Strand* and *Pearson's*, where appeared the first series-stories built around larger-than-life characters like Conan Doyle's Sherlock Holmes. The U.S. pulps would have been unthinkable without their series characters, and without all those magazine-story "templates" which had been laid down, principally in

Britain, in the 1880s and 1890s: the detective story, the horror story, the scientific romance, the mystery- swashbuckler, the short seafaring yarn, the "situation comedy," and so on — the western story was perhaps the only home-grown American example.)

The first British pulp, as opposed to the slicker "gaslight" magazines, was *The Grand Magazine*, launched by Newnes (publisher of *Tit-Bits* and *The Strand*) in February 1905 and destined to run until 1939. Consisting almost entirely of popular fiction, and printed on low-grade paper similar to that of the U.S. pulps pioneered by Frank Munsey, its legion of yarn-spinners included the likes of William Hope Hodgson, M. P. Shiel, E. Phillips Oppenheim, Rafael Sabatini, P. G. Wodehouse, Bertram Atkey, Edgar Jepson, Agatha Christie... and a former journalist from the East End of London called Edgar Wallace. Just as in America Munsey's pulps inspired many other publishers, such as Street & Smith, to jump on his bandwagon, so in Britain Newnes's first pulp was followed by numerous competitors: *The Novel Magazine* (Pearson, from April 1905), *The Story-Teller* (Cassell, from April 1907), *The Red Magazine* (Harmsworth's Amalgamated Press, from June 1908), *The Weekly Tale-Teller* (Shurey, from May 1909), *The Premier Magazine* (Amalgamated Press, from May 1914), *The Sovereign Magazine* (Hutchinson, from November 1919), *The 20 Story Magazine* (Odham's Press, from July 1922), *Adventure-Story Magazine* (Hutchinson, from September 1922) and many more. Several of the writers named above wrote for these rival magazines too, not least the prolific Edgar Wallace — as did still other stalwarts of British pop fiction, such as William Le Queux, Sax Rohmer, H. De Vere Stacpoole, Agnes & Egerton Castle, "Sapper" (H. C. McNeile), A. M. Burrage, Alice & Claude Askew, Capt. Frank H. Shaw, Richmal Crompton, E. Charles Vivian, Jessie Douglas Kerruish, J. S. Fletcher, Edmund Snell, Ursula Bloom, F. A. M. Webster, Francis H. Sibson, Marjorie Bowen, Peter Cheyney, Barbara Cartland, C. S. Forester — and even, on occasions, H. Rider Haggard and G. K. Chesterton. These were the British pulpsters, or a significant fraction of them at any rate.

The UK pulps, most of which died out with the severe paper shortages of World War II, imported stories from the American pulps too — particularly the fiction of noted transatlantic "mega-pulpsters" like Edgar Rice Burroughs (creator of Tarzan), Max Brand (creator of Dr Kildare), H. Bedford-Jones (Canadian), J. Allan Dunn (British-born, but an erstwhile protege of Jack London in California), Frank L. Packard (another Canadian), Johnston McCulley (creator of Zorro), Achmed Abdullah (Russian- born, British-educated), Beatrice Grimshaw (another Britisher- born, though Papuan- and later Australian-resident) and, probably (though I have yet to establish that he appeared in any UK pulp), Talbot Mundy (still another Britisher who had knocked around the world before settling in the States). To those familiar with the U.S. pulps, names like Burroughs, Brand, Bedford-Jones and Mundy seem synonymous with pulpdom: they were all big producers (mind- bogglingly so in the case of Frederick Faust, a.k.a. Max Brand) who gained huge popularity and are remembered for their close association with pulp magazines — hence my label for them, the Mega-Pulpsters. Curiously, though, Edgar Wallace and most of the other resident Brits who contributed to the UK pulps — Rohmer, Sabatini, Christie, etc — are not thought of as pulpsters in the same sense. This may be because the British pulps are almost totally forgotten, whereas their American equivalents are well- remembered. Or it may because Britain had a stronger trade in cheap hardcover books during the first half of the century (maintained by the demands of the now-defunct circulating libraries, such as Boots the Chemist's), while in America there were comparatively few low-cost boardbacked novels published during the heyday of the pulps — and Wallace et al. are still associated in the public mind with books rather than with pulp magazines. Or it may be because the British mega-pulpsters, just like Conan Doyle and the leading "gaslighters" before them, were peculiarly adept at making the transition to high-paying "big slick" magazines when they came to be published in the USA. (Americans seem to think of Sax Rohmer, for instance, as a writer for the slick weekly *Collier's*, which indeed he was, even though in the UK his Fu Manchu stories were first published on pulp paper. Agatha Christie too is thought of a "slickster": didn't she crack the biggest slick of them all, the *Saturday Evening Post* — as did salty C. S. Forester after her?)

Whatever the reason for pulp enthusiasts' general lack of recognition of the fact, I would contend that the supremely energetic Richard Horatio Edgar Wallace (1875-1932) was the leading figure among Britain's mega-pulpsters —

the most widely- published, the most prolific, and, in his day, the most popular of them all. Not only was he published in virtually all the UK pulps — *The Story-Teller* (where he appeared from 1907), *The Grand Magazine* (where he appeared from 1908), *The Weekly Tale-Teller* (which introduced his "Sanders of the River" stories to the world from 1909), *The Novel Magazine* (which published him from 1912), *The Red Magazine* (which featured him from 1914), *The Happy Mag.* (where his stories rubbed shoulders with Richmal Crompton's "Just William" comedies in the early 1920s), *The Detective Magazine* (from 1922, a title which was virtually created to accommodate him), and so on through to his death in the 1930s — but he conquered large tracts of the American pulps too. He appeared in Street & Smith's *New Story* magazine as early as 1914, and in Munsey's *All-Story Weekly* from at least 1916. Although naturally most of his work appeared in magazines twice over, on both sides of the Atlantic, Wallace was such a big producer that he was able to create original material for both the British and the American pulps. Street & Smith's *Popular Magazine* published his science-fiction thrillers *The Green Rust* (in four parts, 7th-28th August 1919) and *The Day of Uniting* (complete in the issue of 20th July 1921) — the latter well in advance of its first British book publication in 1926 — while the same company's *Detective Story Magazine* serialized his *The Devastating Angel* (18th March-15th April 1922), *The Hairy Arm* (9th February-8th March 1924), *The Sinister Man* (24th May-28th June 1924), *The Ringer* (18th April-23rd May 1925), *Terror Keep*

(6th November-4th December 1926) and *The Clew of the Silver Key* (20th September-25th October 1930), among many others. At the same time he was appearing regularly in such other U.S. pulps as *Flynn's*, *Short Stories* and *Munsey's Magazine*. So omnipresent was he that it is hard to imagine how some of the American pulps of the 1920s, particularly the Street & Smith titles, could have filled their pages in his absence. For a long time, the Three Just Men and Mr J. G. Reeder, along with many other Wallace series characters, helped sustain the U.S. pulp-fiction industry. All this, while his stories were consuming almost equally vast quantities of pulp paper and flooding the railway bookstalls back home in Britain ("Bookstall Salesman: 'Seen the mid-day Wallace, Sir?'" as a famous *Punch* cartoon had it).

Wallace's principal genre was, of course, the creepy crime thriller, full of surprising twists and turns. It is what he is remembered for — all those gaunt strangers, Crimson Circles, sinister men, Fellowships of the Frog, black abbots, yellow snakes, Hands of Power, jokers, brigands, forgers, mixers, ringers, gunners, twisters and squeakers. However, he had several other strings to his bow. He was a successful playwright, and a comic writer of not inconsiderable talent. The many volumes of "Sanders of the River" stories, often casually described as African adventure yarns (which, in a sense, they are) are actually situation comedies wrought with some skill — though, given the racial element, not a type of comedy which has worn well. His well-informed horse-racing stories (Wallace was an inveterate gambler) and "Educated Evans" comedies are highly regarded by some. He also wrote a number of books which contain ingredients of the supernatural or the science-fictional. *Captains of Souls* (1922) is an effective tale of soul-switching. *Private Selby* (1912) and "1925": *The Story of a Fatal Peace* (1915) are future-war novels. *The Fourth Plague* (1913), *The Green Rust* (1919) and *The Day of Uniting* (1926) are about larger-scale disasters (or threatened disasters). The novella *Planetoid 127* (1929) is a piece of boys'-paper science fiction. None of these are major works of the weird or predictive imagination, but they are all competent popular entertainments.

Towards the end of his life, Wallace was working on film scenarios in Hollywood and selling serials to major American slick magazines such as *Cosmopolitan*. So, like Sax Rohmer and Agatha Christie, he too "transcended" the pulps. But the pulp milieu was the one in which he thrived for most of his career, and he remained a pulpster to the core. As a consummate pulp professional, Wallace could turn his hand to almost anything, usually with great skill — clever short stories, craftily- plotted plays, non-fiction, poems, newspaper tipster columns, and above all exciting novels. For one who wrote so fast and copiously, his prose is surprisingly literate. He gave pleasure to millions, and if Pulp has a Pantheon he deserves a place therein.

David Pringle, January 1999

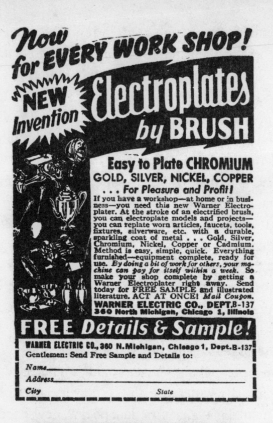

CONTENTS

CONTENTS

THE GREEN RUST

CHAPTER I

THE PASSING OF JOHN MILLINBORN

" I DON'T know whether there's a law that stops my
doing this, Jim; but if there is, you've got to get
round it. You're a lawyer and you know the game.
You're my pal and the best pal I've had, Jim, and you'll
do it for me."

The dying man looked up into the old eyes that were
watching him with such compassion and read their acquies-
cence.

No greater difference could be imagined than existed
between the man on the bed and the slim neat figure who
sat by his side. John Millinborn, broad-shouldered, big-
featured, a veritable giant in frame and even in his last
days suggesting the enormous strength which had been
his in his prime, had been an outdoor man, a man of large
voice and large capable hands; James Kitson had been a
student from his youth up and had spent his manhood
in musty offices, stuffy courts, surrounded by crackling
briefs and calf-bound law-books.

Yet, between these two men, the millionaire ship-builder
and the successful solicitor, utterly different in their tastes
and their modes of life, was a friendship deep and true.
Strange that death should take the strong and leave the
weak; so thought James Kitson as he watched his friend.

" I'll do what can be done, John. You leave a great
responsibility upon the girl—a million and a half of money."

The sick man nodded.

7

" I get rid of a greater one, Jim. When my father died he left a hundred thousand between us, my sister and I. I've turned my share into a million, but that is by the way. Because she was a fairly rich girl and a wilful girl, Jim, she broke her heart. Because they knew she had the money the worst men were attracted to her—and she chose the worst of the worst ! "

He stopped speaking to get his breath.

" She married a plausible villain who ruined her—spent every sou and left her with a mountain of debt and a month-old baby. Poor Grace died and he married again. I tried to get the baby, but he held it as a hostage. I could never trace the child after it was two years old. It was only a month ago I learnt the reason. The man was an international swindler and was wanted by the police. He was arrested in Paris and charged in his true name —the name he had married in was false. When he came out of prison he took his own name—and of course the child's name changed, too."

The lawyer nodded.

" You want me to—— ? "

" Get the will proved and begin your search for Oliva Prédeaux. There is no such person. The girl's name you know, and I have told you where she is living. You'll find nobody who knows Oliva Prédeaux—her father disappeared when she was six—he's probably dead, and her stepmother brought her up without knowing her relationship to me—then she died and the girl has been working ever since she was fifteen."

" She is not to be found ? "

" Until she is married. Watch her, Jim, spend all the money you wish—don't influence her unless you see she is getting the wrong kind of man. . . . "

His voice, which had grown to something of the old strength, suddenly dropped and the great head rolled sideways on the pillow.

Kitson rose and crossed to the door. It opened upon a spacious sitting-room, through the big open windows of which could be seen the broad acres of the Sussex Weald.

A man was sitting in the window-seat, chin in hand,

looking across to the chequered fields on the slope of the downs. He was a man of thirty, with a pointed beard, and he rose as the lawyer stepped quickly into the room.

" Anything wrong ? " he asked.

" I think he has fainted—will you go to him, doctor ? "

The young man passed swiftly and noiselessly to the bedside and made a brief examination. From a shelf near the head of the bed he took a hypodermic syringe and filled it from a small bottle. Baring the patient's side he slowly injected the drug. He stood for a moment looking down at the unconscious man, then came back to the big hall where James Kitson was waiting.

" Well ? "

The doctor shook his head.

" It is difficult to form a judgment," he said quietly, " his heart is all gone to pieces. Has he a family doctor ? "

" Not so far as I know—he hated doctors, and has never been ill in his life. I wonder he tolerated you."

Dr. van Heerden smiled.

" He couldn't help himself. He was taken ill in the train on the way to this place and I happened to be a fellow-passenger. He asked me to bring him here and I have been here ever since. It is strange," he added, " that so rich a man as Mr. Millinborn had no servant travelling with him and should live practically alone in this—well, it is little better than a cottage."

Despite his anxiety, James Kitson smiled.

" He is the type of man who hates ostentation. I doubt if he has ever spent a thousand a year on himself all his life—do you think it is wise to leave him ? "

The doctor spread out his hands.

" I can do nothing. He refused to allow me to send for a specialist and I think he was right. Nothing can be done for him. Still——"

He walked back to the bedside, and the lawyer came behind him. John Millinborn seemed to be in an uneasy sleep, and after an examination by the doctor the two men walked back to the sitting-room.

" The excitement has been rather much for him. I suppose he has been making his will ? "

"Yes," said Kitson shortly.

"I gathered as much when I saw you bring the gardener and the cook in to witness a document," said Dr. van Heerden.

He tapped his teeth with the tip of his fingers—a nervous trick of his.

"I wish I had some strychnine," he said suddenly. "I ought to have some by me—in case."

"Can't you send a servant—or I'll go," said Kitson. "Is it procurable in the village?"

The doctor nodded.

"I don't want you to go," he demurred. "I have sent the car to Eastbourne to get a few things I cannot buy here. It's a stiff walk to the village and yet I doubt whether the chemist would supply the quantity I require to a servant, even with my prescription—you see," he smiled, "I am a stranger here."

"I'll go with pleasure—the walk will do me good," said the lawyer energetically. "If there is anything we can do to prolong my poor friend's life——"

The doctor sat at the table and wrote his prescription and handed it to the other with an apology.

Hill Lodge, John Millinborn's big cottage, stood on the crest of a hill, and the way to the village was steep and long, for Alfronston lay nearly a mile away. Half-way down the slope the path ran through a plantation of young ash. Here John Millinborn had preserved a few pheasants in the early days of his occupancy of the Lodge on the hill. As Kitson entered one side of the plantation he heard a rustling noise, as though somebody were moving through the undergrowth. It was too heavy a noise for a bolting rabbit or a startled bird to make, and he peered into the thick foliage. He was a little near-sighted, and at first he did not see the cause of the commotion. Then:

"I suppose I'm trespassing," said a husky voice, and a man stepped out toward him.

The stranger carried himself with a certain jauntiness, and he had need of what assistance artifice could lend him, for he was singularly unprepossessing. He was a man who might as well have been sixty as fifty. His clothes soiled, torn and greasy, were of good cut. The shirt was filthy, but it was attached to a frayed collar, and the crumpled cravat was ornamented with a cameo pin.

But it was the face which attracted Kitson's attention. There was something inherently evil in that puffed face, in the dull eyes that blinked under the thick black eyebrows. The lips, full and loose, parted in a smile as the lawyer stepped back to avoid contact with the unsavoury visitor.

"I suppose I'm trespassing—good gad! Me trespassing—funny, very funny!" He indulged in a hoarse wheezy laugh and broke suddenly into a torrent of the foulest language that this hardened lawyer had ever heard.

"Pardon, pardon," he said, stopping as suddenly. "Man of the world, eh? You'll understand that when a gentleman has grievances . . ." He fumbled in his waistcoat-pocket and found a black-rimmed monocle and inserted it in his eye. There was an obscenity in the appearance of this foul wreck of a man which made the lawyer feel physically sick.

"Trespassing, by gad!" He went back to his first conceit and his voice rasped with malignity. "Gad! If I had my way with people! I'd slit their throats, I would, sir. I'd stick pins in their eyes—red-hot pins. I'd boil them alive——"

Hitherto the lawyer had not spoken, but now his repulsion got the better of his usually equable temper.

"What are you doing here?" he asked sternly. "You're on private property—take your beastliness elsewhere."

The man glared at him and laughed.

"Trespassing!" he sneered. "Trespassing! Very good—your servant, sir!"

He swept his derby hat from his head (the lawyer saw that he was bald), and turning, strutted back through the plantation the way he had come. It was not the way out and Kitson was half-inclined to follow and see the man off the estate. Then he remembered the urgency of his errand and continued his journey to the village. On his way back he looked about, but there was no trace of the unpleasant intruder. Who was he? he wondered. Some broken derelict with nothing but the memory of former vain splendours and the rags of old fineries, nursing a dear hatred for some more fortunate fellow.

Nearly an hour had passed before he again panted up to the levelled shelf on which the cottage stood.

The doctor was sitting at the window as Kitson passed.

"How is he?"

"About the same. He had one paroxysm. Is that the strychnine? I can't tell you how much obliged I am to you."

He took the small packet and placed it on the window-ledge and Mr. Kitson passed into the house.

"Honestly, doctor, what do you think of his chance?" he asked.

Dr. van Heerden shrugged his shoulders.

"Honestly, I do not think he will recover consciousness."

"Heavens!"

The lawyer was shocked. The tragic suddenness of it all stunned him. He had thought vaguely that days, even weeks, might pass before the end came.

"Not recover consciousness?" he repeated in a whisper.

Instinctively he was drawn to the room where his friend lay and the doctor followed him.

John Millinborn lay on his back, his eyes closed, his face a ghastly grey. His big hands were clutching at his throat, his shirt was torn open at the breast. The two windows, one at each end of the room, were wide, and a gentle breeze blew the casement curtains. The lawyer stooped, his eyes moist, and laid his hand upon the burning forehead.

"John, John," he murmured, and turned away, blinded with tears.

He wiped his face with a pocket-handkerchief and walked to the window, staring out at the serene loveliness of the scene. Over the weald a great aeroplane droned to the sea. The green downs were dappled white with grazing flocks, and beneath the windows the ordered beds blazed and flamed with flowers, crimson and gold and white.

As he stood there the man he had met in the plantation came to his mind and he was half-inclined to speak to the doctor of the incident. But he was in no mood for the description and the speculation which would follow. Restlessly he paced into the bedroom. The sick man had not moved and again the lawyer returned. , He thought of the girl, that girl whose name and relationship with John Millinborn he alone knew. What use would she make of the millions which, all unknown to her, she would soon inherit ? What——

" Jim, Jim ! "

He turned swiftly.

It was John Millinborn's voice.

" Quick—come. . . ."

The doctor had leapt into the room and made his way to the bed.

Millinborn was sitting up, and as the lawyer moved swiftly in the doctor's tracks he saw his wide eyes staring.

" Jim, he has . . ."

His head dropped forward on his breast and the doctor lowered him slowly to the pillow.

" What is it, John ? Speak to me, old man. . . ."

" I'm afraid there is nothing to be done," said the doctor as he drew up the bedclothes.

" Is he dead ? " whispered the lawyer fearfully.

" No—but——"

He beckoned the other into the big room and, after a glance at the motionless figure, Kitson followed.

" There's something very strange—who is that ? "

He pointed through the open window at the clumsy figure of a man who was blundering wildly down the slope which led to the plantation.

Kitson recognized the man immediately. It was the uninvited visitor whom he had met in the plantation. But there was something in the haste of the shabby man, a hint of terror in the wide-thrown arms, that made the lawyer forget his tragic environment.

" Where has he been ? " he asked.

" Who is he ? "

The doctor's face was white and drawn as though he, too, sensed some horror in that frantic flight.

Kitson walked back to the room where the dying man lay, but was frozen stiff upon the threshold.

" Doctor—doctor ! "

The doctor followed the eyes of the other. Something was dripping from the bed to the floor—something red and horrible. Kitson set his teeth and, stepping to the bedside, pulled down the covers.

He stepped back with a cry, for from the side of John Millinborn protruded the ivory handle of a knife.

CHAPTER II

THE DRUNKEN MR. BEALE

DR. VAN HEERDEN'S surgery occupied one of the four shops which formed the ground floor of the Krooman Chambers. This edifice had been erected by a wealthy philanthropist to provide small model flats for the professional classes who needed limited accommodation and a good address (they were in the vicinity of Oxford Street) at a moderate rental. Like many philanthropists, the owner had wearied of his hobby and had sold the block to a syndicate, whose management on more occasions than one had been the subject of police inquiry.

They had then fallen into the hands of an intelligent woman, who had turned out the undesirable tenants, furnished the flats plainly, but comfortably, and had let them to tenants who might be described as solvent, but honest. Krooman Chambers had gradually rehabilitated itself in the eyes of the neighbourhood.

Dr. van Heerden had had his surgery in the building for six years. During the war he was temporarily under suspicion for sympathies with the enemy, but no proof was adduced of his enmity and, though he had undoubtedly been born on the wrong side of the Border at Cranenburg, which is the Prussian frontier station on the Rotterdam-Cologne line, his name was undoubtedly van Heerden, which was Dutch. Change the " van " to " von," said the carping critics, and he was a Hun, and undoubtedly Germany was full of von Heerens and von Heerdens.

The doctor lived down criticism, lived down suspicion, and got together a remunerative practice. He had the largest flat in the building, one room of which was fitted up as a laboratory, for he had a passion for research. The mysterious murder of John Millinborn had given him a certain advertisement which had not been without its advantages. The fact that he had been in attendance on the millionaire had brought him a larger fame.

His theories as to how the murder had been committed by some one who had got through the open window whilst the two men were out of the room had been generally accepted, for the police had found footmarks on the flower-beds, over which the murderer must have passed. They had not, however, traced the seedy-looking personage whom Mr. Kitson had seen. This person had disappeared as mysteriously as he had arrived.

Three months after the murder the doctor stood on the steps of the broad entrance-hall which led to the flats, watching the stream of pedestrians passing. It was six o'clock in the evening and the streets were alive with shop-girls and workers on their way home from business.

He smoked a cigarette and his interest was, perhaps, more apparent than real. He had attended his last surgery case and the door of the " shop," with its sage-green windows, had been locked for the night.

His eyes wandered idly to the Oxford Street end of the thoroughfare, and suddenly he started. A girl was walking toward him. At this hour there was very little wheeled traffic, for Lattice Street is almost a cul-de-sac, and she had taken the middle of the road. She was dressed with that effective neatness which brings the wealthy and the work-girl to a baffling level, in a blue serge costume of severe cut ; a plain white linen coat-collar and a small hat, which covered, but did not hide, a mass of hair which, against the slanting sunlight at her back, lent the illusion of a golden nimbus about her head.

The eyes were deep-set and wise with the wisdom which is found alike in those who have suffered and those who have watched suffering. The nose was straight, the lips scarlet and full. You might catalogue every feature of Oliva Cresswell and yet arrive at no satisfactory explanation for her charm.

Not in the clear ivory pallor of complexion did her charm lie. Nor in the trim figure with its promising lines, nor in the poise of head nor pride of carriage, nor in the ready laughter that came to those quiet eyes. In no one particular quality of attraction did she excel. Rather was her charm the charm of the perfect agglomeration of all those characteristics which men find alluring and challenging.

She raised her hand with a free unaffected gesture, and greeted the doctor with a flashing smile.

" Well, Miss Cresswell, I haven't seen you for quite a long time."

" Two days," she said solemnly, " but I suppose doctors who know all the secrets of nature have some very special drug to sustain them in trials like that."

" Don't be unkind to the profession," he laughed, " and don't be sarcastic, to one so young. By the way, I have never asked you did you get your flat changed ? "

She shook her head and frowned.

" Miss Millit says she cannot move me."

" Abominable," he said, and was annoyed. " Did you tell her about Beale ? "

She nodded vigorously.

" I said to her, says I," she had a trick of mimicry and dropped easily into the southern English accent, " ' Miss Millit, are you aware that the gentleman who lives opposite to me has been, to my knowledge, consistently drunk for two months—ever since he came to live at Kroomans ? ' ' Does he annoy you ? ' says she. ' Drunken people always annoy me,' says I. ' Mr. Beale arrives home every evening in a condition which I can only describe as deplorable.' "

" What did she say ? "

The girl made a little grimace and became serious.

" She said if he did not speak to me or interfere with me or frighten me it was none of my business, or something to that effect." She laughed helplessly. " Really, the flat is so wonderful and so cheap that one cannot afford to get out—you don't know how grateful I am to you, doctor, for having got diggings here at all—Miss Millit isn't keen on single young ladies."

She sniffed and laughed.

" Why do you laugh ? " he asked.

" I was thinking how queerly you and I met."

The circumstances of their meeting had indeed been curious. She was employed as a cashier at one of the great West End stores. He had made some sort of purchase and made payment in a five-pound note which had proved to be counterfeit. It was a sad moment for the girl when the forgery was discovered, for she had to make up the loss from her own pocket and that was no small matter.

Then the miracle had happened. The doctor had arrived full of apologies, had presented his card and explained. The note was one which he had been keeping as a curiosity. It has been passed on him and was such an excellent specimen that he intended having it framed but it had got mixed up with his other money.

" You started by being the villain of the piece and ended by being my good fairy," she said. " I should never have known there was a vacancy here but for you. I should not have been admitted by the proper Miss Millit but for the terror of your name."

She dropped her little hand lightly on his shoulder. It was a gesture of good-comradeship.

She half-turned to go when an angry exclamation held her.

" What is it ? Oh, I see—No. 4 ! "

She drew a little closer to the doctor's side and watched with narrowing lids the approaching figure.

" Why does he do it—oh, why does he do it ? " she demanded impatiently. " How can a man be so weak, so wretchedly weak ? There's nothing justifies that ! "

" That " was apparently trying to walk the opposite
kerb as though it were a tight-rope. Save for a certain
disorder of attire, a protruding necktie and a muddy hat,
he was respectable enough. He was young and, under
other conditions, passably good looking. But with his
fair hair streaming over his forehead and his hat at the
back of his head he lacked fascination. His attempt,
aided by a walking-stick used as a balancing-pole, to keep
his equilibrium on six inches of kerbing, might have been
funny to a less sensitive soul than Oliva's.

He slipped, recovered himself with a little whoop, slipped
again, and finally gave up the attempt, crossing the road
to his home.

He recognized the doctor with a flourish of his hat.

" Glorious weather, my Escu-escu-lapius," he said,
with a little slur in his voice but a merry smile in his eye ;
" simply wonderful weather for bacteria trypanosomes
(got it) an' all the jolly little microbes."

He smiled at the doctor blandly, ignoring the other's
significant glance at the girl, who had drawn back so that
she might not find herself included in the conversation.

" I'm goin' to leave you, doctor," he went on, " goin'
top floor, away from the evil smells of science an' fatal
lure of beauty. Top floor jolly stiff climb when a fellow's
all lit up like the Hotel Doodledum—per arduis ad astra
—through labour to the stars—fine motto. Flying Corps'
motto—my motto. Goo' night ! "

Off came his hat again and he staggered up the broad
stone stairs and disappeared round a turn. Later they
heard his door slam.

" Awful—and yet——"

" And yet ? " echoed the doctor.

" I thought he was funny. I nearly laughed. But
how terrible ! He's so young and he has had a decent
education."

She shook her head sadly.

Presently she took leave of the doctor and made her
way upstairs. Three doors opened from the landing.
Numbers 4, 6 and 8.

She glanced a little apprehensively at No. 4 as she passed,

but there was no sound or sign of the reveller, and she passed into No. 6 and closed the door.

The accommodation consisted of two rooms, a bed- and a sitting-room, a bath-room and a tiny kitchen. The rent was remarkably low, less than a quarter of her weekly earnings, and she managed to live comfortably.

She lit the gas-stove and put on the kettle and began to lay the table. There was a "tin of something" in the diminutive pantry, a small loaf and a jug of milk, a tomato or two and a bottle of dressing—the high tea to which she sat down (a little flushed of the face and quite happy) was seasoned with content. She thought of the doctor and accounted herself lucky to have so good a friend. He was so sensible, there was no "nonsense" about him. He never tried to hold her hand as the stupid buyers did, nor make clumsy attempts to kiss her as one of the partners had done.

The doctor was different from them all. She could not imagine him sitting by the side of a girl in a bus pressing her foot with his, or accosting her in the street with a "Haven't we met before?"

She ate her meal slowly, reading the evening newspaper and dreaming at intervals. It was dusk when she had finished and she switched on the electric light. There was a shilling-in-the-slot meter in the bath-room that acted eccentrically. Sometimes one shilling would supply light for a week, at other times after two days the lights would flicker spasmodically and expire.

She remembered that it was a perilous long time since she had bribed the meter and searched her purse for a shilling. She found that she had half-crowns, florins and sixpences, but she had no shillings. This, of course, is the chronic condition of all users of the slot-meters, and she accepted the discovery with the calm of the fatalist. She considered. Should she go out and get change from the obliging tobacconist at the corner or should she take a chance?

"If I don't go out you will," she said addressing the light, and it winked ominously.

She opened the door and stepped into the passage, and

as she did so the lights behind her went out. There was
one small lamp on the landing, a plutocratic affair independent of shilling meters. She closed the door behind
her and walked to the head of the stairs. As she passed
No. 4, she noted the door was ajar and she stopped. She
did not wish to risk meeting the drunkard, and she turned
back.

Then she remembered the doctor, he lived in No. 8.
Usually when he was at home there was a light in his hall
which showed through the fanlight. Now, however, the
place was in darkness. She saw a card on the door and
walking closer she read it in the dim light.

> BACK AT 12. WAIT.

He was out and was evidently expecting a caller. So
there was nothing for it but to risk meeting the exuberant
Mr. Beale. She flew down the stairs and gained the street
with a feeling of relief.

The obliging tobacconist, who was loquacious on the
subject of Germans and Germany, detained her until
her stock of patience was exhausted; but at last she made
her escape. Half-way across the street she saw the figure
of a man standing in the dark hallway of the chambers,
and her heart sank.

" Matilda, you're a fool," she said to herself.

Her name was not Matilda, but in moments of self-
depreciation she was wont to address herself as such.

She walked boldly up to the entrance and passed through.
The man she saw out of the corner of her eye but did not
recognize. He seemed as little desirous of attracting
attention as she. She thought he was rather stout and
short, but as to this she was not sure. She raced up the
stairs and turned on the landing to her room. The door
of No. 4 was still ajar—but what was much more import-

ant, so was her door. There was no doubt about it, between the edge of the door and the jamb there was a good two inches of space, and she distinctly remembered not only closing it, but also pushing it to make sure that it was fast. What should she do ? To her annoyance she felt a cold little feeling inside her and her hands were trembling.

" If the lights were only on I'd take the risk," she thought ; but the lights were not on and it was necessary to pass into the dark interior and into a darker bath-room—a room which is notoriously adaptable for murder—before she could reach the meter.

" Rubbish, Matilda ! " she scoffed quaveringly, " go in, you frightened little rabbit—you forgot to shut the door, that's all."

She pushed the door open and with a shiver stepped inside.

Then a sound made her stop dead. It was a shuffle and a creak such as a dog might make if he brushed against the chair.

" Who's there ? " she demanded.

There was no reply.

" Who's there ? "

She took one step forward and then something reached out at her. A big hand gripped her by the sleeve of her blouse and she heard a deep breathing.

She bit her lips to stop the scream that arose, and with a wrench tore herself free, leaving a portion of a sleeve in the hands of the unknown.

She darted backward, slamming the door behind her. In two flying strides she was at the door of No. 4, hammering with both her fists.

" Drunk or sober he is a man ! Drunk or sober he is a man ! " she muttered incoherently.

Only twice she beat upon the door when it opened suddenly and Mr. Beale stood in the doorway.

" What is it ? "

She hardly noticed his tone.

" A man—a man, in my flat," she gasped, and showed her torn sleeve, " a man . . . ! "

He pushed her aside and made for the door.

" The key ? " he said quickly.

With trembling fingers she extracted it from her pocket. " One moment."

He disappeared into his own flat and presently came out holding an electric torch. He snapped back the lock, put the key in his pocket and then, to her amazement, he slipped a short-barrelled revolver from his hip-pocket.

With his foot he pushed open the door and she watched him vanish into the gloomy interior.

Presently came his voice, sharp and menacing :

" Hands up ! "

A voice jabbered something excitedly and then she heard Mr. Beale speak.

" Is your light working ?—you can come in, I have him in the dining-room."

She stepped into the bath-room, the shilling dropped through the aperture, the screw grated as she turned it and the lights sprang to life.

In one corner of the room was a man, a white-faced, sickly looking man with a head too big for his body. His hands were above his head, his lower lip trembled in terror.

Mr. Beale was searching him with thoroughness and rapidity.

" No gun, all right, put your hands down. Now turn out your pockets."

The man said something in a language which the girl could not understand, and Mr. Beale replied in the same tongue. He put the contents, first of one pocket then of the other, upon the table, and the girl watched the proceedings with open eyes.

" Hello, what's this ? "

Beale picked up a card. Thereon was scribbled a figure which might have been 6 or 4.

" I see," said Beale, " now the other pocket—you understand English, my friend ? "

Stupidly the man obeyed. A leather pocket-case came from an inside pocket and this Beale opened.

Therein was a small packet which resembled the familiar wrapper of a seidlitz powder. Beale spoke sharply in a

language which the girl realized was German, and the
man shook his head. He said something which sounded
like " No good," several times.

" I'm going to leave you here alone for awhile," said
Beale, " my friend and I are going downstairs together
—I shall not be long."

They went out of the flat together, the little man with
the big head protesting, and she heard their footsteps
descending the stairs. Presently Beale came up alone
and walked into the sitting-room. And then the strange
unaccountable fact dawned on her—he was perfectly sober.

His eyes were clear, his lips firm, and the fair hair whose
tendencies to bedragglement had emphasized his disgrace
was brushed back over his head. He looked at her so
earnestly that she grew embarrassed.

" Miss Cresswell," he said quietly. " I am going to
ask you to do me a great favour."

" If it is one that I can grant, you may be sure that I
will," she smiled, and he nodded.

" I shall not ask you to do anything that is impossible
in spite of the humorist's view of women," he said. " I
merely want you to tell nobody about what has happened
to-night."

" Nobody ? " she looked at him in astonishment. " But
the doctor——"

" Not even the doctor," he said with a twinkle in his
eye. " I ask you this as a special favour—word of honour ? "

She thought a moment.

" I promise," she said. " I'm to tell nobody about that
horrid man from whom you so kindly saved me——"

He lifted his head.

" Understand this, Miss Cresswell, please," he said :
' I don't want you to be under any misapprehension
about that ' horrid man '—he was just as scared as you,
and he would not have harmed you. I have been waiting
for him all the evening."

" Waiting for him ? "

He nodded again.

" Where ? "

" In the doctor's flat," he said calmly, " you see, the

doctor and I are deadly rivals. We are rival scientists, and I was waiting for the hairy man to steal a march on him."

"But, but—how did you get in."

"I had this key," he said holding up a small key, "remember, word of honour! The man whom I have just left came up and wasn't certain whether he had to go in No. 8, that's the doctor's, or No. 6—*and the one key fits both doors*!"

He inserted the key which was in the lock of her door and it turned easily.

"And this is what I was waiting for—it was the best the poor devil could do."

He lifted the paper package and broke the seals. Unfolding the paper carefully he laid it on the table, revealing a teaspoonful of what looked like fine green sawdust.

"What is it?" she whispered fearfully.

Somehow she knew that she was in the presence of a big elementary danger—something gross and terrible in its primitive force.

"That," said Mr. Beale, choosing his words nicely, "that is a passable imitation of the Green Rust, or, as it is to me, the Green Terror."

"The Green Rust? What is the Green Rust—what can it do?" she asked in bewilderment.

"I hope we shall never know," he said, and in his clear eyes was a hint of terror.

CHAPTER III

PUNSONBY'S DISCHARGE AN EMPLOYEE

OLIVA CRESSWELL rose with the final despairing buzz of her alarm clock and conquered the almost irresistible temptation to close her eyes, just to see what it felt like. Her first impression was that she had had no sleep all night. She remembered going to bed at one and turning from side to side until three. She remembered deciding that the best thing to do was to get up, make some tea and watch the sun rise, and that whilst she was deciding whether such a step was romantic or just silly, she must have gone to sleep.

Still, four hours of slumber is practically no slumber to a healthy girl and she swung her pyjama-ed legs over the side of the bed and spent quite five minutes in a fatuous admiration of her little white feet. With an effort she dragged herself to the bath-room and let the tap run. Then she put on the kettle. Half an hour later she was feeling well but unenthusiastic.

When she became fully conscious, which was on her way to business, she realized she was worried. She had been made a party to a secret without her wish—and the drunken Mr. Beale, that youthful profligate, had really forced this confidence upon her. Only, and this she re-called with a start which sent her chin jerking upward (she was in the bus at the time and the conductor, thinking she was signalling him to stop, pulled the bell), only Mr. Beale was surprisingly sober and masterful for one so weak of character.

Ought she to tell the doctor—Dr. van Heerden, who had been so good a friend of hers ? It seemed disloyal, it was disloyal, horribly disloyal to him, to hide the fact that Mr. Beale had actually been in the doctor's room at night.

But was it a coincidence that the same key opened her door and the doctor's ? If it were so, it was an embar-rassing coincidence. She must change the locks without delay.

The bus set her down at the corner of Punsonby's great block. Punsonby's is one of the most successful and at the same time one of the most exclusive dress-houses in London, and Oliva had indeed been fortunate in securing her present position, for employment at Punsonby's was almost equal to Government employment in its permanency, as it was certainly more lucrative in its pay.

As she stepped on to the pavement she glanced up at

the big ornate clock. She was in good time, she said
to herself, and was pushing open the big glass door through
which employees pass to the various departments when a
hand touched her gently on the arm.

She turned in surprise to face Mr. Beale, looking particularly smart in a well-fitting grey suit, a grey felt hat
and a large bunch of violets in his buttonhole.

" Excuse me, Miss Cresswell," he said pleasantly, " may
I have one word with you ? "

She looked at him doubtfully.

" I rather wish you had chosen another time and another
place, Mr. Beale," she said frankly.

He nodded.

" I realize it is rather embarrassing," he said, " but
unfortunately my business cannot wait. I am a business
man, you know," he smiled, " in spite of my dissolute
habits."

She looked at him closely, for she thought she detected
a gentle mockery behind his words, but he was not smiling
now.

" I won't keep you more than two minutes," he went
on, " but in that two minutes I have a great deal to tell
you. I won't bore you with the story of my life."

This time she saw the amusement in his eyes and smiled
against her will, because she was not feeling particularly
amused.

" I have a business in the city of London," he said,
" and again I would ask you to respect my confidence.
I am a wheat expert."

" A wheat expert ? " she repeated with a puzzled frown.

" It's a queer job, isn't it ? but that's what I am. I
have a vacancy in my office for a confidential secretary.
It is a nice office, the pay is good, the hours are few and
the work is light. I want to know whether you will accept
the position."

She shook her head, regarding him with a new interest,
from which suspicion was not altogether absent.

" It is awfully kind of you, Mr. Beale, and adds another
to the debts I owe you," she said, " but I have no desire
to leave Punsonby's. It is work I like, and although I

am sure you are not interested in my private business"
—he could have told her that he was very much interested
in her private business, but he refrained—" I do not mind
telling you that I am earning a very good salary and I
have no intention or desire to change my situation."

His eyes twinkled.

" Ah well, that's my misfortune," he said, " there
are only two things I can say. The first is that if you
work for me you will neither be distressed nor annoyed
by any habits of mine which you may have observed and
which may perhaps have prejudiced you against me.   In
the second place, I want you to promise me that if you
ever leave Punsonby's you will give me the first offer of
your services."

She laughed.

" I think you are very funny, Mr. Beale, but I feel sure
that you mean what you say, and that you would confine
your—er—little eccentricities to times outside of business hours.   As far as leaving Punsonby's is concerned I
promise you that I will give you the first offer of my
invaluable services if ever I leave.   And now I am afraid
I must run away.   I am awfully obliged to you for what
you did for me last night."

He looked at her steadily in the eye.

" I have no recollection of anything that happened
last night," he said, " and I should be glad if your memory
would suffer the same lapse."

He shook hands with her, lifted his hat and turned
abruptly away, and she looked after him till the boom of
the clock recalled her to the fact that the head of the
firm of Punsonby was a stickler for punctuality.

She went into the great cloak-room and hung up her
coat and hat.   As she turned to the mirror to straighten
her hair she came face to face with a tall, dark girl who
had been eyeing her thoughtfully.

" Good morning," said Oliva, and there was in her
tone more of politeness than friendship, for although
these two girls had occupied the same office for more than
a year, there was between them an incompatibility which
no length of acquaintance could remove.

Hilda Glaum was of Swiss extraction, and something of a mystery. She was good looking in a sulky, saturnine way, but her known virtues stopped short at her appearance. She neither invited nor gave confidence, and in this respect suited Oliva, but unlike Oliva, she made no friends, entered into none of the periodical movements amongst the girls, was impervious to the attractions of the river in summer and of the Proms in winter, neither visited nor received.

" 'Morning," replied the girl shortly; then: " Have you been upstairs ? "

" No—why ? "

" Oh, nothing."

Oliva mounted to the floor where her little office was. She and Hilda dealt with the registered mail, extracted and checked the money that came from the post-shoppers and sent on the orders to the various departments.

Three sealed bags lay on her desk, and a youth from the postal department waited to receive a receipt for them. This she scribbled, after comparing the numbers attached to the seals with those inscribed on the boy's receipt-book.

For some reason Hilda had not followed her, and she was alone and had tumbled the contents of the first bag on to her desk when the managing director of Punsonby's made a surprising appearance at the glass-panelled door of her office.

He was a large, stout and important-looking man, bald and bearded. He enjoyed an episcopal manner, and had a trick of pulling back his head when he asked questions, as though he desired to evade the full force of the answer.

He stood in the doorway and beckoned her out, and she went without any premonition of what was in store for her.

" Ah, Miss Cresswell," he said. " I—ah—am sorry I did not see you before you had taken off your coat and hat. Will you come to my office ? "

" Certainly, Mr. White," said the girl, wondering what had happened.

He led the way with his majestic stride, dangling a pair of pince-nez by their cord, as a fastidious person might carry a mouse by its tail, and ushered her into his rosewood-panelled office.

"Sit down, sit down, Miss Cresswell," he said, and seating himself at his desk he put the tips of his fingers together and looked up to the ceiling for inspiration. "I am afraid, Miss Cresswell," he said, "that I have—ah—an unpleasant task."

"An unpleasant task, Mr. White?" she said, with a sinking feeling inside her.

He nodded.

"I have to tell you that Punsonby's no longer require your services."

She rose to her feet, looking down at him open-mouthed with wonder and consternation.

"Not require my services?" she said slowly. "Do you mean that I am discharged?"

He nodded again.

"In lieu of a month's notice I will give you a cheque for a month's salary, plus the unexpired portion of this week's salary."

"But why am I being discharged? Why? Why?"

Mr. White, who had opened his eyes for a moment to watch the effect of his lightning stroke, closed them again.

"It is not the practice of Punsonby's to give any reason for dispensing with the services of its employees," he said oracularly, "it is sufficient that I should tell you that hitherto you have given every satisfaction, but for reasons which I am not prepared to discuss we must dispense with your services."

Her head was in a whirl. She could not grasp what had happened. For five years she had worked in the happiest circumstances in this great store, where everybody had been kind to her and where her tasks had been congenial. She had never thought of going elsewhere. She regarded herself, as did all the better-class employees, as a fixture.

"Do I understand," she asked, "that I am to leave —at once?"

Mr. White nodded. He pushed the cheque across the table and she took it up and folded it mechanically.

"And you are not going to tell me why?"

Mr. White shook his head.

"Punsonby's do nothing without a good reason," he said solemnly, feeling that whatever happened he must make a good case for Punsonby's, and that whoever was to blame for this unhappy incident it was not an august firm which paid its fourteen per cent. with monotonous regularity. "We lack—ah—definite knowledge to proceed any further in this matter than—in fact, than we have proceeded. Definite knowledge" (the girl was all the more bewildered by his cumbersome diplomacy) "definite knowledge was promised but has not—in fact, has not come to hand. It is all very unpleasant—very unpleasant," and he shook his head.

She bowed and turning, walked quickly from the room, passed to the lobby where her coat was hung, put on her hat and left Punsonby's for ever.

It was when she had reached the street that, with a shock, she remembered Beale's words and she stood stock-still, pinching her lip thoughtfully. Had he known? Why had he come that morning, hours before he was ordinarily visible—if the common gossip of Krooman Mansions be worthy of credence?—and then as though to cap the amazing events of the morning she saw him. He was standing on the corner of the street, leaning on his cane, smoking a long cigarette through a much longer holder, and he seemed wholly absorbed in watching a linesman, perched high above the street, repairing a telegraph wire.

She made a step toward him, but stopped. He was so evidently engrossed in the acrobatics of the honest workman in mid-air that he could not have seen her and she turned swiftly and walked the other way.

She had not reached the end of the block before he was at her side.

"You are going home early, Miss Cresswell," he smiled.

She turned to him.

"Do you know why?" she asked.

"I don't know why—unless——"

"Unless what?"

"Unless you have been discharged," he said coolly.

Her brows knit.

"What do you know about my discharge?" she asked.

"Such things are possible," said Mr. Beale.

"Did you know I was going to be discharged?" she asked again.

He nodded.

"I didn't exactly know you would be discharged this morning, but I had an idea you would be discharged at [some time or other. That is why I came with my offer."

"Which, of course, I won't accept," she snapped.

"Which, of course, you have accepted," he said quietly. "Believe me, I know nothing more than that Punsonby's have been prevailed upon to discharge you. What reason induced them to take that step, honestly I don't know."

"But why did you think so?"

He was grave of a sudden.

"I just thought so," he said. "I am not going to be mysterious with you and I can only tell you that I had reasons to believe that some such step would be taken."

She shrugged her shoulders wearily.

"It is quite mysterious enough," she said. "Do you seriously want me to work for you?"

He nodded.

"You didn't tell me your city address."

"That is why I came back," he said.

"Then you knew I was coming out?"

"I knew you would come out some time in the day."

She stared at him.

"Do you mean to tell me that you would have waited all day to give me your address?"

He laughed.

"I only mean this," he replied, "that I should have waited all day."

It was a helpless laugh which echoed his.

" My address is 342 Lothbury," he went on, " 342. You
may begin work this afternoon and——" He hesitated.

" And ? " she repeated.

" And I think it would be wise if you didn't tell your
friend, the doctor, that I am employing you."

He was examining his finger-nails attentively as he
spoke, and he did not meet her eye.

" There are many reasons," he went on. " In the
first place, I have blotted my copy-book, as they say, in
Krooman Mansions, and it might not rebound to your
credit."

" You should have thought of that before you asked
me to come to you," she said.

" I thought of it a great deal," he replied calmly.

There was much in what he said, as the girl recognized.
She blamed herself for her hasty promise, but somehow
the events of the previous night had placed him on a
different footing, had given him a certain indefinable position to which the inebriate Mr. Beale had not aspired.

" I am afraid I am rather bewildered by all the mystery
of it," she said, " and I don't think I will come to the
office to-day. To-morrow morning, at what hour ? "

" Ten o'clock," he said, " I will be there to explain
your duties. Your salary will be £5 a week. You will
be in charge of the office, to which I very seldom go, by
the way, and your work will be preparing statistical returns
of the wheat-crops in all the wheat-fields of the world for
the last fifty years."

" It sounds thrilling," she said, and a quick smile flashed
across his face.

" It is much more thrilling than you imagine," were his
parting words.

She reached Krooman Mansions just as the doctor was
coming out, and he looked at her in surprise.

" You are back early ! "

Should she tell him ? There was no reason why she
shouldn't. He had been a good friend of hers and she felt
sure of his sympathy. It occurred to her at that moment
that Mr. Beale had been most unsympathetic, and had
not expressed one word of regret.

" Yes, I've been discharged," she exclaimed.

" Discharged ? Impossible ! "

She nodded.

" To prove that it is possible it has happened," she said cheerfully.

" My dear girl, this is monstrous ! What excuse did they give ? "

" None." This was said with a lightness of tone which did not reflect the indignation she felt at heart.

" Did they give you no reason ? "

" They gave me none. They gave me my month's cheque and just told me to go off, and off I came like the well-disciplined wage-earner I am."

" But it is monstrous," he said indignantly. " I will go and see them. I know one of the heads of the firm —at least, he is a patient of mine."

" You will do nothing of the kind," she replied firmly. " It really doesn't matter."

" What are you going to do ? By Jove ! " he said suddenly, " what a splendid idea ! I want a clinical secretary."

The humour of it got the better of her, and she laughed in his face.

" What is the joke ? " he asked.

" Oh, I am so sorry, doctor, but you mustn't think I am ungrateful, but I am beginning to regard myself as one of the plums in the labour market."

" Have you another position ? " he asked quickly.

" I have just accepted one," she said, and he did not disguise his disappointment, which might even have been interpreted, were Oliva more conceited, into absolute chagrin.

" You are very quick," said he, and his voice had lost some of its enthusiasm. " What position have you taken ? "

" I am going into an office in the city," she said.

" That will be dull. If you have settled it in your mind, of course, I cannot alter your decision, but I would be quite willing to give you £5 or £6 a week, and the work would be very light."

She held out her hand, and there was a twinkle in her eye.

"London is simply filled with people who want to give me £5 a week for work which is very light; really I am awfully grateful to you, doctor."

She felt more cheerful as she mounted the stairs than she thought would have been possible had such a position been forecast and had she to speculate upon the attitude of mind with which she would meet such a misfortune.

Punsonby's, for all the humiliation of her dismissal, seemed fairly unimportant. Some day she would discover the circumstances which had decided the high gods who presided over the ready-made clothing business in their action.

She unlocked the door and passed in, not without a comprehensive and an amused glance which took in the sober front doors of her new employer and her would-be employer.

"Sarah, your luck's in," she said, as she banged the door—Sarah was the approving version of Matilda. "If the wheezy man fires you, be sure there'll be a good angel waiting on the doorstep to offer you £20 a week for 'phoning the office once a day."

It occurred to her that it would be wise to place on record her protest against her summary dismissal, and she went to the little bookshelf-writing-table where she kept her writing-material to indite the epistle whilst she thought of it. It was one of those little fumed-oak contraptions where the desk is formed by a hinged flap which serves when not in use to close the desk.

She pulled out the two little supports, inserted the key in the lock, but it refused to turn, for the simple reason that it was unlocked. She had distinctly remembered that morning locking it after putting away the bill which had arrived with the morning post.

She pulled down the flap slowly and stared in amazement at the little which it hid. Every pigeon-hole had been ransacked and the contents were piled up in a confused heap. The two tiny drawers in which she kept stamps and nibs were out and emptied.

CHAPTER IV

THE LETTERS THAT WERE NOT THERE

SHE made a rapid survey of the documents. They were unimportant, and consisted mainly of letters from the few girl friends she had made during her stay at Punsonby's—old theatre programmes, recipes copied from newspapers and bunches of snapshots taken on her last summer excursion.

She arranged the things in some sort of rough order and made an inspection of her bedroom. Here, too, there was evidence that somebody had been searching the room. The drawers of her dressing-table were open, and though the contents had been little disturbed, it was clear that they had been searched. She made another discovery. The window of the bedroom was open at the bottom. Usually it was open half-way down from the top, and was fastened in that position by a patent catch. This precaution was necessary, because the window looked upon a narrow iron parapet which ran along the building and communicated with the fire-escape. She looked out. Evidently the intruder had both come and gone this way, and as evidently her return had disturbed him in his inspection, for it was hardly likely he would leave her papers and bureau in that state of confusion.

She made a brief inspection of the drawers in the dressing-table, and so far as she could see nothing was missing. She went back to the writing-bureau, mechanically put away the papers, little memorandum-books and letters which had been dragged from their pigeon-holes, then resting her elbow on the desk she sat, chin in hand, her pretty forehead wrinkled in a frown, recalling the events of the morning.

Who had searched her desk? What did they hope to discover? She had no illusions that this was the work of a common thief. There was something behind all this, something sinister and terrifying.

What association had the search with her summary

dismissal and what did the pompous Mr. White mean when he talked about definite knowledge? Definite knowledge of what? She gave it up with a shrug. She was not as much alarmed as disturbed. Life was grating a little, and she resented this departure from the smooth course which it had hitherto run. She resented the intrusion of Mr. Beale, who was drunk one moment and sober the next, who had offices in the city which he did not visit and who took such an inordinate interest in her affairs, and she resented him all the more because, in some indefinable way, he had shaken her faith—no, not shaken her faith, that was too strong a term—he had pared the mild romance which Dr. van Heerden's friendship represented.

She got up from the table and paced the room, planning her day. She would go out to lunch and indulge in the dissipation of a matinee. Perhaps she would stay out to dinner and come back—she shivered unconsciously and looked round the room. Somehow she did not look forward to an evening spent alone in her flat.

" Matilda, you're getting maudlin," she said, " you are getting romantic, too. You are reading too many sensational novels and seeing too many sensational films."

She walked briskly into her bedroom, unhooked a suit from the wardrobe and laid it on the bed.

At that moment there came a knock at the door. She put down the clothes-brush which was in her hand, walked out into the hall, opened the door and stepped back. Three men stood in the passage without. Two were strangers with that curious official look which the plain-clothes policeman can never wholly eradicate from his bearing. The third was Mr. White, more pompous and more solemn than ever.

" Miss Cresswell? " asked one of the strangers.

" That is my name."

" May we come inside? I want to see you."

She led the way to her little sitting-room. Mr. White followed in the rear.

" Your name is Oliva Cresswell. You were recently employed by Punsonby's, Limited, as cashier."

"That is true," she said, wondering what was coming next.

"Certain information was laid against you," said the spokesman, "as a result of which you were discharged from the firm this morning?"

She raised her eyebrows in indignant surprise.

"Information laid against me?" she said haughtily. "What do you mean?"

"I mean, that a charge was made against you that you were converting money belonging to the firm to your own use. That was the charge, I believe, sir?" He turned to Mr. White.

Mr. White nodded slowly.

"It is a lie. It is an outrageous lie," cried the girl, turning flaming eyes upon the stout managing director of Punsonby's. "You know it's a lie, Mr. White! Thousands of pounds have passed through my hands and I have never—oh, it's cruel."

"If you will only keep calm for a little while, miss," said the man, who was not unused to such outbreaks, "I will explain that at the moment of your dismissal there was no evidence against you."

"No definite knowledge of your offence," murmured Mr. White.

"And now?" demanded the girl.

"Now we have information, miss, to the effect that three registered letters, containing in all the sum of £63——"

"Fourteen and sevenpence," murmured Mr. White.

"Sixty-three pounds odd," said the detective, "which were abstracted by you yesterday are concealed in this flat."

"In the left-hand bottom drawer of your bureau," murmured Mr. White. "That is the definite knowledge which has come to us—it is a great pity."

The girl stared from one to the other.

"Three registered envelopes," she said incredulously; "in this flat?"

"In the bottom drawer of your bureau," mumbled Mr. White, who stood throughout the interview with his

eyes closed, his hands clasped in front of him, a picture
of a man performing a most painful act of duty.

" I have a warrant——" began the detective.

" You need no warrant," said the girl quietly, " you
are at liberty to search this flat or bring a woman to search
me. I have nothing in these rooms which I am ashamed
that you should see."

The detective turned to his companion.

" Fred," he said, " just have a look over that writing-
bureau. Is it locked, miss ? "

She had closed and locked the secretaire and she handed
the man the key. The detective who had done the speaking passed into the bedroom, and the girl heard him pulling out the drawers. She did not move from where she
stood confronting her late employer, still preserving his
attitude of somnolent detachment.

" Mr. White," she asked quietly, " I have a right to
know who accused me of stealing from your firm."

He made no reply.

" Even a criminal has a right to that, you know," she
said, recovering some of her poise. " I suppose that you
have been missing things for quite a long while—people
always miss things for quite a long while before the thief
is discovered, according to the Sunday papers."

" I do not read newspapers published on the Lord's
Day," said Mr. White reproachfully. " I do not know
the habits of the criminal classes, but as you say, and I
fear I must convey the gist of your speech to the officers
of the law, money has been missed from your department
for a considerable time. As to your accuser, acting as
—ah—as a good citizen and performing the duties which
are associated with good-citizenship, I cannot reveal his,
her, or their name."

She was eyeing him curiously with a gleam of dormant
laughter in her clear eyes. Then she heard a hurried
footstep in the little passage and remembered that the
door had been left open and she looked round.

The new-comer was Dr. van Heerden.

" What is this I hear ? " he demanded fiercely, addressing White. " You dare accuse Miss Cresswell of theft ? "

" My dear doctor," began White.

" It is an outrage," said the doctor. " It is disgraceful, Mr. White. I will vouch for Miss Cresswell with my life."

The girl stopped him with a laugh.

" Please don't be dramatic, doctor. It's really a stupid mistake. I didn't know you knew Mr. White."

" It is a disgraceful mistake," said the doctor violently. " I am surprised at you, White."

Mr. White could not close his eyes any tighter than they were closed. He passed the responsibility for the situation upon an invisible Providence with one heaving shrug of his shoulders.

" It is awfully kind of you to take this interest, doctor," said the girl, putting out her hands to him, " it was just like you."

" Is there anything I can do ? " he asked earnestly. " You can depend upon me to the last shilling if any trouble arises out of this."

" No trouble will arise out of it," she said. " Mr. White thinks that I have stolen money and that that money is hidden in the flat—by the way, who told you that I had been accused ? "

For a moment he was taken aback ; then :

" I saw the police officers go into your flat. I recognized them, and as they were accompanied by White, and you had been dismissed this morning, I drew my own conclusions."

It was at this moment that the detective came back from the bedroom.

" There's nothing there," he said.

Mr. White opened his eyes to their fullest extent.

" In the bottom drawer of the bureau ? " he asked incredulously.

" Neither in the bottom drawer nor the top drawer," said the detective. " Have you found anything, Fred ? "

" Nothing," said the other man.

" Have a look behind those pictures."

They turned up the corners of the carpets, searched her one little bookcase, looked under the tables, an unnecessary and amusing proceeding in the girl's eyes till the detective explained with that display of friendliness which all policemen show to suspected persons whom they do not at heart suspect, it was not an uncommon process for criminals to tack the proceeds of bank-note robberies to the underside of the table.

"Well, miss," said the detective at last, with a smile, "I hope we haven't worried you very much. What do you intend doing, sir?" He addressed White.

"Did you search the bottom drawer of the bureau?" said Mr. White again.

"I searched the bottom drawer of the bureau, the top drawer and the middle drawer," said the detective patiently. "I searched the back of the bureau, the trinket-drawer, the trinket-boxes——"

"And it was not there?" said Mr. White, as though he could not believe his ears.

"It was not there. What I want to know is, do you charge this young lady? If you charge her, of course you take all the responsibility for the act, and if you fail to convict her you will be liable to an action for false arrest."

"I know, I know, I know," said Mr. White, with remarkable asperity in one so placid. "No, I do not charge her. I am sorry you have been inconvenienced"—he turned to the girl in his most majestic manner—"and I trust that you bear no ill-will."

He offered a large and flabby hand, but Oliva ignored it.

"Mind you don't trip over the mat as you go out,' she said, "the passage is rather dark."

Mr. White left the room, breathing heavily.

"Excuse me one moment," said the doctor in a low voice. "I have a few words to say to White."

"Please don't make a fuss," said Oliva, "I would rather the matter dropped where it is."

He nodded, and strode out after the managing director of Punsonby's. They made a little group of four.

"Can I see you in my flat for a moment, Mr. White?"

"Certainly," said Mr. White cheerfully.

"You don't want us any more?" asked the detective.

" No," said Mr. White ; then : " Are you quite sure you searched the bottom drawer of the bureau ? "

" Perfectly sure," said the detective irritably, " you don't suppose I've been at this job for twenty years and should overlook the one place where I expected to find the letters."

Mr. White was saved the labour of framing a suitable retort, for the door of Mr. Beale's flat was flung open and Mr. Beale came forth. His grey hat was on the back of his head and he stood erect with the aid of the door-post, surveying with a bland and inane smile the little knot of men.

" Why," he said jovially, " it's the dear old doctor, and if my eyes don't deceive me, it's the jolly old Archbishop."

Mr. White brindled. That he was known as the Archbishop in the intimate circles of his acquaintances afforded him a certain satisfaction. That a perfect stranger, and a perfectly drunken stranger at that, should employ a nickname which was for the use of a privileged few, distressed him.

" And," said the swaying man by the door, peering through the half-darkness : " Is it not Detective-Sergeant Peterson and Constable Fairbank ? Welcome to this home of virtue."

The detective-sergeant smiled but said nothing. The doctor fingered his beard indecisively, but Mr. White essayed to stride past, his chin in the air, ignoring the greeting, but Mr. Beale was too quick for him. He lurched forward, caught the lapels of the other's immaculate frock-coat and held himself erect thereby.

" My dear old Whitey," he said.

" I don't know you, sir," cried Mr. White, " will you please unhand me ? "

" Don't know me, Whitey ? Why you astonishing old thing ! "

He slipped his arm over the other's shoulder in an attitude of affectionate regard. " Don't know old Beale ? "

" I never met you before," said Mr. White, struggling to escape.

" Bless my life and soul," said Mr. Beale, stepping back,
shocked and hurt, " I call you to witnesh, Detective-
Sergeant Peterson and amiable Constable Fairbank and
learned Dr. van Heerden, that he has denied me. And
it has come to this," he said bitterly. and leaning his head
against the door-post he howled like a dog.

" I say, stop your fooling, Beale," said the doctor angrily,
" there's been very serious business here, and I should
thank you not to interfere."

Mr. Beale wiped imaginary tears from his eyes, grasped
Mr. White's unwilling hand and shook it vigorously, staggered back to his flat and slammed the door behind him.

" Do you know that man ? " asked the doctor, turning
to the detective.

" I seem to remember his face," said· the sergeant.
" Come on, Fred. Good morning, gentlemen."

They waited till the officers were downstairs and out
of sight, and then the doctor turned to the other and in
a different tone from any he had employed, said :

" Come into my room for a moment, White," and Mr.
White followed him obediently.

They shut the door and passed into the study, with
its rows of heavily bound books, its long table covered
with test-tubes and the paraphernalia of medical research.

" Well," said. White, dropping into a chair, " what
happened ? "

" That is what I want to know," said the doctor.

He took a cigarette from a box on the table and lit it
and the two men looked at one another without speaking.

" Do you think she had the letters and hid them ? "

" Impossible," replied the doctor briefly.

White grunted, took a cigar from a long leather case,
bit off the end savagely and reached out his hand for a
match.

" ' The best-laid schemes of mice and men ! ' " he quoted.

" Oh, shut up," said the doctor savagely.

He was pacing the study with long strides. He stopped
at one end of the room staring moodily through the window,
his hands thrust in his pockets.

" I wonder what happened," he said again. " Well,

that can wait. Now just tell me exactly how matters
stand in regard to you and Punsonby's."

"I have all the figures here," said Mr. White, as he
thrust his hand into the inside pocket of his frock-coat,
"I can raise £40,000 by debentures and—hello, what's
this ?"

He drew from his pocket a white packet, fastened about
by a rubber band. This he slipped off and gasped, for
in his hands were three registered letters, and they were
addressed to Messrs. Punsonby, and each had been slit
open.

CHAPTER V

THE MAN WITH THE BIG HEAD

NO. 342, Lothbury, is a block of business offices somewhat unpretentious in their approach but of surprising depth and importance when explored. Oliva
Cresswell stood for awhile in the great lobby, inspecting
the names of the occupants, which were inscribed on porcelain slips in two big frames on each wall of the vestibule.

After a lengthy search she discovered the name of the
Beale Agency under the heading "fourth floor" and
made her way to the elevator.

Mr. Beale's office was at the end of a seemingly interminable corridor and consisted, as she was to find, of an
outer and an inner chamber. The outer was simply
furnished with a table, two chairs and a railed fence bisected
with a little wooden gateway.

A boy sat at one table, engaged in laborious exercise
on a typewriter with one finger of one hand.

He jumped up as she came through the door.

"Miss Cresswell ?" he asked. "Mr. Beale will see
you."

He opened the wicket-gate and led the way to a door
marked "Private."

It was Beale who opened the door in response to the knock.

"Come in, Miss Cresswell," he said cheerily, "I didn't expect you for half an hour."

"I thought I'd start well," she smiled.

She had had many misgivings that morning, and had spent a restless night debating the wisdom of engaging herself to an employer whose known weakness had made his name a by-word. But a promise was a promise and, after all, she told herself, her promise was fulfilled when she had given the new work a trial.

"Here is your desk," he said, indicating a large office table in the centre of the room, "and here is my little library. You will note that it mainly consists of agricultural returns and reports—do you read French?" She nodded. "Good, and Spanish—that's rather too much to expect, isn't it?"

"I speak and read Spanish very well," she said. "When I was a little girl I lived around in Paris, Lyons, and Barcelona—my first regular work—the first I was paid for—was in the Anglo-Spanish Cable office in Barcelona."

"That's lucky," he said, apparently relieved, "though I could have taught you the few words that it is necessary you should know to understand the Argentine reports. What I particularly want you to discover—and you will find two or three hundred local guide-books on that shelf at the far end of the room, and these will help you a great deal—is the exact locations of all the big wheat-growing districts, the number of hectares under cultivation in normal times, the method by which the wheat areas are divided—by fences, roads, etc.—the average size of the unbroken blocks of wheatland and, if possible, the width of the roads or paths which divide them."

"Gracious!" she cried in dismay.

"It sounds a monumental business, but I think you will find it simple. The Agricultural Department of the United States Government, for instance, tabulate all those facts. For example, they compel farmers in certain districts to keep a clear space between each lot so that in case of the crops being fired, the fire may be isolated. Canada, the Argentine and Australia have other methods."

She had seated herself at the desk and was jotting down a note of her duties.

" Anything more ? " she asked.

" Yes—I want the names of the towns in the centre of the wheat-growing areas, a list of the hotels in those towns. The guide-books you will find up to date, and these will inform you on this subject. Particularly do I want hotels noted where automobiles can be hired, the address of the local bank and the name of the manager and, where the information is available, the name of the chief constable, sheriff or chef d'gendarmerie in each district."

She looked up at him, her pencil poised.

" Are you serious—of course, I'll do all this, but somehow it reminds me of a story I once read——"

" I know it," said Beale promptly, " it is ' The Case of the Red-Haired Man,' one of Doyle's stories about a man who, to keep him away from his shop, was employed on the useless task of copying the *Encyclopædia Britannica* —no, I am asking you to do serious work, Miss Cresswell— work which I do not want spoken about."

He sat on the edge of the table, looking down at her, and if his eyes were smiling it was because that was their natural expression. She had never seen them when they did not hold the ghost of some joke inwardly enjoyed.

But her instinct told her that he was very much in earnest and that the task he had set her was one which had reason behind it.

" Take the districts first and work up the hotels, et cetera," he suggested, " you will find it more interesting than a novel. Those little books," he pointed to the crowded shelf by the window, " will carry you to stations and ranches and farms all over the world. You shall be wafted through Manitoba, and cross the United States from New England to California. You will know Sydney and Melbourne and the great cornland at the back of beyond. And you'll sit in cool patios and sip iced drinks with Señor Don Perfecto de Cuba who has ridden in from

his rancio to inquire the price of May wheat, or maybe
you'll just amble through India on an elephant, sleeping
in bungalows, listening to the howling of tigers, mos-
quitoes——"

"Now I know you're laughing at me," she smiled.

"Not altogether," he said quietly; then: "Is there
any question you'd like to ask me? By the way, the
key of the office is in the right-hand drawer; go to lunch
when you like and stay away as long as you like. Your
cheque will be paid you every Friday morning."

"But where——?" She looked round the room.
"Where do you work?"

"I don't work," he said promptly, "you do the work
and I get the honour and glory. When I come in I will
sit on the edge of your desk, which is not graceful but
it is very comfortable. There is one question I meant
to ask you. You said you were in a cable office—do you
add to your accomplishments a working knowledge of
the Morse Code?"

She nodded.

"I can see you being useful. If you need me "—he
jerked his head toward a telephone on a small table—" call
8761 Gerrard."

"And where is that?" she asked.

"If I thought you were anything but a very sane young
lady, I should tell you that it is the number of my favourite
bar," he said gravely. "I will not, however, practise
that harmless deception upon you."

Again she saw the dancing light of mischief in his eyes.

"You're a queer man," she said, "and I will not make
myself ridiculous by speaking to you for your good."

She heard his soft laughter as the door closed behind
him and, gathering an armful of the guide-books, she
settled down for a morning's work which proved even
more fascinating than his fanciful pictures had suggested.
She found herself wondering to what use all this information she extracted could be put. Was Mr. Beale really a
buyer or was he interested in the sale of agricultural machinery? Why should he want to know that Jonas Scobbs
was the proprietor of Scobbs' Hotel and General Emporium

in the town of Red Horse Valley, Alberta, and what significance attached to the fact that he had an automobile
for hire or that he ran a coach every Wednesday to Regina ?

Then she . fell to speculating upon the identity and
appearance of this man who bore this weird name of
Scobbs.   She pictured him an elderly man with chin
whiskers who wore his pants thrust into top-boots.   And
why was Red Horse Valley so called ?   These unexpected
and, to her, hitherto unknown names of places and people
set in train most interesting processions of thought that
slid through the noisy jangle of traffic, and coloured the
drab walls of all that was visible of the City of London
through the window with the white lights and purple
shadows of dream prairies.

When she looked at her watch—being impelled to that
act by the indescribable sensation of hunger—she was
amazed to discover that it was three o'clock.

She jumped up and went to the outer office in search
of the boy who, she faintly remembered, had erupted
into her presence hours before with a request which she
had granted without properly hearing.   He was not in
evidence.   Evidently his petition had also been associated
with the gnawing pangs which assail boyhood at one
o'clock in the afternoon.

She was turning back to her office, undecided as to
whether she should remain until his return or close the
office entirely, when the shuffle of feet brought her round.

The outer office was partitioned from the entrance by
a long " fence," the farther end of which was hidden by
a screen of wood and frosted glass.   It was from behind
that screen that the noise came and she remembered that
she had noted a chair there—evidently a place where
callers waited.

" Who is there ? " she asked.

There was a creak as the visitor rose.

" Eggscuse, mattam," said a wheezy voice, " I gall to
eng-vire for Mister Peale, isn't it ? "

He shuffled forward into view, a small man with a
dead white face and a head of monstrous size.

She was bereft of speech and could only look at him,

for this was the man she had found in her rooms the night
before her dismissal—the man who carried the Green Rust.

Evidently he did not recognize her.

" Mister Peale, he tolt me, I must gall him mit der
telephone, but der nomber she vas gone oudt of mine
head ! "

He blinked at her with his short-sighted eyes and laid
a big hairy hand on the gate.

" You must—you mustn't come in," she said breathlessly. " I will call Mr. Beale—sit—sit down again."

" Sch," he said obediently, and shuffled back to his
chair, " dell him der Herr Brofessor it was."

The girl took up the telephone receiver with a shaking
hand and gave the number. It was Beale's voice that
answered her.

" There's a man here," she said hurriedly, " a—a—the
man—who was in my room—the Herr Professor."

She heard his exclamation of annoyance.

" I'm sorry," and if she could judge by the inflection
of his voice his sorrow was genuine. " I'll be with you
in ten minutes—he's quite a harmless old gentleman——"

" Hurry, please."

She heard the " click " of his receiver and replaced
her own slowly. She did not attempt to go back to the
outer office, but waited by the closed door. She recalled
the night, the terror of that unknown presence in her
darkened flat, and shuddered. Then Beale, surprisingly
sober, had come in and he and the " burglar " had gone
away together.

What had these two, Mr. Beale and the " Herr Professor," in common ? She heard the snap of the outer
door, and Beale's voice speaking quickly. It was probably German—she had never acquired the language and
hardly recognized it, though the guttural " Zu befel, Herr
Peale " was distinct.

She heard the shuffle of the man's feet and the closing
of the outer door and then Beale came in, and his face
was troubled.

" I can't tell you how sorry I am that the old man called
—I'd forgotten that he was likely to come."

She leant against the table, both hands behind her.

" Mr. Beale," she said, " will you give me straight-forward answers to a number of plain questions ? "

He nodded.

" If I can," he said.

" Is the Herr Professor a friend of yours ? "

" No—I know him and in a way I am sorry for him. He is a German who pretends to be Russian. Immensely poor and unprepossessing to a painful degree, but a very clever scientist. In fact, a truly great analytical chemist who ought to be holding a good position. He told me that he had the best qualifications, and I quite believe him, but that his physical infirmities, his very freakishness had ruined him."

Her eyes softened with pity—the pity of the strong for the weak, of the beautiful for the hideous.

" If that is true——" she began, and his chin went up. " I beg your pardon, I know it is true. It is tragic, but —did you know him before you met him in my room ? "

He hesitated.

" I knew him both by repute and by sight," he said. " I knew the work he was engaged on and I guessed why he was engaged. But I had never spoken to him."

" Thank you—now for question number two. You needn't answer unless you wish."

" I shan't," he said.

" That's frank, anyway. Now tell me, Mr. Beale, what is all this mystery about ? What is the Green Rust ? Why do you pretend to be a—a drunkard when you're not one ? " (It needed some boldness to say this, and she flushed with the effort to shape the sentence.) " Why are you always around so providentially when you're needed, and," here she smiled (as he thought) deliciously, " why weren't you round yesterday, when I was nearly arrested for theft ? "

He was back on the edge of the table, evidently his favourite resting-place, she thought, and he ticked her questions off on his fingers.

" Question number one cannot be answered. Question number two, why do I pretend to be a—a drunkard ? " he mimicked her audaciously. "There are other things which intoxicate a man beside love and beer, Miss Cresswell."

"How gross!" she protested. "What are they?"

"Work, the chase, scientific research and the first spring scent of the hawthorn," he said solemnly. "As to the third question, why was I not around when you were nearly arrested? Well, I was around. I was in your flat when you came in and escaped along the fire parapet."

"Mr. Beale!" she gasped. "Then it was you—you are a detective!"

"I turned your desk and dressing-chest upside down? Yes, it was I," he said without shame, ignoring the latter part of the sentence. "I was looking for something."

"You were looking for something?" she repeated. "What were you looking for?"

"Three registered envelopes which were planted in your flat yesterday morning," he said, "and what's more I found 'em!"

She put her hand to her forehead in bewilderment.

"Then you——"

"Saved you from a cold, cold prison cell. Have you had any lunch? Why, you're starving!"

"But——"

"Bread and butter is what you want," said the practical Mr. Beale, "with a large crisp slice of chicken and stacks of various vegetables."

And he hustled her from the office.

CHAPTER VI

MR. SCOBBS OF RED HORSE VALLEY

MR. WHITE, managing director of Punsonby's Store, was a man of simple tastes. He had a horror of extravagance and it was his boast that he had never ridden in a taxi-cab save as the guest of some other person who paid. He travelled by tube or omnibus from the Bays-water Road, where he lived what he described as his pri-vate life. He lunched in the staff dining-room, punctili-ously paying his bill ; he dined at home in solitary state, for he had neither chick nor child, heir or wife. Once an elder sister had lived with him and had died (according to the popularly accepted idea) of slow starvation, for he was a frugal man.

It seems the fate of apparently rich and frugal men that they either die and leave their hoardings to the State or else they disappear, leaving behind them monumental debts. The latter have apparently no vices ; even the harassed accountant who disentangles their estates cannot discover the channel through which their hundreds of thousands have poured. The money has gone and, if astute detectives bring back the defaulter from the pleas-ant life which the Southern American cities offer to rich idlers, he is hopelessly vague as to the method by which it went.

Mr. Lassimus White was the managing director and general manager of Punsonby's. He held, or was sup-posed to hold, a third of the shares in that concern, shares which he had inherited from John Punsonby, his uncle, and the founder of the firm. He drew a princely salary and a substantial dividend, he was listed as a debenture holder and was accounted a rich man.

But Mr. White was not rich. His salary and his divi-dends were absorbed by a mysterious agency which called itself the Union Jack Investment and Mortgage Corpora-tion, which paid premiums on Mr. White's heavy life in-surance and collected the whole or nearly the whole of his income. His secret, well guarded as it was, need be no secret to the reader. Mr. White, who had never touched a playing-card in his life and who grew apoplectic at the sin and shame of playing the races, was an inveterate gambler. His passion was for Sunken Treasure Syndicates, formed to recover golden ingots from ships of the Spanish Armada ; for companies that set forth to harness the horse-power of the sea to the services of commerce ; for optimistic companies that discovered radium mines in the Ural Mountains—anything which promised a steady three hundred per cent. per annum on an initial investment had an irresistible attraction for Mr. White, who argued that some day something would really fulfil expectations and his losses would be recovered.

In the meantime he was in the hands of Moss Ibramovitch, trading as the Union Jack Investment and Mortgage Corporation, licensed and registered as a moneylender according to law. And being in the hands of this gentleman, was much less satisfactory and infinitely more expensive than being in the hands of the bankruptcy officials.

In the evening of the day Oliva Cresswell had started working for her new employer, Mr. White stalked forth from his gloomy house and his departure was watched by the two tough females who kept house for him, with every pleasure. He strutted eastward swinging his umbrella, his head well back, his eyes half-closed, his massive waistcoat curving regally. His silk hat was pushed back from his forehead and the pince-nez he carried, but so seldom wore, swung from the cord he held before him in that deadmouse manner which important men affect.

He had often been mistaken for a Fellow of the Royal Society, so learned and detached was his bearing. Yet no speculation upon the origin of species or the function of the nebulæ filled his mind.

At a moment of great stress and distraction, Dr. van Heerden had arisen above his horizon, and there was something in Dr. van Heerden's manner which inspired confidence and respect. They had met by accident at a meeting held to liquidate the Shining Strand Alluvial Gold Mining Company—a concern which had started forth in the happiest circumstances to extract the fabulous riches which had been discovered by an American philanthropist (he is now selling Real Estate by correspondence) on a Southern Pacific island.

Van Heerden was not a shareholder, but he was intensely interested in the kind of people who subscribe for shares in Dreamland Gold mines. Mr. White had attended incognito—his shares were held in the name of his lawyer, who was thinking seriously of building an annex to hold the unprofitable scrip.

Mr. White was gratified to discover a kindred soul who believed in this kind of speculation.

It was to the doctor's apartment that he was now walking. That gentleman met him in the entrance and accompanied him to his room. There was a light in the fanlight of Oliva's flat, for she had brought some of her work home to finish, but Mr. Beale's flat was dark.

This the doctor noted before he closed his own door, and switched on the light.

" Well, White, have you made up your mind ? " he demanded without preliminary.

" I—ah—have and I—ah—have not," said the cautious adventurer. " Forty thousand is a lot of money—a fortune, one might say—yes, a fortune."

" Have you raised it ? "

Mr. White sniffed his objection to this direct examination.

" My broker has very kindly realized the debentures —I am—ah—somewhat indebted to him, and it was necessary to secure his permission and—yes, I have the money at my bank."

He gazed benignly at the other, as one who conferred a favour by the mere bestowal of his confidences.

" First, doctor—forgive me if I am a little cautious ; first I say, it is necessary that I should know a little more about your remarkable scheme, for remarkable I am sure it is."

The doctor poured out a whisky and soda and passed the glass to his visitor, who smilingly waved it aside.

" Wine is a mocker," he said, " nothing stronger than cider has ever passed my lips—pray do not be offended."

" And yet I seem to remember that you held shares in the Northern Saloon Trust," said the doctor, with a little curl of his bearded lips.

" That," said Mr. White hastily, " was a purely commercial—ah—affair. In business one must exploit even the—ah—sins and weaknesses of our fellows."

" As to my scheme," said the doctor, changing the

subject, " I'm afraid I must ask you to invest in the dark.
I can promise you that you will get your capital back a
hundred times over. I realize that you have heard that
sort of thing before, and that my suggestion has all the
appearance of a confidence trick, except that I do not
offer you even the substantial security of a gold brick.
I may not use your money—I believe that I shall not.
On the other hand, I may. If it is to be of any use to me
it must be in my hands very soon—to-morrow."

He wandered restlessly about the room as he spoke,
and jerked his sentences out now to Mr. White's face,
now over his shoulder.

" I will tell you this," he went on, " my scheme within
the narrow interpretation of the law is illegal—don't
mistake me, there is no danger to those who invest in
ignorance. I will bear the full burden of responsibility.
You can come in or you can stay out, but if you come in
I shall ask you never to mention the name of the enterprise to a living soul."

" The Green Rust Syndicate ? " whispered Mr. White
fearfully. " What—ah—is Green Rust ? "

" I have offered the scheme to my—to a Governme t.
But they are scared of touching it. Scared, by Jove ! "
He threw up his arms to the ceiling and his voice trembled
with passion. " Germany scared ! And there was a
time when Europe cringed at the clank of the Prussian
sword ! When the lightest word of Potsdam set ministries
trembling in Petrograd and London. You told me the
other day you were a pacifist during the war and that
you sympathized with Prussia in her humiliation. I am
a Prussian, why should I deny it ? I glory in the religion
of might—I believe it were better that the old civilization
were stamped into the mud of oblivion than that Prussian
Kultur should be swept away by the licentious French,
the mercenary English——"

" British," murmured Mr. White.

" And the dollar-hunting Yankees—but I'm making
a fool of myself."

With an effort be regained his calm.

' The war's over and done with. As I say, I offered

my Government my secret. They thought it good but
could not help me. They were afraid that the League
would come to learn they were supporting it. They'll
help me in other ways—innocent ways. If this scheme
goes through they will put the full resources of the State
at my disposal."

Mr. White rose, groped for his hat and cleared his throat.

" Dr.—ah—van Heerden, you may be sure that I shall
—ah—respect your confidence. With your very natural
indignation I am in complete sympathy.

" But let us forget, ah—that you have spoken at all
about the scheme in any detail—especially in so far as
to its legality or otherwise. Let us forget, sir "—Mr. White
thrust his hand into the bosom of his coat, an attitude
he associated with the subtle rhetoric of statesmanship.
" Let us forget all, save this, that you invite me to subscribe £40,000 to a syndicate for—ah—let us say model
dwellings for the working classes, and that I am willing
to subscribe, and in proof of my willingness will send you
by the night's post a cheque for that amount. Good
night, doctor."

He shook hands, pulled his hat down upon his head,
opened the door and ran into the arms of a man whose
hand was at that moment raised to press the electric bell-
push by the side of the door.

Both started back.

" Excuse me," mumbled Mr. White, and hurried down
the stairs.

Dr. van Heerden glared at the visitor, white with rage.

" Come in, you fool ! " he hissed, and half-dragged the
man into his room, " what made you leave Scotland ? "

" Scotland I hate ! " said the visitor huskily. " Sticking
a fellow away in the wilds of the beastly mountains, eh ?
That's not playing the game, my cheery sportsman."

" When did you arrive ? " asked van Heerden quickly.

" Seven p.m. Travelled third class ! Me ! Is it not
the most absurd position for a man of my parts—third
class, with foul and common people—I'd like to rip them
all up—I would, by heavens ! "

The doctor surveyed the coarse, drink-bloated face,

the loose, weak mouth, half-smiled at the vanity of the
dangling monocle and pointed to the decanter.

"You did wrong to come," he said, "I have arranged
your passage to Canada next week."

"I'll not go!" said the man, tossing down a drink
and wiping his lips with a not over-clean handkerchief.
"Curse me, van Heerden, why should I hide and fly
like a—a——"

"Like a man who escaped from Cayenne," suggested
the doctor, "or like a man who is wanted by the police
of three countries for crimes ranging from arson to wilful
murder."

The man shuddered.

"All fair fights, my dear fellow," he said more mildly,
"if I hadn't been a boastful, drunken sot, you wouldn't
have heard of 'em—you wouldn't, curse you. I was mad!
I had you in my hand like that!" He closed a not over-
clean fist under van Heerden's nose. "I saw it all, all,
I saw you bullying the poor devil, shaking some secret out
of him, I saw you knife him——"

"Hush!" hissed van Heerden. "You fool—people
can hear through these walls."

"But there are no windows to see through," leered
the man, "and I *saw*! He came out of his death-trance
to denounce you, by Jove! I heard him shout and I
saw you run in and lay him down—lay him down! Lay
him out is better! You killed him to shut his mouth,
my bonnie doctor!"

Van Heerden's face was as white as a sheet, but the
hand he raised to his lips was without a tremor.

"You were lucky to find me that night, dear lad," the
man went on. "I was in a mind to split on you."

"You have no cause to regret my finding you, Jackson,"
said the doctor. "I suppose you still call yourself by
that name?"

"Yes, Jackson," said the other promptly. "Jack—
son, son of Jack. Fine name, eh—good enough for me
and good enough for anybody else. Yes, you found me
and done me well. I wish you hadn't. How I wish you
hadn't."

" Ungrateful fool ! " said van Heerden. " I probably saved your life—hid you in Eastbourne, took you to London, whilst the police were searching for you."

" For me ! " snarled the other. " A low trick, by the Everlasting Virtues—— ! "

" Don't be an idiot—whose word would they have taken, yours or mine ? Now let's talk—on Thursday next you sail for Quebec. . . ."

He detailed his instructions at length and the man called Jackson, mellowed by repeated visits to the decanter, listened and even approved.

On the other side of the hallway, behind the closed door, Oliva Cresswell, her dining-table covered with papers and books, was working hard.

She was particularly anxious to show Mr. Beale a sample of her work in the morning and was making a fair copy of what she had described to him that afternoon as her " hotel list."

" They are such queer names," she said ; " there is one called Scobbs of Red Horse Valley—Scobbs ! "

He had laughed.

" Strangely enough, I know Mr. Scobbs, who is quite a personage in that part of the world. He owns a chain of hotels in Western Canada. You mustn't leave him out."

Even had she wished to, or even had the name been overlooked once, she could not have escaped it. For Jonas Scobbs was the proprietor of Scobbs' Hotel in Falling Star City ; of the Bellevue in Snakefence, of the Palace Hotel in Portage.

After awhile it began to lose its novelty and she accepted the discovery of unsuspected properties of Mr. Scobbs as inevitable.

She filled in the last ruled sheet and blotted it, gathered the sheets together and fastened them with a clip.

She yawned as she rose and realized that her previous night's sleep had been fitful.

She wondered as she began to undress if she would dream of Scobbs or—no, she didn't want to dream of big-headed men with white faces, and the thought awoke a doubt

in her mind. Had she bolted the door of the flat ? She
went along the passage in her stockinged feet, shot the
bolts smoothly and was aware of voices outside. They
came to her clearly through the ventilator above the fanlight.

She heard the doctor say something and then a voice
which she had not heard before.

" Don't worry—I've a wonderful memory, by Jove ! . . ."

The murmur of the doctor did not reach her, but——

" Yes, yes . . . Scobbs' Hotel, Red Horse Valley
. . . know the place well . . . good night, dear old
thing. . . ."

A door banged, an uncertain footstep died away in the
well of the stairs below, and she was left to recover from
her amazement.

CHAPTER VII

PLAIN WORDS FROM MR. BEALE

OLIVA CRESSWELL did not feel at all sleepy, so
she discovered, by the time she was ready for bed.
To retire in that condition of wakefulness meant another
sleepless night, and she slipped a kimono over her, found
a book and settled into the big wicker-chair under the
light for the half-hour's reading which would reduce
her to the necessary state of drowsiness. The book at
any other time would have held her attention, but now
she found her thoughts wandering. On the other side
of the wall (she regarded it with a new interest) was the
young man who had so strangely intruded himself into her
life. Or was he out ? What would a man like that do
with his evenings ? He was not the sort of person who
could find any pleasure in making a round of music-halls
or sitting up half the night in a card-room.

She heard a dull knock, and it came from the wall.

Mr. Beale was at home then, he had pushed a chair against the wall, or he was knocking in nails at this hour of the night.

"Thud—thud—thud"—a pause—"thud, tap, thud, tap."

The dull sound was as if made by a fist, the tap by a finger-tip.

It was repeated.

Suddenly the girl jumped up with a little laugh. He was signalling to her and had sent "O.C."—her initials.

She tapped three times with her finger, struck once with the flat of her hand and tapped again. She had sent the "Understood" message.

Presently he began and she jotted the message on the margin of her book.

"Most urgent : Don't use soap. Bring it to office."

She smiled faintly. She expected something more brilliant in the way of humour even from Mr. Beale. She tapped "acknowledged" and went to bed.

"Matilda, my innocent child," she said to herself, as she snuggled up under the bed-clothes, "exchanging midnight signals with a lodger is neither proper nor lady-like."

She had agreed with herself that in spite of the latitude she was allowed in the matter of office hours, that she would put in an appearance punctually at ten. This meant rising not later than eight, for she had her little household to put in order before she left.

It was the postman's insistent knocking at eight-thirty that woke her from a dreamless sleep, and, half-awake, she dragged herself into her dressing-gown and went to the door.

"Parcel, miss," said the invisible official, and put into the hand that came round the edge of the door a letter and a small package. She brought them to the sitting-room and pulled back the curtains. The letter was type-written and was on the note-paper of a well-known firm of perfumers. It was addressed to " Miss Olivia Cresswell," and ran :

"DEAR MADAME,—

"We have pleasure in sending you for your use a sample cake of our new Complexion Soap, which we trust will meet with your approval."

"But how nice," she said, and wondered why she had been singled out for the favour. She opened the package. In a small carton, carefully wrapped in the thinnest of paper, was an oval tablet of lavender-coloured soap that exhaled a delicate fragrance.

"But how nice," she said again, and put the gift in the bath-room.

This was starting the day well—a small enough foundation for happiness, yet one which every woman knows, for happiness is made up of small and acceptable things and, given the psychological moment, a bunch of primroses has a greater value than a rope of pearls.

In her bath she picked up the soap and dropped it back in the tidy again quickly.

"Don't use soap; bring it to office."

She remembered the message in a flash. Beale had known that this parcel was coming then, and his "most urgent" warning was not a joke. She dressed quickly, made a poor breakfast and was at the office ten minutes before the hour.

She found her employer waiting, sitting in his accustomed place on the edge of the table in her office. He gave her a little nod of welcome, and without a word stretched out his hand.

"The soap?" she asked.

He nodded.

She opened her bag.

"Good," he said. "I see you have kept the wrappings, and that, I presume, is the letter which accompanied the —what shall I say—gift? Don't touch it with your bare hand," he said quickly. "Handle it with the paper."

He pulled his gloves from his pocket and slipped them on, then took the cake of soap in his hand and carried it to the light, smelt it and returned it to its paper.

"Now let me see the letter."

She handed it to him, and he read it.

"From Brandan, the perfumers. They wouldn't be in it, but we had better make sure."

He walked to the telephone and gave a number, and the girl heard him speaking in a low tone to somebody at the other end. Presently he put down the receiver and walked back, his hands thrust into his pockets.

"They know nothing about this act of generosity," he said.

By this time she had removed her coat and hat and hung them up, and had taken her place at her desk. She sat with her elbows on the blotting-pad, her chin on her clasped hands, looking up at him.

"I don't think it's fair that things should be kept from me any longer," she said. "Many mysterious things have happened in the past few days, and since they have all directly affected me, I think I am entitled to some sort of explanation."

"I think you are," said Mr. Beale, with a twinkle in his grey eyes, "but I am not prepared to explain everything just yet. Thus much I will tell you, that had you used this soap this morning, by the evening you would have been covered from head to foot in a rather alarming and irritating rash."

She gasped.

"But who dared to send me this ? "

He shrugged his shoulders.

"Who knows ? But first let me ask you this, Miss Cresswell. Suppose to-night when you had looked at yourself in the glass you had discovered your face was covered with red blotches and, on further examination, you found your arms and, indeed, the whole of your body similarly disfigured, what would you have done ? "

She thought for a moment.

"Why, of course, I should have sent for the doctor."

"Which doctor ? " he asked carelessly.

"Doctor van Heerden—oh ! " She looked at him resentfully. "You don't suggest that Doctor van Heerden sent that hideous thing to me ? "

"I don't suggest anything," said Mr. Beale coolly.

"I merely say that you would have sent for a doctor, and that that doctor would have been Doctor van Heerden. I say further, that he would have come to you and been very sympathetic, and would have ordered you to remain in bed for four or five days. I think, too," he said, looking up at the ceiling and speaking slowly, as though he were working out the possible consequence in his mind, "that he would have given you some very palatable medicine."

"What are you insinuating?" she asked quietly.

He did not reply immediately.

"If you will get out of your mind the idea that I have any particular grievance against Doctor van Heerden, that I regard him as a rival, a business rival let us say, or that I have some secret grudge against him, and if in place of that suspicion you would believe that I am serving a much larger interest than is apparent to you, I think we might discuss"—he smiled—"even Doctor van Heerden without such a discussion giving offence to you."

She laughed.

"I am really not offended. I am rather distressed, if anything," she said, knitting her brows. "You see, Doctor van Heerden has always been most kind to me."

Beale nodded.

"He got you your rooms at the flats," he replied quietly; "he was also ready to give you employment the moment you were providentially discharged from Punsonby's. Does it not strike you, Miss Cresswell, that every kind act of Doctor van Heerden's has had a tendency to bring you together, into closer association, I mean? Does it not appear to you that the net result of all the things that might have happened to you in the past few days would have been to make you more and more dependent upon Doctor van Heerden? For example, if you had gone into his employ as he planned that you should?"

"Planned!" she gasped.

His face was grave now and the laughter had gone out of his eyes.

"Planned," he said quietly. "You were discharged from Punsonby's at Doctor van Heerden's instigation."

"I will not believe it!"

"That will not make it any less the fact," said Mr. Beale. "You were nearly arrested—again at Doctor van Heerden's instigation. He was waiting for you when you came back from Punsonby's, ready to offer you his job. When he discovered you had already engaged yourself he telephoned to White, instructing him to have you arrested so that you might be disgraced and might turn to him, your one loyal friend."

She listened speechless. She could only stare at him and could not even interrupt him. For her shrewd woman instinct told her so convincingly that even her sense of loyalty could not eject the doubt which assailed her mind, that if there was not truth in what he was saying there was at least probability.

"I suggest even more," Beale went on. "I suggest that for some purpose, Doctor van Heerden desires to secure a mental, physical and moral ascendancy over you. In other words, he wishes to enslave you to his will."

She looked at him in wonder and burst into a peal of ringing laughter.

"Really, Mr. Beale, you are too absurd," she said.

"Aren't I?" he smiled. "It sounds like something out of a melodrama."

"Why on earth should he want to secure a mental ascendancy over me? Do you suggest——" She flushed.

"I suggest nothing any longer," said Beale, slipping off from the end of the table. "I merely make a statement of fact. I do not think he has any designs on you, within the conventional meaning of that phrase, indeed, I think he wants to marry you—what do you think about that?"

She had recovered something of her poise, and her sense of humour was helping her out of a situation which, without such a gift, might have been an embarrassing one.

"I think you have been seeing too many plays and reading too many exciting books, Mr. Beale," she said. "I confess I have never regarded Doctor van Heerden as a possible suitor, and if I thought he was I should be immensely flattered. But may I suggest to you that there are other ways of winning a girl than by giving her nettle-rash!"

They laughed together.

' All right," he said, swinging up his hat, " proceed with the good work and seek out the various domiciles of Mr. Scobbs."

Then she remembered.

" Do you know—— ? "

He was at the door when she spoke and he stopped and turned.

" The name of Mr. Scobbs gives me a cold shiver."

" Why ? "

" Answer me this," she said : " why should I who have never heard of him before until yesterday hear his name mentioned by a perfect stranger ? "

The smile died away from his face.

" Who mentioned him ! No, it isn't idle curiosity," he said in face of her derisive finger.   " I am really serious. Who mentioned his name ? "

" A visitor of Doctor van Heerden's. I heard them talking through the ventilator when I was bolting my door."

" A visitor to Doctor van Heerden, and he mentioned Mr. Scobbs of Red Horse Valley," he said half to himself. " You didn't see the man ? "

" No."

" You just heard him. No names were mentioned ? "

" None," she said. " Is it a frightfully important matter ? "

" It is rather," he replied.   " We have got to get busy," and with this cryptic remark he left her.

The day passed as quickly as its predecessor. The tabulation at which she was working grew until by the evening there was a pile of sheets in the left-hand cupboard covered with her fine writing. She might have done more but for the search she had to make for a missing report to verify one of her facts. It was not on the shelf, and she was about to abandon her search and postpone the confirmation till she saw Beale, when she noticed a cupboard beneath the shelves. It was unlocked and she opened it and found, as she had expected, that it was full of books, amongst which was the missing documentation she sought.

With a view to future contingencies, she examined the contents of the cupboard and was arrested by a thin volume which bore no inscription or title on its blank cover. She opened it, and on the title page read : " The Millinborn Murder." The author's name was not given and the contents were made up of very careful analysis of evidence given by the various witnesses at the inquest, and plans and diagrams with little red crosses to show where every actor in that tragedy had been.

She read the first page idly and turned it. She was half-way down the second page when she uttered a little exclamation, for a familiar name was there, the name of Dr. van Heerden.

Fascinated, she read the story to the end, half-expecting that the name of Mr. Beale would occur.

There were many names all unknown to her and one that occurred with the greatest frequency was that of James Kitson. Mr. Beale did not appear to have played any part. She read for an hour, sitting on the floor by the cupboard. She reached the last page, closed the book and slipped it back in the cupboard. She wondered why Beale had preserved this record and whether his antagonism to the doctor was founded on that case. At first she thought she identified him with the mysterious man who had appeared in the plantation before the murder, but a glance back at the description of the stranger dispelled that idea. For all the reputation he had, Mr. Beale did not have "an inflamed, swollen countenance, colourless bloodshot eyes," nor was he bald.

She was annoyed with herself that she had allowed her work to be interrupted, and in penance decided to remain on until six instead of five o'clock as she had intended. Besides, she half expected that Mr. Beale would return, and was surprised to discover that she was disappointed that he had not.

At six o'clock she dismissed the boy, closed and locked the office, and made her way downstairs into the crowded street.

To her surprise she heard her name spoken, and turned to face Dr. van Heerden.

"I have been waiting for you for nearly an hour," he said with good-humoured reproach.

"And your patients are probably dying like flies," she countered.

It was in her mind to make some excuse and go home alone, but curiosity got the better of her and impelled her to wait to discover the object of this unexpected visitation.

"How did you know where I was working?" she asked, as the thought occurred to her.

He laughed.

"It was a very simple matter. I was on my way to a patient and I saw you coming out to lunch," he said, "and as I found myself in the neighbourhood an hour ago I thought I would wait and take you home. You are doing a very foolish thing," he added.

"What do you mean—in stopping to talk to you when I ought to be on my way home to tea?"

"No, in engaging yourself to a man like Beale. You know the reputation he has! My dear girl, I was shocked when I discovered who your employer was."

"I don't think you need distress yourself on my account, doctor," she said quietly. "Really, Mr. Beale is quite pleasant—in his lucid moments," she smiled to herself.

She was not being disloyal to her employer. If he chose to encourage suspicion in his mode of life he must abide by the consequences.

"But a drunkard, faugh!" The exquisite doctor shivered. "I have always tried to be a friend of yours, Miss Cresswell, and I hope you are going to let me continue to be, and my advice to you in that capacity is—give Mr. Beale notice."

"How absurd you are!" she laughed. "There is no reason in the world why I should do anything of the sort. Mr. Beale has treated me with the greatest consideration."

"What is he, by the way?" asked the doctor.

"He's an agent of some sort," said the girl, "but I am sure you don't want me to discuss his business. And now I must go, doctor, if you will excuse me."

"One moment," he begged. "I have a cab here. Won't you come and have tea somewhere?"

"Where is somewhere?" she asked.

"The Grand Alliance?" he suggested.

She nodded slowly.

CHAPTER VIII

THE CRIME OF THE GRAND ALLIANCE

THE hotel and the café of the Grand Alliance was London's newest rendezvous. Its great palm-court was crowded at the tea-hour and if, as the mysterious Mr. Beale had hinted, any danger was to be apprehended from Dr. van Heerden, it could not come to her in that most open of public places.

She had no fear, but that eighth sense of armed caution, which is the possession of every girl who has to work for her living and is conscious of the perils which await her on every side, reviewed with lightning speed all the possibilities and gave her the passport of approval.

It was later than she had thought. Only a few tables were occupied, but he had evidently reserved one, for immediately on his appearance the waiter with a smirk led him to one of the alcoves and pulled back a chair for the girl. She looked round as she stripped her gloves. The place was not unfamiliar to her. It was here she came at rare intervals, when her finances admitted of such an hilarious recreation, to find comfort for jangled nerves, to sit and sip her tea to the sound of violins and watch the happy crowd at her leisure, absorbing something of the happiness they diffused.

The palm-court was a spacious marble hall, a big circle of polished pillars supporting the dome, through the tinted glass of which the light was filtered in soft hues upon the marble floor below.

"Doctor," she said, suddenly remembering, "I have been reading quite a lot about you to-day."

He raised his eyebrows.

"About me?"

She nodded, smiling mischievously.

"I didn't know that you were such a famous person —I have been reading about the Millinborn murder."

"You have been reading about the Millinborn murder?" he said steadily, looking into her eyes. "An unpleasant case and one I should like to forget."

"I thought it was awfully thrilling," she said. "It read like a detective story without a satisfactory end."

He laughed.

"What a perfectly gruesome subject for tea-table talk," he said lightly, and beckoned the head-waiter. "You are keeping us waiting, Jaques."

"Doctor, it will be but a few minutes," pleaded the waiter, and then in a low voice, which was not so low that it did not reach the girl. "We have had some trouble this afternoon, doctor, with your friend."

"My friend?"

The doctor looked up sharply.

"Whom do you mean?"

"With Mr. Jackson."

"Jackson," said the doctor, startled. "I thought he had left."

"He was to leave this morning by the ten o'clock train, but he had a fainting-fit. We recovered him with brandy and he was too well, for this afternoon he faint again."

"Where is he now?" asked van Heerden, after a pause.

"In his room, monsieur. To-night he leave for Ireland —this he tell me—to catch the mail steamer at Queenstown."

"Don't let him know I am here," said the doctor. He turned to the girl with a shrug.

"A dissolute friend of mine whom I am sending out to the colonies," he said.

"Won't you go and see him?" she asked. "He must be very ill if he faints."

"I think not," said Dr. van Heerden quietly, "these

little attacks are not serious—he had one in my room the other night. It is a result of over-indulgence, and six months in Canada will make a man of him."

She did not reply. With difficulty she restrained an exclamation. So that was the man who had been in the doctor's room and who was going to Red Horse Valley! She would have dearly loved to supplement her information about Mr. Scobbs, proprietor of many hotels, and to have mystified him with her knowledge of Western Canada, but she refrained.

Instead, she took up the conversation where he had tried to break it off.

" Do you know Mr. Kitson ? "

" Kitson ? Oh yes, you mean the lawyer man," he replied reluctantly. " I know him, but I am afraid I don't know much that is good about him. Now, I'm going to tell you, Miss Cresswell "—he leant across the table and spoke in a lower tone—" something that I have never told to a human being. You raised the question of the Millinborn murder. My view is that Kitson, the lawyer, knew much more about that murder than any man in this world. If there is anybody who knows more it is Beale."

" Mr. Beale ? " she said incredulously.

" Mr. Beale," he repeated. " You know the story of the murder : you say you have read it. Millinborn was dying and I had left the room with Kitson when somebody entered the window and stabbed John Millinborn to the heart. I have every reason to believe that that murder was witnessed by this very man I am sending to Canada. He persists in denying that he saw anything, but later he may change his tune."

A light dawned upon her.

" Then Jackson is the man who was seen by Mr. Kitson in the plantation ? "

" Exactly," said the doctor.

" But I don't understand," she said, perplexed. " Aren't the police searching for Jackson ? "

" I do not think that it is in the interests of justice that they should find him," he said gravely. " I place the utmost reliance on him. I am sending Mr. Jackson to a farm in Ontario kept by a medical friend of mine who has made a hobby of dealing with dipsomaniacs."

He met her eyes unfalteringly.

"Dr. van Heerden," she said slowly, "you are sending Mr. Jackson to Red Horse Valley."

He started back as if he had been struck in the face, and for a moment was inarticulate.

"What—what do you know?" he asked incoherently.

His face had grown white, his eyes tragic with fear. She was alarmed at the effect of her words and hastened to remove the impression she had created.

"I only know that I heard Mr. Jackson through the ventilator of my flat, saying good-bye to you the other night. He mentioned Red Horse Valley——"

He drew a deep breath and was master of himself again, but his face was still pale.

"Oh, that," he said, "that is a polite fiction. Jackson knows of this inebriates' home in Ontario and I had to provide him with a destination. He will go no farther than——"

"Why, curse my life, if it isn't the doctor!"

At the sound of the raucous voice both looked up. The man called Jackson had hailed them from the centre of the hall. He was well dressed, but no tailor could compensate for the repulsiveness of that puckered and swollen face, those malignant eyes which peered out into the world through two slits. He was wearing his loud-check suit, his new hat was in his hand and the conical-shaped dome of his head glistened baldly.

"I'm cursed if this isn't amiable of you, doctor!"

He did not look at the girl, but grinned complacently upon her angry companion.

"Here I am"—he threw out his arms with an extravagant gesture—"leaving the country of my adoption, if not birth, without one solitary soul to see me off or take farewell of me. I, who have been—well, you know, what I've been, van Heerden. The world has treated me very badly. By heaven! I'd like to come back a billionaire and ruin all of 'em. I'd like to cut their throats and amputate 'em limb from limb, I would like——"

"Be silent!" said van Heerden angrily. "Have you no decency? Do you not realize I am with a lady?"

"Pardon." The man called Jackson leapt up from the chair into which he had fallen and bowed extravagantly in the direction of the girl. "I cannot see your face because of your hat, my dear lady," he said gallantly, "but I am sure my friend van Heerden, whose taste——"

"Will you be quiet?" said van Heerden. "Go to your room and I will come up to you."

"Go to my room!" scoffed the other. "By Jove! I like that! That any whipper-snapper of a sawbones should tell me to go to my room. After what I have been, after the position I have held in society. I have had ambassadors' carriages at my door, my dear fellow, princes of the royal blood, and to be told to go to my room like a naughty little boy! It's too much!"

"Then behave yourself," said van Heerden, "and at least wait until I am free before you approach me again."

But the man showed no inclination to move; rather did this rebuff stimulate his power of reminiscence.

"Ignore me, miss—I have not your name, but I am sure it is a noble one," he said. "You see before you one who in his time has been a squire of dames, by Jove! I can't remember 'em. They must number thousands and only one of them was worth two sous. Yes," he shook his head in melancholy, "only one of 'em. By Jove! The rest were"—he snapped his fingers—"that for 'em!"

The girl listened against her will.

"Jackson!"—and van Heerden's voice trembled with passion—"will you go or must I force you to go?"

Jackson rose with a loud laugh.

"Evidently I am *de trop*," he said with heavy sarcasm. He held out a swollen hand which van Heerden ignored.

"Farewell, mademoiselle." He thrust the hand forward, so that she could not miss it.

She took it, a cold flabby thing which sent a shudder of loathing through her frame, and raised her face to his for the first time.

He let the hand drop. He was staring at her with open mouth and features distorted with horror.

" You ! " he croaked.

She shrunk back against the wall of the alcove, but he made no movement. She sensed the terror and agony in his voice.

" You ! " he gasped. " Mary ! "

" Hang you ! Go ! " roared van Heerden, and thrust him back.

But though he staggered back a pace under the weight of the other's arm, his eyes did not leave the girl's face, and she, fascinated by the appeal in the face of the wreck, could not turn hers away.

" Mary ! " he whispered, " what is your other name ? " With an effort the girl recovered herself.

" My name is not Mary," she said quietly. " My name is Oliva Cresswell."

" Oliva Cresswell," he repeated. " Oliva Cresswell ! " He made a movement toward her but van Heerden barred his way. She heard Jackson say something in a strangled voice and heard van Heerden's sharp " What ! " and there was a fierce exchange of words.

The attention of the few people in the palm-court had been attracted to the unusual spectacle of two men engaged in what appeared to be a struggle.

" Sit down, sit down, you fool ! Sit over there. I will come to you in a minute. Can you swear what you say is true ? "

Jackson nodded. He was shaking from head to foot.

" My name is Prédeaux," he said ; " that is my daughter —I married in the name of Cresswell. My daughter," he repeated. " How wonderful ! "

" What are you going to do ? " asked van Heerden.

He had half-led, half-pushed the other to a chair near one of the pillars of the rotunda.

" I am going to tell her," said the wreck. " What are you doing with her ? " he demanded fiercely.

" That is no business of yours," replied van Heerden sharply.

" No business of mine, eh ! I'll show you it's some business of mine. I am going to tell her all I know about you. I have been a rotter and worse than a rotter." The old flippancy had gone and the harsh voice was vibrant with purpose. " My path has been littered with the wrecks of human lives," he said bitterly, " and they are mostly women. I broke the heart of the best woman in the world, and I am going to see that you don't break the heart of her daughter."

" Will you be quiet ? " hissed van Heerden. " I will go and get her away and then I will come back to you."

Jackson did not reply. He sat huddled up in his chair, muttering to himself, and van Heerden walked quickly back to the girl.

" I am afraid I shall have to let you go back by yourself. He is having one of his fits. I think it is delirium tremens."

" Don't you think you had better send for——" she began. She was going to say " send for a doctor," and the absurdity of the request struck her.

" I think you had better go," he said hastily, with a glance at the man who was struggling to his feet. " I can't tell you how sorry I am that we've had this scene."

" Stop ! "—it was Jackson's voice.

He stood swaying half-way between the chair he had left and the alcove, and his trembling finger was pointing at them.

" Stop ! " he said in a commanding voice. " Stop ! I've got something to say to you. I know . . . he's making you pay for the Green Rust. . . ."

So far he got when he reeled and collapsed in a heap on the floor. The doctor sprang forward, lifted him and carried him to the chair by the pillar. He picked up the overcoat that the man had been wearing and spread it over him.

" It's a fainting-fit, nothing to be alarmed about," he said to the little knot of people from the tables who had gathered about the limp figure. " Jaques "—he called the head-waiter—" get some brandy, he must be kept warm."

" Shall I ring for an ambulance, m'sieur ? "

" It is not necessary," said van Heerden. " He will recover in a few moments. Just leave him," and he walked back to the alcove.

"Who is he?" asked the girl, and her voice was shaking in spite of herself.

"He is a man I knew in his better days," said van Heerden, "and now I think you must go."

"I would rather wait to see if he recovers," she said with some obstinacy.

"I want you to go," he said earnestly; "you would please me very much if you would do as I ask."

"There's the waiter!" she interrupted, "he has the brandy. Won't you give it to him?"

It was the doctor who in the presence of the assembled visitors dissolved a white pellet in the brandy before he forced the clenched teeth apart and poured the liquor to the last drop down the man's throat.

Jackson or Prédeaux, to give him his real name, shuddered as he drank, shuddered again a few seconds later and then went suddenly limp.

The doctor bent down and lifted his eyelid.

"I am afraid—he is dead," he said in a low voice.

"Dead!" the girl stared at him. "Oh no! Not dead!"

Van Heerden nodded.

"Heart failure," he said.

"The same kind of heart failure that killed John Millinborn," said a voice behind him. "The cost of the Green Rust is totalling up, doctor."

The girl swung round. Mr. Beale was standing at her elbow, but his steady eyes were fixed upon van Heerden.

CHAPTER IX

A CRIME AGAINST THE WORLD

"WHAT do you mean?" asked Dr. van Heerden. "I merely repeat the words of the dead man," answered Beale, "heart failure!"

He picked up from the table the leather case which

the doctor had taken from his pocket. There were four little phials and one of these was uncorked.

"Digitalis!" he read. "That shouldn't kill him, doctor."

He looked at van Heerden thoughtfully, then picked up the phial again. It bore the label of a well-known firm of wholesale chemists, and the seal had apparently been broken for the first time when van Heerden opened the tiny bottle.

"You have sent for the police?" Beale asked the agitated manager.

"Oui, m'sieur—directly. They come now, I think."

He walked to the vestibule to meet three men in plain clothes who had just come through the swing-doors. There was something about van Heerden's attitude which struck Beale as strange. He was standing in the exact spot he had stood when the detective had addressed him. It seemed as if something rooted him to the spot. He did not move even when the ambulance men were lifting the body nor when the police were taking particulars of the circumstances of the death. And Beale, escorting the shaken girl up the broad staircase to a room where she could rest and recover, looked back over his shoulder and saw him still standing, his head bent, his fingers smoothing his beard.

"It was dreadful, dreadful," said the girl with a shiver. "I have never seen anybody—die. It was awful."

Beale nodded. His thoughts were set on the doctor. Why had he stood so motionless? He was not the kind of man to be shocked by so normal a phenomenon as death. He was a doctor and such sights were common to him. What was the reason for this strange paralysis which kept him chained to the spot even after the body had been removed?

The girl was talking, but he did not hear her. He knew instinctively that in van Heerden's curious attitude was a solution of Prédeaux's death.

"Excuse me a moment," he said.

He passed with rapid strides from the room, down the broad stairway and into the palm-court.

Van Heerden had gone.

The explanation flashed upon him and he hurried to the spot where the doctor had stood.

On the tessellated floor was a little patch no bigger than a saucer which had been recently washed.

He beckoned the manager.

" Who has been cleaning this tile ? " he asked.

The manager shrugged his shoulders.

" It was the doctor, sare—so eccentric ! He call for a glass of water and he dip his handkerchief in and then lift up his foot and with rapidity incredible he wash the floor with his handkerchief ! "

" Fool ! " snapped Beale. " Oh, hopeless fool ! "

" Sare ! " said the startled manager.

" It's all right, M'sieur Barri," smiled Beale ruefully. " I was addressing myself—oh, what a fool I've been ! "

He went down on his knees and examined the floor.

" I want this tile, don't let anybody touch it," he said.

Of course, van Heerden had stood because under his foot he had crushed the digitalis tablet he had taken from the phial, and for which he had substituted something more deadly. Had he moved, the powdered tablet would have been seen. It was simple—horribly simple.

He walked slowly back to where he had left Oliva.

What followed seemed ever after like a bad dream to the girl. She was stunned by the tragedy which had happened under her eyes and could offer no evidence which in any way assisted the police in their subsequent investigation, the sum of which was ably set forth in the columns of the *Post Record*.

" The tragedy which occurred in the Palm-Court of the Grand Alliance Hotel yesterday must be added to the already long list of London's unravelled mysteries. The deceased, a man named Jackson, has been staying at the hotel for a week and was on the point of departure for Canada. At the last moment Dr. van Heerden, who was assisting the unfortunate man, discovered that Jackson was no other than the wanted man in the Millinborn murder, a crime which most of our readers will recall.

"Dr. van Heerden stated to our representative that the man had represented that he was a friend of the late John Millinborn, but was anxious to get to Canada. He had produced excellent credentials, and Dr. van Heerden, in a spirit of generosity, offered to assist him. At the eleventh hour, however, he was struck with the likeness the man bore to the published description of the missing man in the Millinborn case, and was on the point of telegraphing to the authorities at Liverpool, when he discovered that Jackson had missed the train.

"The present tragedy points to suicide. The man, it will be remembered, collapsed, and Dr. van Heerden rendered first aid, administering to the man a perfectly harmless drug. The post-mortem examination reveals the presence in the body of a considerable quantity of cyanide of potassium, and the police theory is that this was self-administered before the collapse. In the man's pocket was discovered a number of cyanide tablets.

" 'I am satisfied,' said Dr. van Heerden, 'that the man already contemplated the deed, and when I voiced my suspicions in the palm-court he decided upon the action. The presence in his pocket of cyanide —one of the deadliest and quickest of poisons— suggests that he had the project in his mind. I did not see his action or, of course, I should have stopped him ! ' "

Oliva Cresswell read this account in her room two nights following the tragedy and was struck by certain curious inaccuracies, if all that the doctor had told her was true.

Mr. Beale read the account, smiled across the table grimly to the bearded superintendent of the Criminal Investigation Department.

"How does that strike you for ingenuity ? " he said, pushing the paper over the table.

"I have read it," said the other laconically, "I think

we have sufficient evidence to arrest van Heerden. The
tile from the Grand Alliance shows traces of digitalis."

Beale shook his head.

"The case would fall," he said. "What evidence
have you ? We did not confiscate his medicine-case.
He might have dropped a tablet of digitalis by accident.
The only evidence you could convict van Heerden on is
proof that he brought with him cyanide tablets which
he slipped into Prédeaux's pocket. No, we can prove
nothing."

"What is your theory in connection with the crime ? "

"I have many theories," said Mr. Beale, rising and
pacing the room, "and one certainty. I am satisfied that
Millinborn was killed by Doctor van Heerden. He was killed
because, during the absence of Mr. Kitson in the village,
the doctor forced from the dying man a secret which up
till then he had jealously preserved. When Kitson returned
he found his friend, as he thought, *in extremis*, and van
Heerden also thought that John Millinborn would not
speak again. To his surprise Millinborn did speak and
van Heerden, fearful of having his villainy exposed, stabbed
him to the heart under the pretext of assisting him to lie
down.

"Something different occurred at the Grand Alliance
Hotel. A man swoons, immediately he is picked up by
the doctor, who gives him a harmless drug—that is to
say, harmless in small quantities. In five seconds the
man is dead. At the inquest we find he has been poisoned
—cyanide is found in his pocket. And who is this man ?
Obviously the identical person who witnessed the murder
of John Millinborn and whom we have been trying to
find ever since that crime."

"Van Heerden won't escape the third time. His
presence will be a little more than a coincidence," said the
superintendent.

Beale laughed.

"There will be no third time," he said shortly, "van
Heerden is not a fool."

"Have you any idea what the secret was that he wanted
to get from old Millinborn ? " asked the detective.

Beale nodded.

"Yes, I know pretty well," he said, "and in course of time you will know, too."

The detective was glancing over the newspaper account.

"I see the jury returned a verdict of 'Suicide whilst of unsound mind!'" he said. "This case ought to injure van Heerden, anyway."

"That is where you are wrong," said Beale, stopping in his stride, "van Heerden has so manœuvred the Pressmen that he comes out with an enhanced reputation. You will probably find articles in the weekly papers written and signed by him, giving his views on the indiscriminate sale of poisons. He will move in a glamour of romance, and his consulting-rooms will be thronged by new admirers."

"It's a rum case," said the superintendent, rising, "and if you don't mind my saying so, Mr. Beale, you're one of the rummiest men that figure in it. I can't quite make you out. You are not a policeman and yet we have orders from the Foreign Office to give you every assistance. What's the game?"

"The biggest game in the world," said Beale promptly, "a game which, if it succeeds, will bring misery and suffering to thousands, and will bring great businesses tumbling, and set you and your children and your children's children working for hundreds of years to pay off a new national debt."

"Man alive!" said the other, "are you serious?"

Beale nodded.

"I was never more serious in my life," he said, "that is why I don't want the police to be too inquisitive in regard to this murder of Jackson, whose real name, as I say, is Prédeaux. I can tell you this, chief, that you are seeing the development of the most damnable plot that has ever been hatched in the brain of the worst miscreant that history knows. Sit down again. Do you know what happened last year?" he asked.

"Last year?" said the superintendent. "Why, the war ended last year."

"The war ended, Germany was beaten, and had to accept terms humiliating for a proud nation, but fortunately

for her Prussia was not proud, she was merely arrogant.
Her worst blow was the impoverishing conditions which
the Entente Powers imposed. That is to say, they
demanded certain concessions of territory and money which,
added to the enormous interest of war stock which the
Germans had to pay, promised to cripple Prussia for a
hundred years."

" Well ? " said the detective, when the other had stopped.

" Well ? " repeated Beale, with a hard little smile.
" Germany is going to get that money back."

" War ? "

Beale laughed.

" No, nothing so foolish as war. Germany has had
all the war she wants. Oh no, there'll be no war. Do
you imagine that we should go to war because I came
to the Foreign Office with a crazy story. I can tell you
this, that officially the German Government have no knowledge of this plot and are quite willing to repudiate those
people who are engaged in it. Indeed, if the truth be
told, the Government has not contributed a single mark
to bring the scheme to fruition, but when it is working all
the money required will be instantly found. At present
the inventor of this delightful little scheme finds himself
with insufficient capital to go ahead. It is his intention
to secure that capital. There are many ways by which
this can be done. He has already borrowed £40,000 from
White, of Punsonby's."

Superintendent McNorton whistled.

" There are other ways," Beale went on, " and he is
at liberty to try them all except one. The day he secures
control of that fortune, that day I shoot him."

" The deuce you will ? " said the startled Mr. McNorton.

" The deuce I will," repeated Beale.

There was a tap at the door and McNorton rose.

" Don't go," said Beale, " I would like to introduce you
to this gentleman."

He opened the door and a grey-haired man with a lean,
ascetic face came in.

Beale closed the door behind him and led the way to
the dining-room.

" Mr. Kitson, I should like you to know Superintendent McNorton."

The two men shook hands.

" Well ? " said Kitson, " our medical friend seems to have got away with it." He sat at the table, nervously drumming with his fingers. " Does the superintendent know everything ? "

" Nearly everything," replied Beale.

" Nearly everything," repeated the superintendent with a smile, " except this great Green Rust business. There I admit I am puzzled."

" Even I know nothing about that," said Kitson, looking curiously at Beale. " I suppose one of these days you will tell us all about it. It is a discovery Mr. Beale happed upon whilst he was engaged in protecting Miss——" He looked at Beale and Beale nodded—" Miss Cresswell," said Kitson.

" The lady who was present at the murder of Jackson ? "

" There is no reason why we should not take you into our confidence, the more so since the necessity for secrecy is rapidly passing. Miss Oliva Cresswell is the niece of John Millinborn. Her mother married a scamp who called himself Cresswell but whose real name was Prédeaux. He first spent every penny she had and then left her and her infant child."

" Prédeaux ! " cried the detective. " Why you told me that was Jackson's real name."

" Jackson, or Prédeaux, was her father," said Kitson, " it was believed that he was dead ; but after John Millinborn's death I set inquiries on foot and discovered that he had been serving a life sentence in Cayenne and had been released when the French President proclaimed a general amnesty at the close of the war. He was evidently on his way to see John Millinborn the day my unhappy friend was murdered, and it was the recognition of his daughter in the palm-court of the Grand Alliance which produced a fainting-fit to which he was subject."

" But how could he recognize the daughter ? Had he seen her before ? "

For answer Kitson took from his pocket a leather folder

and opened it. There were two photographs. One of a
beautiful woman in the fashion of 25 years before ; and one
a snapshot of a girl in a modern costume, whom McNorton
had no difficulty in recognizing as Oliva Cresswell.

" Yes," he said, " they might be the same person."

" That's the mother on the left," explained Kitson,
" the resemblance is remarkable. When Jackson saw
the girl he called her Mary—that was his wife's name.
Millinborn left the whole of his fortune to Miss Cresswell,
but he placed upon me a solemn charge that she was
not to benefit or to know of her inheritance until she was
married. He had a horror of fortune-hunters. This was
the secret which van Heerden surprised—I fear with
violence—from poor John as he lay dying. Since then he
has been plotting to marry the girl. To do him justice,
I believe that the cold-blooded hound has no other wish
than to secure her money. His acquaintance with White,
who is on the verge of ruin, enabled him to get to know
the girl. He persuaded her to come here and a flat was
found for her. Partly," said the lawyer dryly, " because
this block of flats happens to be her own property and
the lady who is supposed to be the landlady is a nominee
of mine."

" And I suppose that explains Mr. Beale," smiled the
inspector.

" That explains Mr. Beale," said Kitson, " whom I
brought from New York especially to shadow van Heerden
and to protect the girl. In the course of investigations
Mr. Beale has made another discovery, the particulars of
which I do not know."

There was a little pause.

" Why not tell the girl ? " said the superintendent.

Kitson shook his head.

" I have thought it out, and to tell the girl would be
tantamount to breaking my faith with John Millinborn.
No, I must simply shepherd her. The first step we must
take "—he turned to Beale—" is to get her away from
this place. Can't you shift your offices to—say New
York ? "

Beale shook his head.

"I can and I can't," he said. "If you will forgive my saying so, the matter of the Green Rust is of infinitely greater importance than Miss Cresswell's safety."

James Kitson frowned.

"I don't like to hear you say that, Beale."

"I don't like hearing myself say it," confessed the other, "but let me put it this way. I believe by staying here I can afford her greater protection and at the same time put a spoke in the wheel of Mr. van Heerden's larger scheme."

Kitson pinched his lips thoughtfully.

"Perhaps you are right," he said. "Now I want to see this young lady, that is why I have come. I suppose there will be no difficulty?"

"None at all, I think," said Beale. "I will tell her that you are interested in the work she is doing. I might introduce you as Mr. Scobbs," he smiled.

"Who is Scobbs?"

"He is a proprietor of a series of hotels in Western Canada, and is, I should imagine, a most praiseworthy and inoffensive captain of minor industry, but Miss Cresswell is rather interested in him," he laughed. "She found the name occurring in Canadian guide-books and was struck by its quaintness."

"Scobbs," said the lawyer slowly. "I seem to know that name."

"You had better know it if I am going to introduce you as Scobbs himself," laughed Beale.

"Shall I be in the way?" asked the superintendent.

"No, please stay," said Beale. "I would like you to see this lady. We may want your official assistance one of these days to get her out of a scrape."

Mr. Beale passed out of the flat and pressed the bell of the door next to his. There was no response. He pressed it again after an interval, and stepped back to look at the fanlight. No light showed and he took out his watch. It was nine o'clock. He had not seen the girl all day, having been present at the inquest, but he had heard her door close two hours before. No reply came to his second ring, and he went back to his flat.

"She's out," he said. "I don't quite understand it.
I particularly requested her yesterday not to go out after
dark for a day or two."

He walked into his bedroom and opened the window.
The light of day was still in the sky, but he took a small
electric lamp to guide him along the narrow steel balcony
which connected all the flats with the fire-escape. He
found her window closed and bolted, but with the skill
of a professional burglar he unfastened the catch and
stepped inside.

The room was in darkness. He switched on the light
and glanced round. It was Oliva's bedroom, and her
workday hat and coat were lying on the bed. He opened
the long cupboard where she kept her limited wardrobe.
He knew, because it was his business to know, every dress
she possessed. They were all there as, also, were the three
hats which she kept on a shelf. All the drawers of the
bureau were closed and there was no sign of any disorder
such as might be expected if she had changed and gone
out. He opened the door of the bedroom and walked into
the sitting-room, lighting his way across to the electric
switch by means of his lamp.

The moment the light flooded the room he realized that
something was wrong. There was no disorder, but the
room conveyed in some indescribable manner a suggestion
of violence. An object on the floor attracted his attention and he stooped and picked it up. It was a shoe, and
the strap which had held it in place was broken. He
looked at it, slipped it in his pocket and passed rapidly
through the other rooms to the little kitchen and the tiny
bath-room, put on the light in the hall and made a careful
scrutiny of the walls and the floor.

The mat was twisted out of its place, and on the left
side of the wall there were two long scratches. There
was a faint sickly odour.

"Ether," he noted mentally.

He went quickly into the dining-room. The little
bureau-desk was open and a letter half-finished was lying
on the pad, and it was addressed to him and ran :

" DEAR MR. BEALE,—
    Circumstances beyond my control make it necessary
for me to leave to-night for Liverpool."

That was all. It was obviously half finished. He
picked it up, folded it carefully and slipped it in his pocket.
Then he returned to the hall, opened the door and passed
out.

He explained briefly what had happened and crossed
to the doctor's flat, and rang the bell.

CHAPTER X

A FRUITLESS SEARCH

A LIGHT glowed in the hall, the door was opened
and the doctor, in slippers and velvet coat, stood
in the entrance. He showed no resentment nor did he
have time to show it.

" I want a word with you," said Beale.

" Twenty if you wish," said the doctor cheerfully.
" Won't you come in ? "

Beale was half-way in before the invitation was issued
and followed the doctor to his study.

" Are you alone ? " he asked.

" Quite alone. I have very few visitors. In fact, my
last visitor was that unhappy man Jackson."

" When did you see Miss Cresswell last ? "

The doctor raised his eyebrows.

" By what right—— ? " he began.

" Cut all that out," said Beale roughly. " When did
you see Miss Cresswell last ? "

" I have not seen her to-day," said the doctor. " I
have not been out of my flat since I came back from the
inquest."

" I should like to search your flat," said Beale.

"Policeman, eh?" smiled the doctor. "Certainly you can search the flat if you have a warrant."

"I have no warrant, but I shall search your flat."

The doctor's face went dull red.

"I suppose you know you are liable to an action for trespass?"

"I know all about that," said Beale, "but if you have nothing to conceal, Dr. van Heerden, I don't see why you should object."

"I don't object," shrugged the doctor, "search by all means. Where would you like to start? Here?"

He pointed to three upright cases which stood at the end of the room nearest the door.

"You will see nothing very pleasant here, they are anatomical models which have just arrived from Berlin. In fact, I have been trading with the enemy," he smiled. "They are screwed up, but I have a screwdriver here."

Beale hesitated.

"There is only another room," the doctor went on, "my bedroom, but you will not find her there."

Beale twisted round like lightning.

"Her?" he asked. "Who said Her?"

"I gather you are looking for Miss Cresswell," said the doctor coolly. "You are searching for something, and you ask me when I saw her last. Who else could you be looking for?"

"Quite right," he said quietly.

"Let me show you the way." The doctor walked ahead and turned on the light in the inner bedroom.

It was a large apartment, simply furnished with a small steel bed, a hanging wardrobe and a dressing-chest. Beyond that was his bath-room.

Beale was making a casual survey of this when he heard the door of the bedroom click behind him. He turned round, jumped for the door, turned the handle and pulled, but it did not yield. As he did so he thought he heard a mutter of voices.

"Open the door!" he cried, hammering on the panel.

There was no answer. Then:

"Mr. Beale!"

His blood froze at the wild appeal in the tone, for it was the voice of Oliva Cresswell, and it came from the room he had quitted.

He smashed at the panel but it was made of tough oak. His revolver was in his hand and the muzzle was against the lock when the handle turned and the door opened.

" Did you lock yourself in ? " smiled the doctor, looking blandly at the other's pale face.

" Where is the girl, where is Miss Cresswell ? " he demanded. " I heard her voice."

" You are mad, my friend."

" Where is Miss Cresswell ? "

His hand dropped on the other's shoulder and gripped it with a force that made the other shrink. With an oath the doctor flung him off.

" Hang you, you madman ! How should I know ? "

" I heard her voice."

" It was imagination," said the doctor. " I would have opened the door to you before but I had walked out into the passage and had rung Miss Cresswell's bell. I found the door open. I suppose you had been in. I just shut the door and came back here."

Without a word Beale thrust him aside. He had taken one step to the door when he stopped : At the end of the room had been the three long anatomical cases. Now there were only two. One had gone. He did not stop to question the man. He bounded through the door and raced down the stairs. There was no vehicle in sight and only a few pedestrians. At the corner of the street he found a policeman who had witnessed nothing unusual and had not seen any conveyance carrying a box.

As he returned slowly to the entrance of Krooman Mansions something made him look up. The doctor was leaning out of the window smoking a cigar.

" Found her ? " he asked mockingly.

Beale made no reply. He came up the stairs, walked straight through the open door of the doctor's flat and confronted that calm man as he leant against the table, his hands gripping the edge, a cigar in the corner of his mouth and a smile of quiet amusement on his bearded lips.

"Well?" he asked, "did you find her?"

"I did not find her, but I am satisfied that *you* will."

Van Heerden's eyes did not falter.

"I am beginning to think, Mr. Beale, that over-indulgence in alcoholic stimulants has turned your brain," he said mockingly. "You come into my apartment and demand, with an heroic gesture, where I am concealing a beautiful young lady, in whose welfare I am at least as much interested as you, since that lady is my fiancée and is going to be my wife."

There was a pause.

"She is going to be your wife, is she?" said Beale softly. "I congratulate you if I cannot congratulate her. And when is this interesting engagement to be announced?"

"It is announced at this moment," said the doctor. "The lady is on her way to Liverpool, where she will stay with an aunt of mine. You need not trouble to ask me for her address, because I shall not give it to you."

"I see," said Beale.

"You come in here, I repeat, demanding with all the gesture and voice of melodrama, the hiding-place of my fiancée,"—he enunciated the two last words with great relish—"you ask to search my rooms and I give you permission. You lock yourself in through your own carelessness and when I release you you have a revolver in your hand, and are even more melodramatic than ever. I know what you are going to say——"

"You are a clever man," interrupted Beale, "for I don't know myself."

"You were going to say, or you think, that I have some sinister purpose in concealing this lady. Well, to resume my narrative, and to show you your conduct from my point of view, I no sooner release you than you stare like a lunatic at my anatomical cases and dash wildly out, to return full of menace in your tone and attitude. Why?"

"Doctor van Heerden, when I came into your flat there were three anatomical cases at the end of that room.

When I came out there were two. What happened to the third whilst I was locked in the room ? "

Doctor van Heerden shook his head pityingly.

" I am afraid, I am very much afraid, that you are not right in your head," he said, and nodded toward the place where the cases stood.

Beale followed the direction of his head and gasped, for there were three cases.

" I admit that I deceived you when I said they contained specimens. As a matter of fact, they are empty," said the doctor. " If you like to inspect them, you can. You may find some—clue ! "

Beale wanted no invitation. He walked to the cases one by one and sounded them. Their lids were screwed on but the screws were dummies. He found in the side of each a minute hole under the cover of the lid and, taking out his knife, he pressed in the bodkin with which the knife was equipped and with a click the lid flew open. The box was empty. The second one answered the same test and was also empty. The third gave no better result. He flashed his lamp on the bottom of the box, but there was no trace of footmarks.

" Are you satisfied ? " asked the doctor.

" Far from satisfied," said Beale, and with no other word he walked out and down the stairs again.

Half-way down he saw something lying on one of the stairs and picked it up. It was a shoe, the fellow of that which he had in his pocket, and it had not been there when he came up.

*   *   *   *   *

Oliva Cresswell had read the story of the crime in the *Post Record*, had folded up the paper with a little shiver and was at her tiny writing-bureau when a knock came at the door. It was Dr. van Heerden.

" Can I come in for a moment ? " he asked.

She hesitated.

" I shan't eat you," he smiled, " but I am so distressed by what has happened and I feel that an explanation is due to you."

"I shouldn't trouble about that," she smiled, "but if you want to come in, please do."

She closed the door behind him and left the light burning in the hall. She did not ask him to sit down.

"You have seen the account in the *Post Record*?" he asked.

She nodded.

"And I suppose you are rather struck with the discrepancy between what I told you and what I told the reporters, but I feel you ought to know that I had a very special reason for protecting this man."

"Of that I have no doubt," she said coldly.

"Miss Cresswell, you must be patient and kind to me," he said earnestly. "I have devoted a great deal of time and I have run very considerable dangers in order to save you."

"To save me?" she repeated in surprise.

"Miss Cresswell," he asked, "did you ever know your father?"

She shook her head, so impressed by the gravity of his tone that she did not cut the conversation short as she had intended.

"No," she said, "I was a girl when he died. I know nothing of him. Even his own people who brought him up never spoke of him."

"Are you sure he is dead?" he asked.

"Sure? I have never doubted it. Why do you ask me? Is he alive?"

He nodded.

"What I am going to tell you will be rather painful," he said: "your father was a notorious swindler." He paused, but she did not protest.

In her life she had heard many hints which did not redound to her father's credit, and she had purposely refrained from pursuing her inquiries.

"Some time ago your father escaped from Cayenne. He is, you will be surprised to know, a French subject, and the police have been searching for him for twelve months, including our friend Mr. Beale."

"It isn't true," she flamed. "How dare you suggest—— ?"

"I am merely telling you the facts, Miss Cresswell, and you must judge them for yourself," said the doctor. "Your father robbed a bank in France and hid the money in England. Because they knew that sooner or later he would send for you the police have been watching you day and night. Your father is at Liverpool. I had a letter from him this morning. He is dying and he begs you to go to him."

She sat at the table, stunned. There was in this story a hideous probability. Her first inclination was to consult Beale, but instantly she saw that if what the doctor had said was true such a course would be fatal.

"How do I know you are speaking the truth?" she asked.

"You cannot know until you have seen your father," he said. "It is a very simple matter."

He took from his pocket an envelope and laid it before her.

"Here is the address—64 Hope Street. I advise you to commit it to memory and tear it up. After all, what possible interest could I have in your going to Liverpool, or anywhere else for the matter of that?"

"When is the next train?" she asked.

"One leaves in an hour from Euston."

She thought a moment.

"I'll go," she said decidedly.

She was walking back to her room to put on her coat when he called her back.

"There's no reason in the world why you should not write to Beale to tell him where you have gone," he said. "You can leave a note with me and I will deliver it."

She hesitated again, sat down at her desk and scribbled the few lines which Beale had found. Then she twisted round in her chair in perplexity.

"I don't understand it all," she said. "If Mr. Beale is on the track of my father, surely he will understand from this letter that I have gone to meet him."

"Let me see what you have written," said van Heerden coolly, and looked over her shoulder. "Yes, that's enough," he said.

" Enough ? "

" Quite enough. You see, my idea was that you should write sufficient to put him off the track."

" I don't understand you—there's somebody in the passage," she said suddenly, and was walking to the door leading to the hall when he intercepted her.

" Miss Cresswell, I think you will understand me when I tell you that your father is dead, that the story I have told you about Beale being on his track is quite untrue, and that it is necessary for a purpose which I will not disclose to you that you should be my wife."

She sprang back out of his reach, white as death. Instinctively she realized that she was in some terrible danger, and the knowledge turned her cold.

" Your wife ? " she repeated. " I think you must be mad, doctor."

" On the contrary, I am perfectly sane. I would have asked you before, but I knew that you would refuse me. Had our friend Beale not interfered, the course of true love might have run a little more smoothly than it has. Now I am going to speak plainly to you, Miss Cresswell. It is necessary that I should marry you, and if you agree I shall take you away and place you in safe keeping. I will marry you at the registrar's office and part from you the moment the ceremony is completed. I will agree to allow you a thousand a year and I will promise that I will not interfere with you or in any way seek your society."

Her courage had revived during this recital of her future.

" What do you expect me to do," she asked contemptuously—" fall on your neck and thank you, you with your thousand a year and your church-door partings ? No, doctor, if you are sane then you are either a great fool or a great scoundrel. I would never dream of marrying you under any circumstances. And now I think you had better go."

This time he did not stop her as she walked to the door and flung it open. She started back with an exclamation of fear, for there were two men in the hall.

" What do you——"

So far she got when the doctor's arm was round her

and his hand was pressed against her mouth. One of the men was carrying what looked like a rubber bottle with a conical-shaped mouthpiece. She struggled, but the doctor held her in a grip of steel. She was thrown to the ground, the rubber cap of the bottle was pressed over her face, there came a rush of cold air heavily charged with a sickly scent, and she felt life slipping away. . . .

" I think she's off now," said the doctor, lifting up her eyelid, " see if the coast is clear, Gregory, and open the door of my flat."

The man departed. The doctor lifted the unconscious girl in his arms. He was in the hall when he felt her move. Half-conscious as she was, she was struggling to prevent the abduction.

" Quick, the door ! " he gasped.

He carried her across the landing into his room, and the door closed quietly behind him.

CHAPTER XI

THE HOUSE NEAR STAINES

OLIVA CRESSWELL remembered nothing. She did not remember being thrust limply into a long narrow box, nor hearing Beale's voice, nor the click of the door that fastened him in Dr. van Heerden's bedroom. If she cried out, as she did, she had no recollection of the fact.

" Carry her, box and all, to her flat. The door is open," whispered van Heerden to the two men who had made their lightning disappearance into the anatomical cases at the sound of Beale's knock.

" What shall we do ? "

" Wait till I come to you. Hurry ! "

They crossed the landing and passed through the open door of Oliva's flat and the doctor closed the door be-

hind them and returned in time to release the savage
Beale.

He watched him racing down the stairs, darted to the
door of Oliva's rooms, opened it and went in. In ten
seconds she had been lifted from her narrow prison and
laid on her bed, the box had been returned to the place
where it had stood in the doctor's study and the men
had returned to join van Heerden in Oliva's darkened
sitting-room.

Van Heerden had switched on the light in the girl's
room and then noticed for the first time that one of her
shoes was missing. Quickly he slipped off the remaining
shoe.

"You wait here," he told the men, "until you hear
Beale return. Then make your escape. On your way
down leave the shoe on the stairs. It will help to put
our friend off the trail."

Half an hour after the discovery of the shoe on the
stairs Beale went out accompanied by his visitors.

The doctor watched the dark figures disappear into the
night from the window of his sitting-room and made his
way back to the girl's flat. She was lying where he had
left her, feeling dizzy and sick. Her eyes closed in a little
grimace of distaste as he put on the light.

"How does my little friend feel now?" he asked coolly.

She made no reply.

"Really, you must not sulk," he said chidingly, "and
you must get used to being polite because you are going
to see a great deal of me. You had better get up and put
your coat on."

She noticed that he had a medicine glass in his hand,
half-filled with a milky-white liquor.

"Drink this," he said.

She pushed it away.

"Come, drink it," he said, "you don't suppose I want
to poison you, do you? I don't even want to drug you,
otherwise it would have been simple to have given you
a little more ether. Drink it. It will take that hazy
feeling out of your head."

She took the glass with an unsteady hand and swallowed

its contents. It was bitter and hot and burnt her throat, but its effects were magical. In three minutes her mind had cleared and when she sat up she could do so without her head swimming.

" You will now put on your coat and hat, pack a few things that you want for a journey, and come along with me."

" I shall do nothing of the sort," she said, " I advise you to go, Dr. van Heerden, before I inform the police of your outrageous conduct."

" Put on your hat and coat," he repeated calmly, " and don't talk nonsense. You don't suppose that I have risked all that I have risked to let you go at this hour."

" Dr. van Heerden," she said, " if you have any spark of decency or manhood you will leave me."

He laughed a little.

" Now you are talking like a heroine of Lyceum drama," he said. " Any appeal you might make, Miss Cresswell, is a waste of time and a waste of breath. I shall have no hesitation in using violence of the most unpleasant character unless you do as I tell you."

His voice was quiet, but there was about him a convincing air of purpose.

" Where are you going to take me ? " she asked.

" I am going to take you to a place of safety. When I say safety," he added, " I mean safety for me. You yourself need fear nothing unless you act foolishly, in which case you have everything to fear. Disabuse your mind of one thought, Miss Cresswell," he said, " and that is that I am in love with you and that there is any quality or charm in your admirable person which would prevent my cutting your throat if it was necessary for my safety. I am not a brute. I will treat you decently, as well as any lady could wish to be treated, if you do not cross me, but I warn you that if in the street you call for help or attempt to escape you will never know what happened to you."

She stood at the end of her bed, one hand gripping the rail, her white teeth showing against the red lower lip.

" Don't bite your lips, it does not stimulate thought,

I can tell you that as a medical man, and I can also tell you that this is not the moment for you to consider plans for outwitting me. Get your coat and hat on."

His voice was now peremptory, and she obeyed. In a few minutes she was dressed ready for the street. He led the way out and holding her arm lightly they passed out into the street. He turned sharply to the left, the girl keeping in step by his side. To the casual observer, and few could observe them in the gloom of the ill-lit thoroughfares through which they passed, they were a couple on affectionate terms, but the arm locked in hers was the arm of a gaoler, and once when they stood waiting to cross busy Oxford Circus, and she had seen a policeman a few yards away and had cautiously tried to slip her arm from his, she found her wrist gripped with a hand of steel.

At the Marylebone Road end of Portland Place a car was waiting and the doctor opened the door and pushed her in, following immediately.

"I had to keep the car some distance from Krooman Mansions or Beale would have spotted it immediately," he said in an easy conversational tone.

"Where are you taking me?" she asked.

"To a highly desirable residence in the Thames Valley," he said, "in the days when I thought you might be wooed and wed, as the saying goes, I thought it might make an excellent place for a honeymoon." He felt her shrink from him.

"Please don't be distressed, I am rather glad that matters have turned out as they have. I do not like women very much, and I should have been inexpressibly bored if I had to keep up the fiction of being in love with you."

"What do you intend doing?" she asked. "You cannot hope to escape from Mr. Beale. He will find me."

He chuckled.

"As a sleuth-hound, Mr. Beale has his points," he said, "but they are not points which keep me awake at night. I have always suspected he was a detective, and, of course, it was he who planted the registered envelopes on poor old White—that was clever," he admitted handsomely, "but

Beale, if you will excuse my hurting your feelings—and
I know you are half in love with him——"

She felt her face go hot.

"How dare you!" she flamed.

"Don't be silly," he begged. "I dare anything in
these circumstances, the greater outrage includes the
less. If I abdicate you I feel myself entitled to tease
you. No, I think you had better not place too much
faith in Mr. Beale, who doesn't seem to be a member of
the regular police force, and is, I presume, one of those
amateur gentlemen who figure in divorce cases."

She did not reply. Inwardly she was boiling, and she
recognized with a little feeling of dismay that it was not
so much the indignity which he was offering her, as his
undisguised contempt for the genius of Beale, which
enraged her.

They had left the town and were spinning through the
country when she spoke again.

"Will you be kind enough to tell me what you intend
doing?"

He had fallen into a reverie and it was evidently a
pleasant reverie, for he came back to the realities of life
with an air of reluctance.

"Eh? Oh, what am I going to do with you? Why,
I am going to marry you."

"Suppose I refuse?"

"You won't refuse. I am offering you the easiest way
out. When you are married to me your danger is at an
end. Until you marry me your hold on life is somewhat
precarious."

"But why do you insist upon this?" she asked, bewildered. "If you don't love me, what is there in marriage
for you? There are plenty of women who would be
delighted to have you. Why should you want to marry
a girl without any influence or position—a shop-girl, absolutely penniless?"

"It's a whim of mine," he said lightly, "and it's a whim
I mean to gratify."

"Suppose I refuse at the last moment?"

"Then," he said significantly, "you will be sorry.

I tell you, no harm is coming to you if you are sensible.
If you are not sensible, imagine the worst that can happen
to you, and that will be the least. I will treat you so
that you will not think of your experience, let alone talk
of it."

There was a cold malignity in his voice that made her
shudder. For a moment, and a moment only, she was
beaten down by the horrible hopelessness of her situation,
then her natural courage, her indomitable, self-reliance
overcame fear. If he expected an outburst of anger and
incoherent reproach, or if he expected her to break down
into hysterical supplication, he was disappointed. She
had a firm grip upon herself, perfect command of voice
and words.

"I suppose you are one of those clever criminals one
reads about," she said, "prepared for all emergencies,
perfectly self-confident, capable and satisfied that there is
nobody quite so clever as themselves."

"Very likely," he smiled. "It is a form of egotism,"
he said quietly. "I read a book once about criminals.
It was written by an Italian and he said that was the chief
characteristic of them all."

"Vanity? And they always do such clever things and
such stupid things at the same time, and their beautiful
plans are so full of absurd miscalculations, just as yours
are."

"Just as mine are," he said mockingly.

"Just as yours are," she repeated; "you are so satisfied
that because you are educated and you are a scientist,
that you are ever so much more clever than all the rest
of the world."

"Go on," he said. "I like to hear you talking. Your
analysis is nearly perfect and certainly there is a lot of truth
in what you say."

She held down the surging anger which almost choked
her and retained a calm level. Sooner or later she would
find the joint in his harness.

"I suppose you have everything ready?"

"My staff work is always good," he murmured, "marriage licence, parson, even the place where you will

spend your solitary honeymoon after signing a few documents."

She turned toward him slowly. Against the window of the big limousine his head was faintly outlined and she imagined the smile which was on his face at that moment.

" So that is it ! " she said. " I must sign a few documents saying that I married you of my own free will ! "

" No, madam," he said, " the circumstances under which you marry me require no justification and that doesn't worry me in the slightest."

" What documents have I to sign ? " she asked.

" You will discover in time," said he. " Here is the house, unless my eyesight has gone wrong."

The car turned from the road, seemed to plunge into a high hedge, though in reality, as the girl saw for a second as the lamps caught the stone gate-posts, it was the entrance to a drive, and presently came to a stop before a big rambling house. Van Heerden jumped down and assisted her to alight. The house was in darkness, but as they reached the door it was opened.

" Go in," said van Heerden, and pushed her ahead.

She found herself in an old-fashioned hall, the walls panelled of oak, the floor made of closely mortised stone flags. She recognized the man who had admitted them as one of those she had seen in her flat that same night. He was a cadaverous man with high cheekbones and short, bristly black hair and a tiny black moustache.

" I won't introduce you," said the doctor, " but you may call this man Gregory. It is not his name, but it is good enough."

The man smiled furtively and eyed her furtively, took up the candle and led the way to a room which opened off the hall at the farther end.

" This is the dining-room," said van Heerden. " It is chiefly interesting to you as the place where the ceremony will be performed. Your room is immediately above. I am sorry I did not engage a maid for you, but I cannot afford to observe the proprieties or consider your reputation. The fact is, I know no woman I could trust to perform that duty, and you will have to look after yourself."

He led the way upstairs, unlocked a door and passed in. There was one window which was heavily curtained. He saw her glance and nodded.

"You will find the windows barred," he said. "This was evidently the nursery and is admirably suited to my purpose. In addition, I might tell you that the house is a very old one and that it is impossible to walk about the room without the door creaking and, as I spend most of my time in the dining-room below, you will find it extremely difficult even to make preparations for escape without my being aware of the fact."

The room was comfortably furnished. A small fire was alight in the tiny grate and a table had been laid, on which were displayed sandwiches, a thermos flask and a small silver basket of confectionery.

There was a door by the big four-poster bed.

"You may consider yourself fortunate in having the only room in the house with a bath-room attached," he said. "You English people are rather particular about that kind of thing."

"And you German people aren't," she said coolly.

"German?" he laughed. "So you guessed that, did you?"

"Guessed it?"—it was her turn to laugh scornfully. "Isn't the fact self-evident? Who but a Hun——"

His face went a dull red.

"That is a word you must not use to me," he said roughly—"hang your arrogance! Huns! We, who gave the world its kultur, who lead in every department of science, art and literature!"

She stared at him in amazement.

"You are joking, of course," she said, forgetting her danger for the moment in face of this extraordinary phenomenon. "If you are a German, and I suppose you are, and an educated German at that, you don't for a moment imagine you gave the world anything. Why, the Germans have never been anything but exploiters of other men's brains."

From dull red, his face had gone white, his lip was trembling with passion and when he spoke he could scarcely control his voice.

"We were of all people ordained by God to save the world through the German spirit."

So far he got when she burst into a fit of uncontrollable laughter. It was so like all the caricatures of German character she had read or seen depicted. He looked at her, his face distorted with rage, and before she had realized what had happened he had raised his hand and struck her across the mouth.

She staggered back, speechless. To her had happened the most incredible thing in the world, more incredible than her abduction, more incredible than all the villainies known or suspected, in this man.

He stood there glowering at her, unrepentant, half-tempted, it seemed, to repeat the blow. He had struck a woman and was not overwhelmed by shame. All her views of men and things, all her conceptions of the codes which govern mankind in their dealings one with the other, crumbled away. If he had fallen on his knees and asked her pardon, if he had shown any contrition, any fear, any shame, she might have gone back to her old standards.

"You swine cat!" he said in German, "Herr Gott, but I will punish you if you laugh at me!"

She was staring at him in intense curiosity. Her lip was bleeding a little, the red mark of his fingers showed against her white face, but she seemed to have forgotten the pain or the shock of the actual blow and was wholly concerned in this new revelation.

"A Hun," she said, but she seemed to be speaking to herself, "of course he's a Hun. They do that sort of thing, but I never believed it before."

He took a step toward her, but she did not flinch, and he turned and walked quickly from the room, locking the door behind him.

CHAPTER XII

INTRODUCING PARSON HOMO

WHEN Beale left Krooman Mansions with his two companions he had only the haziest idea as to where he should begin his search. Perhaps the personal interest he had in his client, an interest revealed by the momentary panic into which her disappearance had thrown this usually collected young man, clouded his better judgment.

A vague discomfort possessed him and he paused irresolutely at the corner of the street. There was a chance that she might still be concealed in the building, but a greater chance that if he followed one of the three plans which were rapidly forming in his mind he might save the girl from whatever danger threatened her.

" You are perfectly sure you heard her voice ? "

" Certain," replied Beale shortly, " just as I am sure that I smelt the ether."

" She may have been using it for some other purpose. Women put these drugs to all sorts of weird purposes, like cleaning gloves, and——"

" That may be," interrupted Beale, " but I wasn't mistaken about her voice. I am not subject to illusions of that kind."

He whistled. A man who had been lurking in the shadow of a building on the opposite side of the road crossed to him.

" Fenson," said Beale, " watch these flats. If you see a car drive up just go along and stand in front of the door. Don't let anybody enter that car or carry any bundle into that car until you are sure that Miss Cresswell is not one of the party or the bundle. If necessary you can pull a gun—I know it isn't done in law-abiding London," he smiled at Superintendent McNorton, " but I guess you've got to let me do a little law-breaking."

" Go all the way," said the superintendent easily.

" That will do, Fenson. You know Miss Cresswell ? "

"Sure, sir," said the man, and melted back into the shadows.

"Where are you going now?" asked Kitson.

"I am going to interview a gentleman who will probably give me a great deal of information about van Heerden's other residences."

"Has he many?" asked Kitson, in surprise.

Beale nodded.

"He has been hiring buildings and houses for the past three months," he said quietly, "and he has been so clever that I will defy you to trace one of them. All his hiring has been done through various lawyers he has employed, and they are all taken in fictitious names."

"Do you know any of them?"

"Not one," said Beale, with a baffled little laugh, "didn't I tell you he's mighty clever? I got track of two of them but they were the only two where the sale didn't go through."

"What does he want houses for?"

"We shall learn one of these days," said Beale cryptically. "I can tell you something else, gentlemen, and this is more of a suspicion than a certainty, that there is not a crank scientist who has ever gone under through drink or crime in the whole of this country, aye, and America and France, too, that isn't working for him. And now, gentlemen, if you will excuse me——"

"You don't want any assistance?" asked the superintendent.

"I guess not," said Beale, with a smile, "I guess I can manage the Herr Professor."

*　　*　　*　　*　　*

On the south side of the River Thames is a congested and thickly populated area lying between the Waterloo and the Blackfriars Roads. Here old houses, which are gauntly picturesque because of their age, stand cheek-by-jowl with great blocks of model dwellings, which make up in utility all that they lack in beauty. Such dwelling-places have a double advantage. Their rent is low and they are close to the centre of London. Few of the houses

are occupied by one family, and indeed it is the exception
that one family rents in its entirety so much as a
floor.

In a basement room in one of those houses sat two
men as unlike one another as it is possible to conceive.
The room itself was strangely tidy and bare of anything
but the necessary furniture. A camp bed was under the
window in such a position as to give its occupant a view of
the ankles of those people who trod the pavement of the
little street.

A faded cretonne curtain hid an inner and probably
a smaller room where the elder of the men slept. They
sat on either side of a table, a kerosene lamp placed exactly
in the centre supplying light for their various occupations.

The elder of the two was bent forward over a microscope,
his big hands adjusting the focus screw. Presently he
would break off his work of observation and jot down a
few notes in crabbed German characters. His big head,
his squat body, his long ungainly arms, his pale face with
its little wisp of beard, would have been recognized by
Oliva Cresswell, for this was Professor Heyler—" the
Herr Professor," as Beale called him.

The man sitting opposite was cast in a different mould.
He was tall, spare, almost æsthetic. The clean-shaven
face, the well-moulded nose and chin hinted at a refine-
ment which his shabby threadbare suit and his collarless
shirt freakishly accentuated. Now and again he would
raise his deep-set eyes from the book he was reading, survey
the absorbed professor with a speculative glance and then
return to his reading.

They had sat in silence for the greater part of an hour,
when Beale's tap on the door brought the reader round
with narrow eyes.

" Expecting a visitor, professor ? " he asked in German.

" Nein, nein," rambled the old man, " who shall visit
me ? Ah yes "—he tapped his fat forefinger—" I remember, the Fraulein was to call."

He got up and, shuffling to the door, slipped back the
bolt and turned it. His face fell when he saw Beale, and
the man at the table rose.

"Hope I am not disturbing you," said the detective. "I thought you lived alone."

He, too, spoke in the language which the professor understood best.

"That is a friend of mine," said old Heyler uncomfortably, "we live together. I did not think you knew my address."

"Introduce me," said the man at the table coolly.

The old professor looked dubiously from one to the other.

"It is my friend, Herr Homo."

"Herr Homo," repeated Beale, offering his hand, "my name is Beale."

Homo shot a keen glance at him.

"A split! or my criminal instincts fail me," he said, pleasantly enough.

"Split?" repeated Beale, puzzled.

"American I gather from your accent," said Mr. Homo; "pray sit down. 'Split' is the phrase employed by the criminal classes to describe a gentleman who in your country is known as a 'fly cop'!"

"Oh, a detective," smiled Beale. "No, in the sense you mean I am not a detective. At any rate, I have not come on business."

"So I gather," said the other, seating himself, "or you would have brought one of the 'busy fellows' with you. Here again you must pardon the slang but we call the detective the 'busy fellow' to distinguish him from the 'flattie,' who is the regular cop. Unless you should be under any misapprehension, Mr. Beale, it is my duty to tell you that I am a representative of the criminal classes, a fact which our learned friend," he nodded toward the distressed professor, "never ceases to deplore," and he smiled blandly.

They had dropped into English and the professor after waiting uncomfortably for the visitor to explain his business had dropped back to his work with a grunt.

"I am Parson Homo and this is my *pied-à-terre*. We professional criminals must have somewhere to go when we are not in prison, you know."

The voice was that of an educated man, its modulation, the confidence and the perfect poise of the speaker suggested the college man.

"So that you shall not be shocked by revelations I must tell you that I have just come out of prison. I am by way of being a professional burglar."

"I am not easily shocked," said Beale.

He glanced at the professor.

"I see," said Parson Homo, rising, "that I am *de trop*. Unfortunately I cannot go into the street without risking arrest. In this country, you know, there is a law which is called the Prevention of Crimes Act, which empowers the unemployed members of the constabulary who find time hanging on their hands to arrest known criminals on suspicion if they are seen out in questionable circumstances. And as all circumstances are questionable to the unimaginative 'flattie,' and his no less obtuse friend the 'split,' I will retire to the bedroom and stuff my ears with cotton-wool."

"You needn't," smiled Beale, "I guess the professor hasn't many secrets from you."

"Go on guessing, my ingenious friend," said the parson, smiling with his eyes, "my own secrets I am willing to reveal but—*adios*!"

He waved his hand and passed behind the cretonne curtain and the old man looked up from his instrument.

"It is the Donovan Leichmann body that I search for," he said solemnly; "there was a case of sleeping-sickness at the docks, and the Herr Professor of the Tropical School so kindly let me have a little blood for testing."

"Professor," said Beale, sitting down in the place which Parson Homo had vacated and leaning across the table, "are you still working for van Heerden?"

The old man rolled his big head from side to side in an agony of protest.

"Of the learned doctor I do not want to speak," he said, "to me he has been most kind. Consider, Herr Peale, I was starving in this country which hates Germans and regard as a mad old fool and an ugly old devil, and none helped me until the learned doctor discovered me. I am a German, yes. Yet I have no nationality, being absorbed in the larger brotherhood of science. As for me I am indifferent whether the Kaiser or the Socialists live in Potsdam, but I am loyal, Herr Peale, to all who help me. To you, also," he said hastily, " for you have been most kind, and once when in foolishness I went into a room where I ought not to have been you saved me from the police." He shrugged his massive shoulders again. " I am grateful, but must I not also be grateful to the learned doctor ? "

" Tell me this, professor," said Beale, " where can I find the learned doctor to-night ? "

" At his so-well-known laboratory, where else ? " asked the professor.

" Where else ? " repeated Beale.

The old man was silent.

" It is forbidden that I should speak," he said ; " the Herr Doctor is engaged in a great experiment which will bring him fortune. If I betray his secrets he may be ruined. Such ingratitude, Herr Peale ! "

There was a silence, the old professor, obviously distressed and ill at ease, looking anxiously at the younger man.

" Suppose I tell you that the Herr Doctor is engaged in a dangerous conspiracy," said Beale, " and that you yourself are running a considerable risk by assisting him ? "

The big hands were outspread in despair.

" The Herr Doctor has many enemies," mumbled Heyler. " I can tell you nothing, Herr Peale."

" Tell me this," said Beale : " is there any place you know of where the doctor may have taken a lady—the young lady into whose room you went the night I found you ? "

" A young lady ? " The old man was obviously surprised. " No, no, Herr Peale, there is no place where a young lady could go. Ach ! No ! "

" Well," said Beale, after a pause, " I guess I can do no more with you, professor." He glanced round at the cretonne recess : " I won't inconvenience you any longer, Mr. Homo."

The curtains were pushed aside and the æsthetic-looking man stepped out, the half-smile on his thin lips.

"I fear you have had a disappointing visit," he said pleasantly, "and it is on the tip of your tongue to ask me if I can help you. I will save you the trouble of asking—I can't."

Beale laughed.

"You are a bad thought-reader," he said. "I had no intention of asking you."

He nodded to the old man, and with another nod to his companion was turning when a rap came at the door. He saw the two men exchange glances and noted in the face of the professor a look of blank dismay. The knock was repeated impatiently.

"Permit me," said Beale, and stepped to the door.

"Wait, wait," stammered the professor, "if Mr. Peale will permit——"

He shuffled forward, but Beale had turned the latch and opened the door wide. Standing in the entrance was a girl whom he had no difficulty in recognizing as Hilda Glaum, sometime desk companion of Oliva Cresswell. His back was to the light and she did not recognize him.

"Why did you not open more quickly?" she asked in German, and swung the heavy bag she carried into the room, "every moment I thought I should be intercepted. Here is the bag. It will be called for to-morrow——"

It was then that she saw Beale for the first time and her face went white.

"Who—who are you?" she asked; then quickly, "I know you. You are the man Beale. The drunken man——"

She looked from him to the bag at her feet and to him again, then before he could divine her intention she had stooped and grasped the handle of the bag. Instantly all his attention was riveted upon that leather case and its secret. His hand shot out and gripped her arm, but she wrenched herself free. In doing so the bag was carried by the momentum of its release and was driven heavily against the wall. He heard a shivering crash as though a hundred little glasses had broken simultaneously.

Before he could reach the bag she snatched it up, leapt through the open door and slammed it to behind her. His hand was on the latch——

"Put 'em up, Mr. Beale, put 'em up," said a voice behind him. "Right above your head, Mr. Beale, where we can see them."

He turned slowly, his hands rising mechanically to face Parson Homo, who still sat at the table, but he had discarded his Greek book and was handling a business-like revolver, the muzzle of which covered the detective.

"Smells rotten, doesn't it?" said Homo pleasantly.

Beale, too, had sniffed the musty odour, and knew that it came from the bag the girl had wrenched from his grasp. It was the sickly scent of the Green Rust!

CHAPTER XIII

AT DEANS FOLLY

WITH her elbows resting on the broad window-ledge and her cheeks against the cold steel bars which covered the window, Oliva Cresswell watched the mists slowly dissipate in the gentle warmth of the morning sun. She had spent the night dozing in a rocking-chair and at the first light of day she had bathed and redressed ready for any emergency. She had not heard any sound during the night and she guessed that van Heerden had returned to London.

The room in which she was imprisoned was on the first floor at the back of the house and the view she had of the grounds was restricted to a glimpse between two big lilac bushes which were planted almost on a level with her room.

The house had been built on the slope of a gentle rise so that you might walk from the first-floor window on to the grassy lawn at the back of the house but for two import-

ant obstacles, the first being represented by the bars which
protected the window and the second by a deep area,
concrete-lined, which formed a trench too wide to jump.

She could see, however, that the grounds were extensive.
The high wall which, apparently, separated the garden
from the road was a hundred yards away. She knew it
must be the road because of a little brown gate which
from time to time she saw between the swaying bushes.
She turned wearily from the window and sat on the edge
of the bed. She was not afraid—irritated would be a
better word to describe her emotion. She was mystified,
too, and that was an added irritation.

Why should this man, van Heerden, who admittedly
did not love her, who indeed loved her so little that he
could strike her and show no signs of remorse—why did
this man want to marry her ? If he wanted to marry
her, why did he kidnap her ?

There was another question, too, which she had debated
that night. Why did his reference to the American detective, Beale, so greatly embarrass her ?

She had reached the point where even such tremendous
subjects of debate had become less interesting than the
answer to that question which was furnished, when a
knock came to her door and a gruff voice said :

" Breakfast ! "

She unlocked the door and pulled it open. The man
called Gregory was standing on the landing. He jerked
his thumb to the room opposite.

" You can use both these rooms," he said, " but you
can't come downstairs. I have put your breakfast in
there."

She followed the thumb across the landing and found
herself in a plainly furnished sitting-room. The table
had been laid with a respectable breakfast, and until she
had appeased her healthy young appetite she took very
little stock of her surroundings.

The man came up in half an hour to clear away the
table.

" Will you be kind enough to tell me where I am ? "
asked Oliva.

"I am not going to tell you anything," said Gregory.
"I suppose you know that by detaining me here you
are committing a very serious crime?"

"Tell it to the doctor," said the man, with a queer little
smile.

She followed him out to the landing. She wanted to
see what sort of guard was kept and what possibilities
there were of escape. Somehow it seemed easier to make
a reconnaissance now under his very eyes than it had been
in the night, when in every shadow had lurked a menace.

She did not follow him far, however. He put down
the tray at the head of the stairs and reaching out both
his hands drew two sliding doors from the wall and snapped
them in her face. She heard the click of a door and knew
that any chance of escape from this direction was hopeless.
The doors had slid noiselessly on their oiled runners and
had formed for her a little lobby of the landing. She
guessed that the sliding doors had been closed after van
Heerden's departure. She had exhausted all the possibilities of her bedroom and now began an inspection of
the other.

Like its fellow, the windows were barred. There was
a bookshelf, crowded with old volumes, mostly on matters
ecclesiastical or theological. She looked at it thoughtfully.

"Now, if I were clever like Mr. Beale," she said aloud,
"I could deduce quite a lot from this room."

A distant church bell began to clang and she realized
with a start that the day was Sunday. She looked at her
watch and was amazed to see it was nearly eleven. She
must have slept longer than she had thought.

This window afforded her no better view than did that
of the bedroom, except that she could see the gate more
plainly and what looked to be the end of a low-roofed
brick building which had been erected against the wall.
She craned her neck, looking left and right, but the bushes
had been carefully planted to give the previous occupants
of these two rooms greater privacy.

Presently the bell stopped and she addressed herself
again to an examination of the room. In an old-fashioned

sloping desk she found a few sheets of paper, a pen and a bottle half-filled with thick ink. There were also two telegraph forms, and these gave her an idea. She went back to the table in the middle of the room. With paper before her she began to note the contents of the apartment.

"I am trying to be Bealish," she admitted.

She might also have confessed that she was trying to keep her mind off her possibly perilous position and that though she was not afraid she had a fear of fear.

"A case full of very dull good books. That means that the person who lived here before was very serious-minded."

She walked over and examined the titles, pulled out a few books and looked at their title pages. They all bore the same name, "L. T. B. Stringer." She uttered an exclamation. Wasn't there some directory of clergy-men's names?—she was sure this was a clergyman, nobody else would have a library of such weighty volumes.

Her fingers ran along the shelves and presently she found what she wanted—Crocker's Clergy List of 1879. She opened the book and presently found, "Stringe, Laurence Thomas Benjamin, Vicar of Upper Staines, Deans Folly, Upper Reach Village, near Staines."

Her eyes sparkled. Instinctively she knew that she had located her prison. Van Heerden had certainly hired the house furnished, probably from the clergyman or his widow. She began to search the room with feverish haste. Near the window was a cupboard built out. She opened it and found that it was a small service lift, apparently communicating with the kitchen. In a corner of the room was an invalid chair on wheels.

She sat down at the table and reconstructed the char-acter of its occupant. She saw an invalid clergyman who had lived permanently in this part of the house. He was probably wheeled from his bedroom to his sitting-room, and in this cheerless chamber had spent the last years of his life. And this place was Deans Folly? She took up the telegraph form and after a few minutes' deliberation wrote :

"To Beale, Krooman Mansions."

She scratched that out, remembering that he had a telegraphic address and substituted :

" Belocity, London." She thought a moment, then wrote : " Am imprisoned at Deans Folly, Upper Reach Village, near Staines. Oliva." That looked too bold, and she added " Cresswell."

She took a florin from her bag and wrapped it up in the telegraph form. She had no exact idea as to how she should get the message sent to the telegraph office, and it was Sunday, when all telegraph offices would be closed. Nor was there any immediate prospect of her finding a messenger. She supposed that tradesmen came to the house and that the kitchen door was somewhere under her window, but tradesmen do not call on Sundays. She held the little package irresolutely in her hand. She must take her chance to-day. To-morrow would be Monday and it was certain somebody would call.

With this assurance she tucked the message into her blouse. She was in no mood to continue her inspection of the room, and it was only because in looking again from the window she pulled it from its hook that she saw the strange-looking instrument which hung between the window and the service lift. She picked it up, a dusty-looking thing. It consisted of a short vulcanite handle, from which extended two flat steel supports, terminating in vulcanite ear-plates. The handle was connected by a green cord with a plug in the wall.

Oliva recognized it. It was an electrophone. One of those instruments by which stay-at-home people can listen to an opera, a theatrical entertainment or—a sermon. Of course it was a church. It was a very common practice for invalids to be connected up with their favourite pulpit, and doubtless the Rev. Mr. Stringer had derived considerable comfort from this invention.

She dusted the receiver and put them to her ears. She heard nothing. Beneath the plug was a little switch. She turned this over and instantly her ears were filled with a strange hollow sound—the sound which a bad gramophone record makes.

Then she realized that she was listening to a congre-

gation singing. This ceased after awhile and she heard
a cough, so surprisingly near and loud that she started.
Of course, the transmitter would be in the pulpit, she
thought. Then a voice spoke, clear and distinct, yet with
that drawl which is the peculiar property of ministers of
the Established Church. She smiled as the first words
came to her.

"I publish the banns of marriage between Henry Cole-
brook, and Jane Maria Smith both of this parish. This
is the second time of asking." A pause, then: "Also
between Henry Victor Vanden and Oliva Cresswell Prédeaux, both of this parish. This is the third time of
asking. If any of you know cause or just impediment
why these persons should not be joined together in holy
matrimony, ye are to declare it."

She dropped the instrument with a crash and stood
staring down at it. She had been listening to the publication of her own wedding-notice.

"Vanden" was van Heerden. "Oliva Cresswell Prédeaux" was herself. The strangeness of the names meant
nothing. She guessed rather than knew that the false
name would not be any insuperable bar to the ceremony.
She must get away. For the first time she had a horrible
sense of being trapped, and for a few seconds she must
have lost her head, for she tugged at the iron bars, dashed
wildly out and hammered at the sliding door. Presently
her reason took charge. She heard the heavy step of
Gregory on the stairs and recovered her calm by the time
he had unlocked the bar and pulled the doors apart.

"What do you want?" he asked.

"I want you to let me out of here."

"Oh, is that all?" he said sarcastically, and for the
second time that day slammed the door in her face.

She waited until he was out of hearing, then she went
back noiselessly to the sitting-room. She pushed open
the door of the service lift and tested the ropes. There
were two, one which supported the lift and one by which
it was hauled up, and she gathered that these with the
lift itself formed an endless chain.

Gripping both ropes firmly she crept into the confined

space of the cupboard and let herself down hand over hand. She had about twelve feet to descend before she reached the kitchen entrance of the elevator. She squeezed through the narrow opening and found herself in a stone-flagged kitchen. It was empty. A small fire glowed in the grate. Her own tray with all the crockery unwashed was on the dresser, and there were the remnants of a meal at one end of the plain table. She tiptoed across the kitchen to the door. It was bolted top and bottom and locked. Fortunately the key was in the lock, and in two minutes she was outside in a small courtyard beneath the level of the ground.

One end of the courtyard led past another window, and that she could not risk. To her right was a flight of stone steps, and that was obviously the safer way. She found herself in a little park which fortunately for her was plentifully sprinkled with clumps of rhododendrons, and she crept from bush to bush, taking care to keep out of sight of the house. She had the telegram and the money in her hand, and her first object was to get this outside. It took her twenty minutes to reach the wall. It was too high to scale and there was no sign of a ladder. The only way out was the little brown door she had seen from her bedroom window, and cautiously she made her way back, flitting from bush to bush until she came to the place where a clear view of the door and the building to its left could be obtained.

The low-roofed shed she had seen was much longer than she had expected and evidently had recently been built. Its black face was punctured at intervals with square windows, and a roughly painted door to the left of the brown garden gate was the only entrance she could see. She looked for a key but without hope of finding one. She must take her chance, she thought, and a quick run brought her from the cover of the bushes to the brown portal which stood between her and liberty.

With trembling hands she slid back the bolts and turned the handle. Her heart leapt as it gave a little. Evidently it had not been used for years and she found it was only held fast by the gravel which had accumulated beneath it.

Eagerly she scraped the gravel aside with her foot and her hand was on the knob when she heard a muffled voice behind her. She turned and then with a gasp of horror fell back. Standing in the doorway of the shed was a thing which was neither man nor beast. It was covered in a wrap which had once been white but was now dappled with green. The face and head were covered with rubber, two green staring eyes surveyed her, and a great snout-like nose was uplifted as in amazement. She was paralysed for a moment. For the beastliness of the figure was appalling.

Then realizing that it was merely a man whose face was hidden by a hideous mask, she sprang again for the door, but a hand gripped her arm and pulled her back. She heard a cheerful whistle from the road without and remembering the package in her hand she flung it high over the wall and heard its soft thud, and the whistle stop.

Then as the hideous figure slipped his arm about her and pressed a musty hand over her mouth she fainted.

CHAPTER XIV

MR. BEALE SUGGESTS MARRIAGE

" HELD up by a gunman ? " asked James Kitson incredulously, " why, what do you mean ? "

" It doesn't sound right, does it ? " smiled Beale, " especially after McNorton telling us the other day that there was no such thing as a gunman in England. Do you remember his long dissertation on the law-abiding criminals of this little old country ? " he laughed.

" But a gunman," protested Mr. Kitson—" by the way, have you had breakfast ? "

" Hours ago," replied Beale, " but don't let me interrupt you."

Mr. James Kitson pulled his chair to the table and unfolded his napkin. It was almost at this hour that Oliva Cresswell had performed a similar act.

"You are not interrupting me," said Kitson, "go on."

Beale was frowning down at deserted Piccadilly which Mr. Kitson's palatial suite at the Ritz-Carlton overlooked.

"Eh?" he said absently, "oh yes, the gunman—a sure enough gunman."

He related in a few words his experience of the previous night.

"This man Homo," said Kitson, "is he one of the gang?"

Beale shook his head.

"I don't think so. He may be one of van Heerden's ambassadors."

"Ambassadors?"

"I will explain van Heerden's game one of these days and you will understand what I mean," said Beale. "No, I don't think that Parson Homo is being any more than a gentle knight succouring a distressed lady, whether for love of the lady, out of respect for the professor or from a general sense of antagonism to all detectives, I can only speculate. Anyway, he held me until the lady was out of hearing and presumably out of sight. And then there was no need for me to go. I just sat down and talked, and a more amiable and cultured gentleman it would be impossible to meet."

Kitson looked at his companion through narrowed lids.

"Why, that's not like you, Beale," he said. "I thought you were too hot on the scent to waste time."

"So I am," said the other, thrusting his hands deep into his pockets, "that's just what I am." He turned suddenly to the older man. "Mr. Kitson, I've got to know a little more about John Millinborn's will than I know at present."

The lawyer looked up, fixed his glasses and regarded the younger man with a troubled look.

"I'm sorry to jump in on you like this, but I'm rattled.

I don't understand much about the English law, though I know that marriages aren't as easy to make here in London as they are in our country. But here as everywhere else it is fairly difficult to force a girl into marriage against her will, and the marriage of course is not good in law."

He sat down on the arm of a couch, dangling his hat between his legs, and ran his fingers through his hair with a nervous little laugh.

" Here I'm telling you all that I came to ask you."

" Have a cup of tea," said Kitson, with a smile, " everybody in England rushes to tea and I hope I shall get you in the habit."

Beale shook his head.

" You are right about the marriage," Kitson went on, " but I'll give you the law on the subject. A marriage can only be solemnized if due notice is given by the parties who must be resident in the district where it is to take place—three weeks is the period of notice."

" Is there no other way ? "

" Yes. By paying special fees and offering a good and sufficient reason a faculty can be secured from the Archbishop of Canterbury, or rather from his officials, authorizing a marriage without notice. It is called a special licence, and the marriage may occur at any hour and at any place."

" Is there a register of applications ? " asked Beale quickly.

" I've thought of that," nodded the lawyer, " yes, I'm keeping that side under observation. It is difficult because officialdom isn't as obliging as it might be. My own view is that van Heerden will be married in the ordinary way, that is to say by giving notice. To secure his special licence he would be obliged to give his own name and be vouched for ; he can be married in the ordinary way even if he gives a false name, which in all probability he will."

" Would the marriage be legal if it was in a false name ? "

" Absolutely. In English law you may commit an

offence by marrying in a wrong name, but it would not invalidate the marriage."

Stanford Beale sat studying the pattern of the carpet.

"Is there any chance of two special licences being issued to marry the same girl ? " he asked.

"None—why do you ask ? "

Beale did not reply immediately.

"Something Homo said last night when I told him frankly that I was searching for Miss Cresswell. ' Oh,' said he, ' that's the lady that's marrying the doctor.' He wouldn't tell me more. But he gave me an idea to make sure that no special licence is issued to van Heerden. I shall apply for one myself."

The lawyer stared at him.

"To marry the girl ? " he gasped. "But——"

Stanford Beale laughed a little bitterly.

"Say, don't get up in the air, Mr. Kitson—I'm only thinking of Miss Cresswell. A special licence in my name would stop one of van Heerden's paths to easy money. Tell me, and this is what I came to ask you, under Millinborn's will, does the husband benefit directly by the marriage, or is he dependent upon what his wife gives him ? '

"He benefits directly," said Kitson after a pause, "on his marriage he receives exactly one-half of the girl's fortune. That was Millinborn's idea. ' Make the husband independent,' he said, ' do not put him in the humiliating position of dependence on his wife's generosity, and there will be a chance of happiness for them both.' "

"I see—of course, van Heerden knows that. He has only to produce a marriage certificate to scoop in two and a half million dollars—that is half a million in English money. This is the secret of it all. He wants money immediately, and under the terms of the will—— ? "

"He gets it," said Kitson. "If he came to me to-morrow with proof of his marriage, even if I knew that he had coerced the girl into marriage, I must give him his share—van Heerden was pretty thorough when he put my dying friend through his examination." His face hard-

ened. "Heavens, I'd give every penny I had in the world
to bring that fiend to the gallows, Beale!"

His voice shook, and rising abruptly he walked to the
window. Presently he turned. "I think there is something in your idea. Get the licence."

"I will—and marry her," said Beale quickly.

"Marry her—I don't quite understand you?"

For the first time there was suspicion in his voice.

"Mr. Kitson, I'm going to put all my cards on the table,"
said Beale quietly, "will you sit down a moment? There
are certain facts which we cannot ignore. Fact one is
that Oliva Cresswell is in the hands of a man who is absolutely unscrupulous, but has no other object in view than
marriage. Her beauty, her charm, all the attractive
qualities which appeal to most men and to all brutes have
no appeal for him—to him she is just a money proposition.
If he can't marry her, she has no further interest for
him."

"I see that," agreed the lawyer, "but——"

"Wait, please. If we knew where she was we could
stop the marriage and indict van Heerden—but I've an
idea that we shan't locate her until it is too late or nearly
too late. I can't go hunting with a pack of policemen. I
must play a lone hand, or nearly a lone hand. When I
find her I must be in a position to marry her without losing
a moment."

"You mean to marry her to foil van Heerden, and after
—to dissolve the marriage?" asked the lawyer, shaking
his head. "I don't like that solution, Beale—I tell you
frankly, I don't like it. You're a good man and I have
every faith in you, but if I consented, even though I were
confident that you would play fair, which I am, I should
feel that I had betrayed John Millinborn's trust. It isn't
because it is you, my son," he said kindly enough, "but
if you were the Archangel Gabriel I'd kick at that plan.
Marriage is a difficult business to get out of once you are
in it, especially in this country."

Beale did not interrupt the older man.

"Right, and now if you've finished I'll tell you my
scheme," he said, "as I see it there's only a ghost of a

chance of our saving this girl from marriage. I've done my best and we—McNorton and I—have taken all the facts before a judge this morning. We got a special interview with the idea of securing a warrant for van Heerden's arrest. But there is no evidence to convict him on any single charge. We cannot connect him with the disappearance of Miss Cresswell, and although I pointed out that van Heerden admits that he knows where the girl is, the judge said, fairly I thought, that there was no law which compelled a man to divulge the address of his fiancée to one who was a possible rival. The girl is of an age when she can do as she wishes, and as I understand the matter you have no legal status as a guardian."

"None," said James Kitson, "that is our weak point. I am merely the custodian of her money. Officially I am supposed to be ignorant of the fact that Oliva Cresswell is Oliva Prédeaux, the heiress."

"Therefore our hands are tied," concluded Beale quietly. "Don't you see that my plan is the only one—but I haven't told you what it is. There's a man, a criminal, this Parson Homo who can help. I am satisfied that he does not know where the girl is—but he'll help for a consideration. As a matter of fact, he was pulled again. I am seeing him this afternoon."

Mr. Kitson frowned.

"The gunman—how can he help you ? "

"I will tell you. This man, as I say, is known to the police as Parson Homo. Apparently he is an unfrocked priest, one who has gone under. He still preserves the resemblance to a gentleman "—he spoke slowly and deliberately ; "in decent clothes he would look like a parson. I propose that he shall marry me to Miss Cresswell. The marriage will be a fake, but neither the girl nor van Heerden will know this. If my surmise is right, when van Heerden finds she is married he will take no further steps—except, perhaps," he smiled, "to make her a widow. Sooner or later we are bound to get him under lock and key, and then we can tell Miss Cresswell the truth."

"In other words, you intend breaking the law and committing a serious offence," said Kitson, shaking his head. "I can't be a party to that—besides, she may not marry you."

"I see that danger—van Heerden is a mighty clever fellow. He may be married before I trace them."

"You say that Homo doesn't know about the girl, what does he know?"

"He has heard of van Heerden. He has heard probably from the girl Hilda Glaum that van Heerden is getting married—the underworld do not get their news out of special editions—he probably knows too that van Heerden is engaged in some swindle which is outside the parson's line of business."

"Will he help you?"

"Sure," Beale said with quiet confidence, "the man is broke and desperate. The police watch him like a cat, and would get him sooner or later. McNorton told me that much. I have offered him passage to Australia and £500, and he is ready to jump at it."

"You have explained the scheme?"

"I had to," confessed Beale, "there was no time to be lost. To my surprise he didn't like it. It appears that even a double-dyed crook has scruples, and even when I told him the whole of my plan he still didn't like it, but eventually agreed. He has gone to Whitechapel to get the necessary kit. I am putting him up in my flat. Of course, it may not be necessary," he went on, "but somehow I think it will be."

Kitson spread out his hands in despair.

"I shall have to consent," he said, "the whole thing was a mistake from the beginning. I trust you, Stanford," he went on, looking the other in the eye, "you have no feeling beyond an ordinary professional interest in this young lady?"

Beale dropped his eyes.

"If I said that, Mr. Kitson, I should be telling a lie," he said quietly. "I have a very deep interest in Miss Cresswell, but that is not going to make any difference to me and she will never know."

He left soon after this and went back to his rooms. At four o'clock he received a visitor. Parson Homo, cleanly shaved and attired in a well-fitting black coat and white choker, seemed more real to the detective than the Parson Homo he had met on the previous night.

"You look the part all right," said Beale.

"I suppose I do," said the other shortly; "what am I to do next?"

"You stay here. I have made up a bed for you in my study," said Beale.

"I would like to know a little more of this before I go any further," Homo said, "there are many reasons why I want information."

"I have told you the story," said Beale patiently, "and I am going to say right here that I do not intend telling you any more. You carry this thing through and I'll pay you what I agreed. Nobody will be injured by your deception, that I promise you."

"That doesn't worry me so much," said the other coolly, "as——"

There came a knock at the door, an agitated hurried knock, and Beale immediately answered it. It was McNorton, and from force of habit Parson Homo drew back into the shadows.

"All right, Parson," said McNorton, "I knew you were here. What do you make of this?"

He turned to Beale and laid on the table a piece of paper which had been badly crumpled and which he now smoothed out. It was the top half of a telegraph form, the lower half had been torn away.

"'To Belocity, London,'" Beale read aloud.

"That's you," interrupted McNorton, and the other nodded.

"'To Belocity, London,'" he read slowly. "'Am imprisoned at Deans——'"

At this point the remainder of the message had been torn off.

CHAPTER XV

THE GOOD HERR STARDT

" WHERE is the rest ? " said Beale.

"That's the lot," replied McNorton grimly. "It's the only information you will get from this source for twenty-four hours."

"But I don't understand, it is undoubtedly Miss Cresswell's handwriting."

"And 'Belocity' is as undoubtedly your telegraphic address. This paper," he went on, "was taken from a drunken tramp—'hobo' you call 'em, don't you ? "

" Where ? "

"At Kingston-on-Thames," said McNorton—"the man was picked up in the street, fighting drunk, and taken to the police station, where he developed delirium tremens. Apparently he has been on the jag all the week, and to-day's booze finished him off. The local inspector in searching him found this piece of paper in his pocket and connected it with the disappearance of Miss Cresswell, the matter being fresh in his mind, as only this morning we had circulated a new description throughout the home counties. He got me on the 'phone and sent a constable up to town with the paper this afternoon."

"H'm," said Beale, biting his lips thoughtfully, "she evidently gave the man the telegram, telling him to dispatch it. She probably gave him money, too, which was the explanation of his final drunk."

"I don't think that is the case," said McNorton, "he had one lucid moment at the station when he was cross-examined as to where he got the money to get drunk, and he affirmed that he found it wrapped up in a piece of paper. That sounds true to me. She either dropped it from a car or threw it from a house."

" Is the man very ill ? "

"Pretty bad," said the other," you will get nothing out of him before the morning. The doctors had to dope him to get him quiet, and he will be some time before he is right. '

He looked up at the other occupant of the room.

"Well, Parson, you are helping Mr. Beale, I understand?"

"Yes," said the other easily.

"Returning to your old profession, I see," said McNorton. Parson Homo drew himself up a little stiffly.

"If you have anything against me you can pull me for it," he said insolently: "that's your business. As to the profession I followed before I started on that career of crime which brought me into contact with the crude representatives of what is amusingly called 'the law,' is entirely my affair."

"Don't get your wool off, Parson," said the other good-humouredly. "You have lost your sense of humour."

"That's where you are wrong," said Homo coolly: "I have merely lost my sense of decency."

McNorton turned to the other.

"What are you going to do?" he asked.

"'I am imprisoned at Deans,'" repeated Beale. "What 'Deans' have you in this country?"

"There are a dozen of them," replied the police chief: "there's Deansgate in Manchester, Deanston in Perth, Deansboro', Deans Abbey—I've been looking them up, there is a whole crowd of them."

"Are there any 'Deans' near Kingston?"

"None," replied the other.

"Then it is obviously the name of a house," said Beale. "I have noticed that in England you are in the habit of naming rather than numbering your houses, especially in the suburbs." He looked across to Parson Homo, "Can you help?"

The man shook his head.

"If I were a vulgar burglar I might assist you," he said, "but my branch of the profession does not take me to the suburbs."

"We will get a Kingston Directory and go through it," said McNorton; "we have one on the file at Scotland Yard. If——"

Beale suddenly raised his hand to enjoin silence: he had heard a familiar step in the corridor outside.

" That's van Heerden," he said in a low voice, " he has been out all the morning."

" Has he been shadowed ? " asked McNorton in the same tone.

" My man lost him," he said.

He tiptoed along the passage and stood listening behind the door. Presently he heard the doctor's door close and came back.

" I have had the best sleuth in America trailing him," he said, " and he has slipped him every time."

" Anyway," said McNorton, " this telegram disposes of the idea that she has gone to Liverpool. It also settles the question as to whether she went of her own free will. If his name were on that telegram," he said thoughtfully, " I would take a risk and pull him in."

" I will give you something bigger to pull him for," Beale said, " once I have placed Miss Cresswell in safety."

" The Green Rust ? " smiled the police chief.

" The Green Rust," said Beale, but he did not smile, " that's van Heerden's big game. The abduction of Miss Cresswell is merely a means to an end. He wants her money and may want it very badly. The more urgent is his need the sooner that marriage takes place."

" But there is no clergyman in England who would marry them "—it was Homo who interrupted. " My dear friend, that sort of thing is not done except in story books. If the woman refuses her consent the marriage cannot possibly occur. As I understand, the lady is not likely to be cowed."

" That is what I am afraid of," said Beale, " she is all pluck——"

He stopped, for he had heard the doctor's door close. In three strides he had crossed the hallway and was in the corridor, confronting his suave neighbour. Dr. van Heerden, carefully attired, was pulling on his gloves and smiled into the stern face of his rival.

" Well," he asked pleasantly, " any news of Miss Cresswell ? "

" If I had any news of Miss Cresswell you would not be here," said Beale.

" But how interesting," drawled the doctor.   " Where should I be ? "

" You would be under lock and key, my friend," said Beale.

The doctor threw back his head and laughed softly.

" What a lover ! " he said, " and how reluctant to accept his dismissal !   It may ease your mind to know that Miss Cresswell, whom I hope very soon to call Mrs. van Heerden, is perfectly happy, and is very annoyed at your persistence. I had a telegram from her this morning, begging me to come to Liverpool at the earliest opportunity."

" That's a lie," said Beale quietly, " but one lie more or less, I suppose, doesn't count."

" A thoroughly immoral view to take," said the doctor with much severity, " but I see there is nothing to be gained by arguing with you, and I can only make one request."

Beale said nothing but stood waiting.

" It is this," said the doctor, choosing his words with great care : " that you call off the gentleman who has been dogging my footsteps to-day.   It was amusing at first but now it is becoming annoying.   Some of my patients have complained of this man watching their houses."

" You've not seen a patient to-day, van Heerden," said Beale, " and, anyway, I guess you had better get used to being shadowed.   It isn't your first experience."

The doctor looked at him under lowered lids and smiled again.

" I could save your man a great deal of trouble," he said, " and myself considerable exertion by giving him a list of the places where I intend calling."

" He will find that out for himself," said Beale.

" I wish him greater success than he has had," replied the other, and passed on, descending the stairs slowly.

Beale went back to his flat, passed to his bedroom and looked down into the street.   He made a signal to a man at the corner and received an almost imperceptible answer. Then he returned to the two men.

" This fellow is too clever for us, I am afraid, and London

with its tubes, its underground stations and taxi-cabs is a pretty difficult proposition."

"I suppose your man lost him in the tube," said McNorton.

"There are two ways down, the elevator and the stairs, and it is mighty difficult to follow a man unless you know which way he is going."

"But you were interrupted at an interesting moment. What are you going to tell us about the Green Rust?"

"I can only tell you this," said Beale, "that the Green Rust is the greatest conspiracy against the civilized world that has ever been hatched."

He looked sharply at Homo.

"Don't look at me," said the Parson, "I know nothing about it, unless——" He stopped and frowned. "The Green Rust," he repeated, "is that old man Heyler's secret?"

"He's in it," said Beale shortly.

"Is it a swindle of some kind?" asked the Parson curiously. "It never struck me that Heyler was that kind of man."

"There is no swindle in it so far as Heyler's concerned," said Beale, "it is something bigger than a swindle."

A telephone bell rang and he took up the receiver and listened, only interjecting a query or two. Then he hung up the instrument.

"It is as I thought," he said: "the doctor's slipped again. Had a car waiting for him in Oxford Street and when he saw there were no taxi-cabs about, jumped in and was driven eastward."

"Did you get the number of the car?" asked McNorton.

Beale smiled.

"That's not much use," he said, "he's probably got two or three number-plates."

He looked at his watch.

"I'll go along to Kingston," he said.

"I shan't be able to come with you," said McNorton, "I have a meeting with the commissioner at five."

"Before you go," remarked Beale, "you might put your signature to this declaration of my *bona fides*."

He laid on the table a blue foolscap blank.

"What's this?" asked the surprised McNorton, "an application for a special licence—are you going to be married?"

"I hope so," said the other cautiously.

"You don't seem very cheerful about it. I presume you want me to testify to the urgency of the case. I am probably perjuring myself." He signed his name with a flourish. "When are you getting the licence and what's the hurry?"

"I am getting the licence to-morrow," said Beale.

"And the lady's name is—— ? "

"I thought you had noticed it," smiled the other, deftly blotting and folding the form.

"Not Miss Cresswell?" demanded the police chief in surprise.

"Miss Cresswell it is."

"But I thought——"

"There are circumstances which may be brought to your official notice, McNorton," said the detective, "for the present it is necessary to keep my plan a secret."

"Has it anything to do with the Green Rust?" asked the other jokingly.

"A great deal to do with the Green Rust."

"Well, I'll get along," said McNorton. "I will telephone the Kingston police to give you all the assistance possible, but I am afraid you will learn nothing from the tramp till the morning, and perhaps not then."

He took his leave soon after.

"Now, Homo, it is up to you and me," said Beale. "You will have to keep close to me after to-morrow. Make yourself at home here until I come back."

"One moment," said Homo, as Beale rose and gathered up his hat and gloves to depart. "Before you go I want you to understand clearly that I am taking on this job because it offers me a chance that I haven't had since I fell from grace, if you will excuse the *cliché*."

"That I understand," said Beale.

"I may be doing you a very bad turn."

"I'll take that risk," said Beale.

"On your own head be it," said Homo, his hard face creased in a fleeting smile.

Beale's car was waiting, but his departure was unexpectedly delayed. As he passed down the stairs into the vestibule he saw a stranger standing near the door reading the enamelled name-plates affixed to the wall. Something in his appearance arrested Beale. The man was well dressed in the sense that his clothes were new and well cut, but the pattern of the cloth, no less than the startling yellowness of the boots and that unmistakable sign-manual of the foreigner, the shape and colour of the cravat, stamped him as being neither American nor British.

"Can I be of any assistance?" asked Beale. "Are you looking for somebody?"

The visitor turned a pink face to him.

"You are very good," he said with the faint trace of an accent. "I understand that Doctor van Heerden lives here?"

"Yes, he lives here," said Beale, "but I am afraid he is not at home."

He thought it might be a patient or a summons to a patient.

"Not at home?" The man's face fell. "But how unfortunate! Could you tell me where I can find him, my business is immediate and I have come a long way."

From Germany, guessed Beale. The mail train was due at Charing Cross half an hour before.

"I am a friend of Doctor van Heerden and possibly I can assist you. Is the business very important? Does it concern," he hesitated, "the Green Rust?"

He spoke the last sentence in German and the man started and looked at him with mingled suspicion and uncertainty.

"It is a matter of the greatest importance," he repeated, "it is of vital importance."

He spoke in German.

"About the Green Rust?" asked Beale, in the same language.

"I do not know anything of the Green Rust," said the man hurriedly, "I am merely the bearer of a communication which is of the greatest importance." He repeated the words—" the greatest importance."

" If you give me the letter," said Beale, " I will see that it is sent on to him," and he held out his hand with the assurance of one who shared the dearest secrets of the doctor. The stranger's hand wandered to his breast pocket, but came back empty.

" No, it must be given—I must see the doctor himself," he said. " He does not expect me and I will wait."

Beale thought quickly.

" Well, perhaps you will come upstairs to my flat and wait," he said genially, and led the way, and the man, still showing evidence of uneasiness, was ushered into his room, where the sight of the Rev. Parson Homo tended to reassure him.

Would he have tea ? He would not have tea. Would he take coffee ? He would not take coffee. A glass of wine perhaps ? No, he did not drink wine nor beer, nor would he take any refreshment whatever.

" My man," thought the desperate Beale, " I either chloroform you or hit you on the head with the poker, but I am going to see that letter."

As if divining his thought, but placing thereon a wrong construction, the man said :

" I should avail myself of your kindness to deliver my letter to Doctor van Heerden, but of what service would it be since it is only a letter introducing me to the good doctor ? "

" Oh, is that all ? " said Beale, disappointed, and some-how he knew the man spoke the truth.

" That is all," he said, " except of course my message, which is verbal. My name is Stardt, you may have heard the doctor speak of me. We have had some corre-spondence."

" Yes, yes, I remember," lied Beale.

" The message is for him alone, of course, as you will understand, and if I deliver it to you," smiled Herr Stardt, " you should not understand it, because it is one word."

" One word ? " said Beale blankly. " A code—hang ! "

CHAPTER XVI

THE PAWN TICKET

OLIVA CRESSWELL awoke to consciousness as she was being carried up the stairs of the house. She may have recovered sooner, for she retained a confused impression of being laid down amidst waving grasses and of hearing somebody grunt that she was heavier than he thought.

Also she remembered as dimly the presence of Dr. van Heerden standing over her, and he was wearing a long grey dust-coat.

As her captor kicked open the door of her room she scrambled out of his arms and leant against the bed-rail for support.

" I'm all right," she said breathlessly, " it was foolish to faint, but—but you frightened me."

The man grinned, and seemed about to speak, but a sharp voice from the landing called him, and he went out, slamming the door behind him. She crossed to the bath-room, bathed her face in cold water and felt better, though she was still a little giddy.

Then she sat down to review the situation, and in that review two figures came alternately into prominence—van Heerden and Beale.

She was an eminently sane girl. She had had the beginnings of what might have been an unusually fine education, had it not been interrupted by the death of her foster-mother. She had, too, the advantage which the finished young lady does not possess, of having grafted to the wisdom of the schools the sure understanding of men and things which personal contact with struggling humanity can alone give to us.

The great problems of life had been sprung upon her with all their hideous realism, and through all she had retained her poise and her clear vision. Many of the phenomena represented by man's attitude to woman she could understand, but that a man who admittedly did not love her and had no other apparent desire than to rid himself of the incubus of a wife as soon as he was wed, should wish to marry her was incomprehensible. That he had already published the banns of her marriage left her gasping at his audacity. Strange how her thoughts leapt all the events of the morning : the wild rush to escape, the struggle with the hideously masked man, and all that went before or followed, and went back to the night before.

Somehow she knew that van Heerden had told her the truth, and that there was behind this act of his a deeper significance than she could grasp. She remembered what he had said about Beale, and flushed.

"You're silly, Matilda," she said to herself, employing the term of address which she reserved for moments of self-depreciation, "here is a young man you have only met half a dozen times, who is probably a very nice married policeman with a growing family and you are going hot and cold at the suggestion that you're in love with him." She shook her head reproachfully.

And yet upon Beale all her thoughts were centred, and however they might wander it was to Beale they returned. She could analyse that buoyancy which had asserted itself, that confidence which had suddenly become a mental armour, which repelled every terrifying thought, to this faith she had in a man, who in a few weeks before she had looked upon as an incorrigible drunkard.

She had time for thought, and really, though this she did not acknowledge, she desperately needed the occupation of that thought. What was Beale's business ? Why did he employ her to copy out this list of American and Canadian statistics ? Why did he want to know all these hotels, their proprietors, the chief of the police and the like ? She wished she had her papers and books so that she might go on extracting that interminable list.

What would van Heerden do now ? Would her attempted escape change his plans ? How would he overcome the difficulty of marrying a girl who was certain to denounce him in the presence of so independent a witness as a clergyman ? She would die before she married him, she told herself.

She could not rest, and walked about the room examining the framed prints and looking at the books, and occasionally walking to the glass above the dressing-chest to see if any sign was left of the red mark on her cheek where van Heerden's hand had fallen. This exercise gave her a curious satisfaction, and when she saw that the mark had subsided and was blending more to the colour of her skin she felt disappointed. Startled, she analysed this curious mental attitude and again came to Beale. She wanted Beale to see the place. She wanted Beale's sympathy. She wanted Beale's rage—she was sure he would rage.

She laughed to herself and for want of other and better amusement walked to the drawers in the dressing-bureau and examined their contents. They were empty and unlocked save one, which refused to respond to her tug. She remembered she had a small bunch of keys in her bag.

"I am going to be impertinent. Forgive the liberty," she said, as she felt the lock give to the first attempt.

She pulled the drawer open. It contained a few articles of feminine attire and a thick black leather portfolio. She lifted this out, laid it on the table and opened it. It was filled with foolscap. Written on the cover was the word "Argentine" and somehow the writing was familiar to her. It was a bold hand, obviously feminine.

"Where have I seen that before ? " she asked, and knit her forehead.

She turned the first leaf and read :

"Alsigar Hotel, Fournos, Proprietor, Miguel Porcorini. Index 2."

Her mouth opened in astonishment and she ran down the list. She took out another folder. It was marked "Canada," and she turned the leaves rapidly. She recognized this work. It was the same work that Beale had given to her, a list of the hotels, their proprietors and means of conveyance, but there was no reference to the police. And then it dawned upon her. An unusually long description produced certain characteristics of writing which she recognized.

"Hilda Glaum ! " she said. "I wonder what this means ! "

She examined the contents of the drawer again and some of them puzzled her. Not the little stack of handkerchiefs, the folded collars and the like. If Hilda Glaum was in the habit of visiting Deans Folly and used this room it was natural that these things should be here. If this were her bureau the little carton of nibs and the spare note book were to be expected. It was the steel box which set her wondering. This she discovered in the far corner of the drawer. If she could have imagined anything so fantastic she might have believed that the box had been specially made to hold the thing it contained and preserve it from the dangers of fire. The lid, which closed with a spring catch, released by the pressure of a tiny button, was perfectly fitted so that the box was in all probability air-tight.

She opened it without difficulty. The sides were lined with what seemed to be at first sight thick cardboard but which proved on closer inspection to be asbestos. She opened it with a sense of eager anticipation, but her face fell. Save for a tiny square blue envelope at the bottom, the box was empty!

She lifted it in her hand to shake out the envelope and it was then that the idea occurred to her that the box had been made for the envelope, which refused to budge until she lifted one end with a hairpin.

It was unsealed, and she slipped in her finger and pulled out—a pawn ticket!

She had an inclination to laugh which she checked. She examined the ticket curiously. It announced the fact that Messrs. Rosenblaum Bros., of Commercial Road, London, had advanced ten shillings on a "Gents' Silver Hunter Watch," and the pledge had been made in the name of van Heerden!

She gazed at it bewildered. He was not a man who needed ten shillings or ten dollars or ten pounds. Why should he pledge a watch and why having pledged it should he keep the ticket with such care?

Oliva hesitated a moment, then slipped the ticket from its cover, put back the envelope at the bottom of the box and closed the lid. She found a hiding-place for the little square pasteboard before she returned the box and port-folio to the drawer and locked it.

There was a tap at the door and hastily she replaced the key in her bag.

"Come in," she said.

She recognized the man who stood in the doorway as he who had carried her back to the room.

There was a strangeness in his bearing which made her uneasy, a certain subdued hilarity which suggested drunkenness.

"Don't make a noise," he whispered with a stifled chuckle, "if Gregory hears he'll raise fire."

She saw that the key was in the lock on the outside of the door and this she watched. But he made no attempt to withdraw it and closed the door behind him softly.

"My name is Bridgers," he whispered, "van Heerden has told you about me—Horace Bridgers, do you—— ?" He took a little tortoiseshell box from the pocket of his frayed waistcoat and opened it with a little kick of his middle finger. It was half-full of white powder that glittered in a stray ray of sunlight. "Try a sniff," he begged eagerly, "and all your troubles will go—phutt !"

"Thank you, no "—she shook her head, looking at him with a perplexed smile—"I don't know what it is."

"It's the white terror," he chuckled again, "better than the green—not so horribly musty as the green, eh ?"

"I'm not in the mood for terrors of any kind," she said, with a half-smile. She wondered why he had come, and had a momentary hope that he was ignorant of van Heerden's character.

"All right "—he stuffed the box back into his waistcoat pocket—"*you're* the loser, you'll never find heaven on earth !"

She waited.

All the time he was speaking, it seemed to her that he was on the *qui vive* for some interruption from below. He would stop in his speech to turn a listening ear to the door. Moreover, she was relieved to see he made no attempt to advance any farther into the room. That he was under the influence of some drug she guessed. His eyes glittered with unnatural brilliance, his hands, discoloured and uncleanly, moved nervously and were never still.

"I'm Bridgers," he said again. "I'm van Heerden's best man—rather a come down for the best analytical chemist that the school ever turned out, eh? Doing odd jobs for a dirty Deutscher!" He walked to the door, opened it and listened, then tiptoed across the room to her.

"You know," he whispered, "you're van Heerden's girl—what is the game?"

"What is—— ?" she stammered.

"What is the game? What is it all about? I've tried to pump Gregory and Milsom, but they're mysterious. Curse all mysteries, my dear. What is the game? Why are they sending men to America, Canada, Australia and India? Come along and be a pal! Tell me! I've seen the office, I know all about it. Thousands of sealed envelopes filled with steamship tickets and money. Thousands of telegraph forms already addressed. You don't fool me!" He hissed the last words almost in her face. "Why is he employing the crocks and the throw-outs of science? Perrilli, Maxon, Boyd Heyler—and me? If the game's square why doesn't he take the new men from the schools?"

She shook her head, being, by now, less interested in such revelations as he might make, than in her own personal comfort. For his attitude was grown menacing . . . then the great idea came to her. Evidently this man knew nothing of the circumstances under which she had come to the house. To him she was a wilful but willing assistant of the doctor, who for some reason or other it had been necessary to place under restraint.

"I will tell you everything if you will take me back to my home," she said. "I cannot give you proofs here."

She saw suspicion gather in his eyes. Then he laughed.

"That won't wash," he sneered—"you know it all. I can't leave here," he said; "besides, you told me last time that there was nothing. I used to watch you working away at night," he went on to the girl's amazement. "I've sat looking at you for hours, writing and writing and writing."

She understood now. She and Hilda Glaum were of about the same build, and she was mistaken for Hilda by this bemused man who had, in all probability, never seen the other girl face to face.

"What made you run away?" he asked suddenly; but with a sudden resolve she brought him back to the subject he had started to discuss.

"What is the use of my telling you?" she asked. "You know as much as I."

"Only bits," he replied eagerly, "but I don't know van Heerden's game. I know why he's marrying this other girl, everybody knows that. When is the wedding?"

"What other girl?" she asked.

"Cresswell or Prédeaux, whatever she calls herself," said Bridgers carelessly. "She was a store girl, wasn't she?"

"But"—she tried to speak calmly—"why do you think he wants to marry her?"

He laughed softly.

"Don't be silly," he said, "you can't fool me. Everybody knows she's worth a million."

"Worth a million?" she gasped.

"Worth a million." He smacked his lips and fumbled for the little box in his waistcoat pocket. "Try a sniff —you'll know what it feels like to be old man Millinborn's heiress."

There was a sound in the hall below and he turned with an exaggerated start (she thought it theatrical but could not know of the jangled nerves of the drug-soddened man which magnified all sound to an intensity which was almost painful).

He opened the door and slid out—and did not close the door behind him.

Swiftly she followed, and as she reached the landing saw his head disappear down the stairs. She was in a blind panic; a thousand formless terrors gripped her and turned her resolute soul to water. She could have screamed her relief when she saw that the sliding door was half-open—the man had not stopped to close it—and she passed through and down the first flight. He had vanished before she reached the half-way landing and the hall below was empty. It was a wide hall, stone-flagged, with a glass door between her and the open portal.

She flew down the stairs, pulled open the door and ran straight into van Heerden's arms.

CHAPTER XVII

THE JEW OF CRACOW

IF there were committed in London the crime of the century—a crime so tremendous that the names of the chief actors in this grisly drama were on the lips of every man, woman and talkative child in Europe—you might walk into a certain department of Scotland Yard with the assurance that you would not meet within the confining walls of that bureau any police officer who was interested in the slightest, or who, indeed, had even heard of the occurrence save by accident. This department is known as the Parley Voos or P.V. Department, and concerns itself only in suspicious events beyond the territorial waters of Great Britain and Ireland. Its body is on the Thames Embankment, but its soul is at the Central Office, or at the Sûreté or even at the Yamen of the police minister of Pekin.

It is sublimely ignorant of the masters of crime who dwell beneath the shadows of the Yard, but it could tell you, without stopping to look up reference, not only the names of the known gunmen of New York, but the composition of almost every secret society in China.

A Pole had a quarrel with a Jew in the streets of Cracow, and they quarrelled over the only matter which is worthy of quarrel in that part of Poland. The sum in dispute was the comparatively paltry one of 260 Kronen, but when the Jew was taken in a dying condition to the hospital he made a statement which was so curious that the Chief

of Police in Cracow sent it on to Vienna and Vienna sent
it to Berne and Berne scratched its chin thoughtfully and
sent it forward to Paris, where it was distributed to Rio
de Janeiro, New York, and London.

The Assistant Chief of the P.V. Department came out
of his room and drifted aimlessly into the uncomfortable
bureau of Mr. McNorton.

"There's a curious yarn through from Cracow," he
said, "which might interest your friend Beale."

"What is it?" asked McNorton, who invariably found
the stories of the P.V. Department fascinating but profitless.

"A man was murdered," said the P.V. man lightly, as
though that were the least important feature of the story,
"but before he pegged out he made a will or an assign-
ment of his property to his son, in the course of which he
said that none of his stocks—he was a corn factor—were
to be sold under one thousand Kronen a bushel. That's
about £30."

"Corn at £30 a bushel?" said McNorton. "Was he
delirious?"

"Not at all," said the other. "He was a very well-
known man in Cracow, one Zibowski, who during the late
war was principal buying agent for the German Government. The Chief of the Police at Cracow apparently
asked him if he wasn't suffering from illusions, and the man
then made a statement that the German Government
had an option on all the grain in Galicia, Hungary and
the Ukraine at a lower price. Zibowski held out for better
terms. It is believed that he was working with a member
of the German Government who made a fortune in the
war out of army contracts. In fact, he as good as let this
out just before he died, when he spoke in his delirium of
a wonderful invention which was being worked on behalf
of the German Government, an invention called the Green
Rust."

McNorton whistled.

"Is that all?" he said.

"That's all," said the P.V. man. "I seem to remember
that Beale had made one or two mysterious references
to the Rust. Where is he now?"

" He left town last night," replied McNorton.

" Can you get in touch with him ? "

The other shook his head.

" I suppose you are sending on a copy of this communication to the Cabinet," he said—" it may be rather serious. Whatever the scheme is, it is being worked in London, and van Heerden is the chief operator."

He took down his hat and went out in search of Kitson, whom he found in the lobby of the hotel. James Kitson came toward him eagerly.

" Have you news of Beale ? "

" He was at Kingston this morning," said McNorton, " with Parson Homo, but he had left. I was on the 'phone to the inspector at Kingston, who did not know very much and could give me no very definite news as to whether Beale had made his discovery. He interviewed the tramp early this morning, but apparently extracted very little that was helpful. As a matter of fact, I came to you to ask if he had got in touch with you."

Kitson shook his head.

" I want to see him about his Green Rust scare—Beale has gone single-handed into this matter," said the superintendent, shaking his head, " and he has played the lone game a little too long."

" Is it very serious ? "

" It may be an international matter," replied McNorton gravely, " all that we know at present is this. A big plot is on foot to tamper with the food supplies of the world and the chief plotter is van Heerden. Beale knows more about the matter than any of us, but he only gives us occasional glimpses of the real situation. I have been digging out van Heerden's record without, however, finding anything very incriminating. Up to a point he seems to have been a model citizen, though his associates were not always of the best. He has been seen in the company of at least three people with a bad history. Milsom, a doctor, convicted of murder in the 'nineties ; Bridgers, an American chemist with two convictions for illicit trading in drugs ; Gregory—who seems to be his factotum and general assistant, convicted in Manchester for saccharine smuggling; and a girl called Glaum, who is an alien, charged during the war for failing to register."

" But against van Heerden ? "

" Nothing. He has travelled a great deal in America and on the Continent. He was in Spain a few years ago and was suspected of being associated with the German Embassy. His association with the Millinborn murder you know."

" Yes, I know that," said James Kitson bitterly.

" Beale will have to tell us all he knows," McNorton went on, " and probably we can tell him something he doesn't know ; namely, that van Heerden conducts a pretty expensive correspondence by cable with all parts of the world. Something has happened in Cracow which gives a value to all Beale's suspicions."

Briefly he related the gist of the story which had reached him that morning.

" It is incredible," said Kitson when the chief had finished. " It would be humanly impossible for the world to buy at that price. And there is no reason for it. It happens that I am interested in a milling corporation and I know that the world's crops are good—in fact, the harvest will be well above the average. I should say that the Cracow Jew was talking in delirium."

But McNorton smiled indulgently.

" I hope you're right," he said. " I hope the whole thing is a mare's nest and for once in my life I trust that the police clues are as wrong as hell. But, anyway, van Heerden is cabling mighty freely—and I want Beale ! "

But Beale was unreachable. A visit to his apartment produced no results. The " foreign gentleman " who on the previous day had called on van Heerden had been seen there that morning, but he, too, had vanished, and none of McNorton's watchers had been able to pick him up.

McNorton shifted the direction of his search and dropped into the palatial establishment of Punsonby's. He strolled past the grill-hidden desk which had once held Oliva Cresswell, and saw out of the tail of his eye a stranger in her place and by her side the darkly taciturn Hilda Glaum.

Mr. White, that pompous man, greeted him strangely. As the police chief came into the private office Mr. White half-rose, turned deadly pale and became of a sudden bereft of speech. McNorton recognized the symptoms from long acquaintance with the characteristics of detected criminals, and wondered how deeply this pompous man was committed to whatever scheme was hatching.

" Ah—ah—Mr. McNorton ! " stammered White, shaking like a leaf, " won't you sit down, please ? To what—to what," he swallowed twice before he could get the words out, " to what am I indebted ? "

" Just called in to look you up," said McNorton genially. "Have you been losing any more—registered letters lately ? "

Mr. White subsided again into his chair.

" Yes, yes—no, I mean," he said, " no—ah—thank you. It was kind of you to call, inspector——"

" Superintendent," corrected the other good-humouredly.

" A thousand pardons, superintendent," said Mr. White hastily, " no, sir, nothing so unfortunate."

He shot a look half-fearful, half-resentful at the police officer.

" And how is your friend Doctor van Heerden ? "

Mr. White twisted uncomfortably in his chair. Again his look of nervousness and apprehension.

" Mr.—ah—van Heerden is not a friend of mine," he said, " a business acquaintance," he sighed heavily, " just a business acquaintance."

The White he had known was not the White of to-day. The man looked older, his face was more heavily lined and his eyes were dark with weariness.

" I suppose he's a pretty shrewd fellow," he remarked carelessly. " You are interested in some of his concerns, aren't you ? "

" Only one, only one," replied White sharply, " and I wish to Heaven——"

He stopped himself.

" And you wish you weren't, eh ? "

Again the older man wriggled in his chair.

" Doctor van Heerden is very clever," he said ; " he has

great schemes, in one of which I am—ah—financially interested, That is all—I have put money into his—ah —syndicate, without, of course, knowing the nature of the work which is being carried out. That I would impress upon you."

"You are a trusting investor," said the good-humoured McNorton.

"I am a child in matters of finance," admitted Mr. White, but added quickly, "except, of course, in so far as the finance of Punsonby's, which is one of the soundest business concerns in London, Mr. McNorton. We pay our dividends regularly and our balance sheets are a model for the industrial world."

"So I have heard," said McNorton dryly. "I am interested in syndicates, too. By the way, what is Doctor van Heerden's scheme?"

Mr. White shrugged his shoulders.

"I haven't the slightest idea," he confessed with a melancholy smile. "I suppose it is very foolish of me, but I have such faith in the doctor's genius that when he came to me and said: "My dear White, I want you to invest a few thousand in one of my concerns,' I said: ' My dear doctor, here is my cheque, don't bother me about the details but send in my dividends regularly.' Ha! ha!"

His laugh was hollow, and would not have deceived a child of ten.

"So you invested £40,000——" began McNorton.

"Forty thousand!" gasped Mr. White, "how did you know?"

He went a trifle paler.

"These things get about," said McNorton, "as I was going to say, you invested £40,000 without troubling to discover what sort of work the syndicate was undertaking. I am not speaking now as a police officer, Mr. White," he went on, and White did not disguise his relief, "but as an old acquaintance of yours."

"Say friend," said the fervent Mr. White. "I have always regarded you, Mr. McNorton, as a friend of mine. Let me see, how long have we known one another? I

think the first time we met was when Punsonby's was
burgled in '93."

"It's a long time," said McNorton; "but don't let us
get off the subject of your investment, which interests me
as a friend. You gave Doctor van Heerden all this money
without even troubling to discover whether his enterprise
was a legal one. I am not suggesting it was illegal," he
said, as White opened his mouth to protest, "but it seems
strange that you did not trouble to inquire."

"Oh, of course, I inquired, naturally I inquired, Mr.
McNorton," said White eagerly, "it was for some chemical
process and I know nothing about chemistry. I don't
mind admitting to you," he lowered his voice, though there
was no necessity, "that I regret my investment very much.
We business men have many calls. We cannot allow
our money to be tied up for too long a time, and it
happens—ah—that just at this moment I should be
very glad, very glad indeed, to liquidate that investment."

McNorton nodded. He knew a great deal more about
White's financial embarrassments than that gentleman
gave him credit for. He knew, for example, that the
immaculate managing director of Punsonby's was in the
hands of moneylenders, and that those moneylenders
were squeezing him. He suspected that all was not well
with Punsonby's. There had been curious rumours in the
City amongst the bill discounters that Punsonby's "paper"
left much to be desired.

"Do you know the nationality of van Heerden?" he
asked.

"Dutch," replied Mr. White promptly.

"Are you sure of this?"

"I would stake my life on it," answered the heroic
Mr. White.

"As I came through to your office I saw a young lady
at the cashier's desk—Miss Glaum, I think her name is.
Is she Dutch, too?"

"Miss Glaum—·ah—well Miss Glaum." White hesitated.
"A very nice, industrious girl, and a friend of Doctor
van Heerden's. As a matter of fact, I engaged her

at his recommendation. You see, I was under an obligation to the doctor. He had—ah—attended me in my illness."

That this was untrue McNorton knew. White was one of those financial shuttlecocks which shrewd moneylenders toss from one to the other. White had been introduced by van Heerden to capital in a moment of hectic despair and had responded when his financial horizon was clearer by pledging his credit for the furtherance of van Heerden's scheme.

"Of course you know that as a shareholder in van Heerden's syndicate you cannot escape responsibility for the purposes to which your money is put," he said, as he rose to go. "I hope you get your money back."

"Do you think there is any doubt?" demanded White, in consternation.

"There is always a doubt about getting money back from syndicates," said McNorton cryptically.

"Please don't go yet." Mr. White passed round the end of his desk and intercepted the detective with unexpected agility, taking, so to speak, the door out of his hands and closing it. "I am alarmed, Mr. McNorton," he said, as he led the other back to his chair, "I won't disguise it. I am seriously alarmed by what you have said. It is not the thought of losing the money, oh dear, no. Punsonby's would not be ruined by—ah—a paltry £40,000. It is, if I may be allowed to say so, the sinister suggestion in your speech, inspector—superintendent I mean. Is it possible"—he stood squarely in front of McNorton, his hands on his hips, his eyeglass dangling from his fastidious fingers and his head pulled back as though he wished to avoid contact with the possibility, "is it possible that in my ignorance I have been assisting to finance a scheme which is—ah—illegal, immoral, improper and contrary—ah—to the best interests of the common weal?"

He shook his head as though he were unable to believe his own words.

"Everything is possible in finance," said McNorton with a smile. "I am not saying that Doctor van Heerden's syndicate is an iniquitous one, I have not even seen a copy of his articles of association. Doubtless you could oblige me in that respect."

"I haven't got such a thing," denied Mr. White vigorously, "the syndicate was not registered. It was, so to speak, a private concern."

"But the exploitation of Green Rust?" suggested the superintendent, and the man's face lost the last vestige of colour it possessed.

"The Green Rust?" he faltered. "I have heard the phrase. I know nothing——"

"You know nothing, but suspect the worst," said McNorton. "Now I am going to speak plainly to you. The reason you know nothing about this syndicate of van Heerden's is because you had a suspicion that it was being formed for an illegal purpose—please don't interrupt me— you know nothing because you did not want to know. I doubt even whether you deceived yourself. You saw a chance of making big money, Mr. White, and big money has always had an attraction for you. There isn't a fool's scheme that was ever hatched in a back alley bar that you haven't dropped money over. And you saw a chance here, more tangible than any that had been presented to you."

"I swear to you——" began White.

"The time has not come for you to swear anything," said McNorton sternly, "there is only one place where a man need take his oath, and that is on the witness-stand. I will tell you this frankly, that we are as much in the dark as you pretend to be. There is only one man who knows or guesses the secret of the Green Rust, and that man is Beale."

"Beale!"

"You have met the gentleman, I believe? I hope you don't have to meet him again. The Green Rust may mean little. It may mean no more than that you will lose your money, and I should imagine that is the least which will happen to you. On the other hand, Mr. White, I do not disguise from you the fact that it may also mean your death at the hands of the law."

White made a gurgling noise in his throat and held on to the desk for support.

" I have only the haziest information as to what it is all about, but somehow "—McNorton knit his brows in a frown and was speaking half to himself—" I seem to feel that it is a bad business—a damnably bad business."

He took up his hat from the table and walked to the door.

" I don't know whether to say au revoir or good-bye," he said with twitching lips.

" Good-bye—ah—is a very good old-fashioned word," said Mr. White, in an heroic attempt to imitate the other's good humour.

CHAPTER XVIII

BRIDGERS BREAKS LOOSE

DR. VAN HEERDEN sat by the side of the big four-poster bed, where the girl lay, and his cold blue eyes held a spark of amusement.

" You look very foolish," he said.

Oliva Cresswell turned her head sharply so as to remove the man from her line of vision.

More than this she could not do, for her hands and feet were strapped, and on the pillow, near her head, was a big bath-towel saturated with water which had been employed in stifling her healthy screams which marked her return to understanding.

" You look very foolish," said the doctor, chewing at the end of his cigar, " and you look no more foolish than you have been. Bridgers let you out, eh ? Nice man, Mr. Bridgers ; what had he been telling you ? "

She turned her head again and favoured him with a stare. Then she looked at the angry red mark on her wrists where the straps chafed.

" How Hun-like ! " she said ; but this time he smiled.

"You will not make me lose my temper again, Little-wife-to-be," he mocked her; "you may call me Hun or Heinz or Fritz or any of the barbarous and vulgar names which the outside world employ to vilify my countrymen, but nothing you say will distress or annoy me. To-morrow you and I will be man and wife."

"This is not Germany," she said scornfully. "You cannot make a woman marry you against her will, this is——"

"The land of the free," he interrupted suavely. "Yes —I know those lands, on both sides of the Atlantic. But even there curious things happen. And you're going to marry me—you will say ' Yes ' to the sleek English clergy-man when he asks you whether you will take this man to be your married husband, to love and cherish and all that sort of thing, you'll say ' Yes.' "

"I shall say ' No ! ' " she said steadily.

"You will say ' Yes,' " he smiled. "I had hoped to be able to give sufficient time to you so that I might per-suade you to act sensibly. I could have employed argu-ments which I think would have convinced you that there are worse things than marriage with me."

"I cannot think of any," she replied coldly.

"Then you are singularly dense," said the doctor. "I have already told you the conditions under which that marriage will take place. There might be no marriage, you know, and a different end to this adventure," he said, significantly, and she shivered.

He said nothing more for five minutes, simply sitting biting at the cigar between his teeth and looking at her blankly, as though his thoughts were far away and she was the least of the problems which confronted him.

"I know it is absurd to ask you," he said suddenly, "but I presume you have not devoted any of your studies to the question of capital punishment. I see you haven't; but there is one interesting fact about the execution of criminals which is not generally known to the public, and it is that in many countries, my own for example, before a man is led to execution he is doped with a drug which I will call ' Bromocine.' Does that interest you ? "

She made no reply, and he laughed quietly.

"It should interest you very much," he said. "The effect of Bromocine," he went on, speaking with the quiet precision of one who was lecturing on the subject to an interested audience, "is peculiar. It reduces the subject to a condition of extreme lassitude, so that really nothing matters or seems to matter. Whilst perfectly conscious the subject goes obediently to his death, behaves normally and does just what he is told—in fact, it destroys the will."

"Why do you tell me this?" she asked, a sudden fear gripping her heart.

He half-turned in his chair, reached out his hand and took a little black case from the table near the window. This he laid on the bed and opened, and she watched him, fascinated. He took a tiny bottle containing a colourless liquid, and with great care laid it on the coverlet. Then he extracted a small hypodermic syringe and a needle-pointed nozzle. He uncorked the bottle, inserted the syringe and filled it, then he screwed on the needle, pressed the plunger until a fine jet leapt in the air, then he laid it carefully back in the case.

"You say you will not marry me and I presume that you would make a scene when I bring in the good English parson to perform the ceremony. I had hoped," he said apologetically, "to have given you a wedding with all the pomp and circumstance which women, as I understand, love. Failing that, I hoped for a quiet wedding in the little church out yonder." He jerked his head toward the window. "But now I am afraid that I must ask his reverence to carry out the ceremony in this house."

He rose, leant over her and deftly pulled back her sleeve.

"If you scream I shall smother you with the towel," he said. "This won't hurt you very much. As I was going to say, you will be married here because you are in a delicate state of health and you will say 'Yes.'"

She winced as the needle punctured the skin.

"It won't hurt you for very long," he said calmly. "You will say 'Yes,' I repeat, because I shall tell you to say 'Yes.'"

Suddenly the sharp pricking pain in her arm ceased. She was conscious of a sensation as though her arm was being blown up like a bicycle tyre, but it was not unpleasant. He withdrew the needle and kept his finger pressed upon the little red wound where it had gone in.

"I shall do this to you again to-night," he said, "and you will not feel it at all, and to-morrow morning, and you will not care very much what happens. I hope it will not be necessary to give you a dose to-morrow afternoon."

"I shall not always be under the influence of this drug," she said between her teeth, "and there will be a time of reckoning for you, Dr. van Heerden."

"By which time," he said calmly, "I shall have committed a crime so wonderful and so enormous that the mere offence of 'administering a noxious drug'—that is the terminology which describes the offence—will be of no importance and hardly worth the consideration of the Crown officers. Now I think I can unfasten you." He loosened and removed the straps at her wrists and about her feet and put them in his pocket.

"You had better get up and walk about," he said, "or you will be stiff. I am really being very kind to you if you only knew it. I am too big to be vindictive. And, by the way, I had an interesting talk with your friend, Mr. Beale, this afternoon, a persistent young man who has been having me shadowed all day." He laughed quietly. "If I hadn't to go back to the surgery for the Bromocine I should have missed our very interesting conversation. That young man is very much in love with you"—he looked amusedly at the growing red in her face. "He is very much in love with you," he repeated. "What a pity! What a thousand pities!"

"How soon will this drug begin to act?" she asked.

"Are you frightened?"

"No, but I should welcome anything which made me oblivious to your presence—you are not exactly a pleasant companion," she said, with a return to the old tone he knew so well.

"Content yourself, little person," he said with simulated affection. "You will soon be rid of me."

"Why do you want to marry me?"

"I can tell you that now," he said: "Because you are a very rich woman and I want your money, half of which comes to me on my marriage."

"Then the man spoke the truth!" She sat up suddenly, but the effort made her head swim.

He caught her by the shoulders and laid her gently down.

"What man—not that babbling idiot, Bridgers?" He said something, but instantly recovered his self-posses sion. "Keep quiet," he said with professional sternness. "Yes, you are the heiress of an interesting gentleman named John Millinborn."

"John Millinborn!" she gasped. "The man who was murdered!"

"The man who was killed," he corrected. "'Murder' is a stupid, vulgar word. Yes, my dear, you are his heiress. He was your uncle, and he left you something over six million dollars. That is to say he left *us* that colossal sum."

"But I don't understand. What does it mean?"

"Your name is Prédeaux. Your father was the ruffian——"

"I know, I know," she cried. "The man in the hotel. The man who died. My father!"

"Interesting, isn't it?" he said calmly, "like something out of a book. Yes, my dear, that was your parent, a dissolute ruffian whom you will do well to forget. I heard John Millinborn tell his lawyer that your mother died of a broken heart, penniless, as a result of your father's cruelty and unscrupulousness, and I should imagine that that was the truth."

"My father!" she murmured.

She lay, her face as white as the pillow, her eyes closed.

"John Millinborn left a fortune for you—and I think that you might as well know the truth now—the money was left in trust. You were not to know that you were an heiress until you were married. He was afraid of some fortune-hunter ruining your young life as Prédeaux ruined your mother's. That was thoughtful of him. Now I don't intend ruining your life, I intend leaving you with half your uncle's fortune and the capacity for enjoying all that life can hold for a high-spirited young woman."

" I'll not do it, I'll not do it, I'll not do it," she muttered.

He rose from the chair and bent over her.

" My young friend, you are going to sleep," he said to himself, waited a little longer and left the room, closing the door behind him.

He descended to the hall and passed into the big dining-hall beneath the girl's bedroom. The room had two occupants, a stout, hairless man who had neither hair, eyebrows, nor vestige of beard, and a younger man.

" Hello, Bridgers," said van Heerden addressing the latter, " you've been talking."

" Well, who doesn't ? " snarled the man.

He pulled the tortoiseshell box from his pocket, opened the lid and took a pinch from its contents, snuffling the powder luxuriously.

" That stuff will kill you one of these days," said van Heerden.

" It will make him better-tempered," growled the hairless man. " I don't mind people who take cocaine as long as they are taking it. It's between dopes that they get on my nerves."

" Dr. Milsom speaks like a Christian and an artist," said Bridgers, with sudden cheerfulness. " If I didn't dope, van Heerden, I should not be working in your beastly factory, but would probably be one of the leading analytical chemists in America. But I'll go back to do my chore," he said rising. " I suppose I get a little commission for restoring your palpitating bride ? Milsom tells me that it is she. I thought it was the other dame—the Dutch girl. I guess I was a bit dopey."

Van Heerden frowned.

" You take too keen an interest in my affairs," he said.

" Aw ! You're getting touchy. If I didn't get interested in something I'd go mad," chuckled Bridgers.

He had reached that stage of cocaine intoxication when the world was a very pleasant place indeed and full of subject for jocularity.

"This place is getting right on my nerves," he went on, "couldn't I go to London? I'm stagnating here. Why, some of the stuff I cultivated the other day wouldn't react. Isn't that so, Milsom? I get so dull in this hole that all bugs look alike to me."

Van Heerden glanced at the man who was addressed as Dr. Milsom and the latter nodded.

"Let him go back," he said, "I'll look after him. How's the lady?" asked Milsom when they were alone.

The other made a gesture and Dr. Milsom nodded.

"It's good stuff," he said. "I used to give it to lunatics in the days of long ago."

Van Heerden did not ask him what those days were. He never pryed too closely into the early lives of his associates, but Milsom's history was public property. Four years before he had completed a "life sentence" of fifteen years for a crime which had startled the world in '99.

"How are things generally?" he asked.

Van Heerden shrugged his shoulders.

"For the first time I am getting nervous," he said. "It isn't so much the fear of Beale that rattles me, but the sordid question of money. The expenses are colossal and continuous."

"Hasn't your—Government"—Milsom balked at the word—"haven't your friends abroad moved in the matter yet?"

Van Heerden shook his head.

"I am very hopeful there," he said. "I have been watching the papers very closely, especially the Agrarian papers, and, unless I am mistaken, there is a decided movement in the direction of support. But I can't depend on that. The marriage must go through to-morrow."

"White is getting nervous, too," he went on. "He is pestering me about the money I owe him, or rather the syndicate owes him. He's on the verge of ruin."

Milsom made a little grimace.

"Then he'll squeal," he said, "those kind of people always do. You'll have to keep him quiet. You say the marriage is coming off to-morrow?"

"I have notified the parson," said van Heerden. "I

told him my fiancée is too ill to attend the church and the ceremony must be performed here."

Milsom nodded. He had risen from the table and was looking out upon the pleasant garden at the rear of the house.

"A man could do worse than put in three or four weeks here," he said. "Look at that spread of green."

He pointed to an expanse of waving grasses, starred with the vari-coloured blossoms of wild flowers.

"I was never a lover of nature," said van Heerden, carelessly.

Milsom grunted.

"You have never been in prison," he said cryptically. "Is it time to give your lady another dose?"

"Not for two hours," said van Heerden. "I will play you at piquet."

The cards were shuffled and the hands dealt when there was a scamper of feet in the hall, the door burst open and a man ran in. He was wearing a soiled white smock and his face was distorted with terror.

"M'sieur, m'sieur," he cried, "that imbecile Bridgers!"

"What's wrong?" Van Heerden sprang to his feet.

"I think he is mad. He is dancing about the grounds, singing, and he has with him the preparation!"

Van Heerden rapped out an oath and leapt through the door, the doctor at his heels. They took the short cut and ran up the steps leading from the well courtyard, and bursting through the bushes came within sight of the offender.

But he was not dancing now. He was standing with open mouth, staring stupidly about him.

"I dropped it, I dropped it!" he stammered.

There was no need for van Heerden to ask what he had dropped, for the green lawn which had excited Milsom's admiration was no longer to be seen. In its place was a black irregular patch of earth which looked as though it had been blasted in the furnaces of hell, and the air was filled with the pungent mustiness of decay.

CHAPTER XIX

OLIVA IS WILLING

IT seemed that a grey curtain of mist hung before Oliva's eyes. It was a curtain spangled with tiny globes of dazzling light which grew from nothing and faded to nothing. Whenever she fixed her eyes upon one of these it straightway became two and three and then an unaccountable quantity.

She felt that she ought to see faces of people she knew, for one half of her brain had cleared and was calmly diagnosing her condition, but doing so as though she were somebody else. She was emerging from a drugged sleep; she could regard herself in a curious impersonal fashion which was most interesting. And people who are drugged see things and people. Strange mirages of the mind arise and stranger illusions are suffered. Yet she saw nothing save this silvery grey curtain with its drifting spots of light and heard nothing except a voice saying, "Come along, come along, wake up." A hundred, a thousand times this monotonous order was repeated, and then the grey curtain faded and she was lying on the bed, her head throbbing, her eyes hot and prickly, and two men were looking down at her, one of them a big barefaced man with a coarse mouth and sunken eyes.

"Was it my father really?" she asked drowsily.

"I was afraid of that second dose you gave her last night," said Milsom. "You are getting a condition of coma and that's the last thing you want."

"She'll be all right now," replied van Heerden, but his face was troubled. "The dose was severe—yet she seemed healthy enough to stand a three-minim injection."

Milsom shook his head.

"She'll be all right now, but she might as easily have died," he said. "I shouldn't repeat the dose."

"There's no need," said van Heerden.

"What time is it?" asked the girl, and sat up. She felt very weak and weary, but she experienced no giddiness.

"It is twelve o'clock; you have been sleeping since seven last night. Let me see if you can stand. Get up."

She obeyed meekly. She had no desire to do anything but what she was told. Her mental condition was one of complete dependence, and had she been left to herself she would have been content to lie down again.

Yet she felt for a moment a most intense desire to propound some sort of plan which would give this man the money without going through a marriage ceremony. That desire lasted a minute and was succeeded by an added weariness as though this effort at independent thought had added a new burden to her strength. She knew and was mildly amazed at the knowledge that she was under the influence of a drug which was destroying her will, yet she felt no particular urge to make a fight for freedom of determination. "Freedom of determination." She repeated the words, having framed her thoughts with punctilious exactness, and remembered that that was a great war phrase which one was constantly discovering in the newspapers. All her thoughts were like this—they had the form of marshalled language, so that even her speculations were punctuated.

"Walk over to the window," said the doctor, and she obeyed, though her knees gave way with every step she took. "Now come back—good, you're all right."

She looked at him, and did not flinch when he laid his two hands on her shoulders.

"You are going to be married this afternoon—that's all right, isn't it?"

"Yes," she said, "that is all right."

"And you'll say 'yes' when I tell you to say 'yes,' won't you?"

"Yes, I'll say that," she said.

All the time she knew that this was monstrously absurd. All the time she knew that she did not wish to marry this man. Fine sentences, pompously framed, slowly formed in her mind such as : "This outrage will not go unpunished, comma, and you will suffer for this, comma, Dr. van Heerden, full stop."

But the effort of creating the protest exhausted her so that she could not utter it. And she knew that the words were stilted and artificial, and the working-cells of her brain whispered that she was recalling and adapting something she had heard at the theatre. She wanted to do the easiest thing, and it seemed absurdly easy to say "yes."

"You will stay here until the parson comes," said van Heerden, "and you will not attempt to escape, will you?"

"No, I won't attempt to escape," she said.

"Lie down."

She sat on the bed and swung her feet clear of the ground, settling herself comfortably.

"She'll do," said van Heerden, satisfied. "Come downstairs, Milsom, I have something to say to you."

So they left her, lying with her cheek on her hand, more absorbed in the pattern on the wall-paper than in the tremendous events which threatened.

"Well, what's the trouble?" asked Milsom, seating himself in his accustomed place by the table.

"This," said van Heerden, and threw a letter across to him. "It came by one of my scouts this morning— I didn't go home last night. I cannot risk being shadowed here."

Milsom opened the letter slowly and read:

"A man called upon you yesterday afternoon and has made several calls since. He was seen by Beale, who cross-examined him. Man calls himself Stardt, but is apparently not British. He is staying at Saraband Hotel, Berners Street."

"Who is this?" asked Milsom.

"I dare not hope——" replied the doctor, pacing the room nervously.

"Suppose you dared, what form would your hope take?"

"I told you the other day," said van Heerden, stopping before his companion, "that I had asked my Government to assist me. Hitherto they have refused, that is why

I am so desperately anxious to get this marriage through. I must have money. The Paddington place costs a small fortune—you go back there to-night, by the way——"

Milsom nodded.

"Has the Government relented?" he asked.

"I don't know. I told you that certain significant items in the East Prussian newspapers seemed to hint that they were coming to my assistance. They have sent no word to me, but if they should agree they would send their agreement by messenger."

"And you think this may be the man?"

"It is likely."

"What have you done?"

"I have sent Gregory up to see the man. If he is what I hope he may be, Gregory will bring him here—I have given him the password."

"What difference will it make?" asked Milsom. "You are on to a big fortune, anyway."

"Fortune?" The eyes of Dr. van Heerden sparkled and he seemed to expand at the splendour of the vision which was conjured to his eyes.

"No fortune which mortal man has ever possessed will be comparable. All the riches of all the world will lie at my feet. Milliards upon milliards——"

"In fact, a lot of money," said the practical Dr. Milsom. "'Umph! I don't quite see how you are going to do it. You haven't taken me very much into your confidence, van Heerden."

"You know everything."

Milsom chuckled.

"I know that in the safe of my office you have a thousand sealed envelopes addressed, as I gather, to all the scallywags of the world, and I know pretty well what you intend doing; but how do you benefit? And how do I benefit?"

Van Heerden had recovered his self-possession.

"You have already benefited," he said shortly, "more than you could have hoped."

There was an awkward pause; then Milsom asked:

"What effect is it going to have upon this country?"

"It will ruin England," said van Heerden fervently, and the old criminal's eyes narrowed.

"'Umph!" he said again, and there was a note in his voice which made van Heerden look at him quickly.

"This country hasn't done very much for you," he sneered.

"And I haven't done much for this country—yet," countered the other.

The doctor laughed.

"You're turning into a patriot in your old age," he said.

"Something like that," said Milsom easily. "There used to be a fellow at Portland—you have probably run across him—a clever crook named Homo, who used to be a parson before he got into trouble."

"I never met the gentleman, and talking of parsons," he said, looking at his watch, "our own padre is late. But I interrupted you."

"He was a man whose tongue I loathed, and he hated me poisonously," said Milsom, with a little grimace, "but he used to say that patriotism was the only form of religion which survived penal servitude. And I suppose that's the case. I hate the thought of putting this country in wrong."

"You'll get over your scruples," said the other easily. "You are putting yourself in right, anyway. Think of the beautiful time you're going to have, my friend."

"I think of nothing else," said Milsom, "but still——" He shook his head.

Van Heerden had taken up the paper he had brought down and was reading it, and Milsom noted that he was perusing the produce columns.

"When do we make a start?"

"Next week," said the doctor. "I want to finish up the Paddington factory and get away."

"Where will you go?"

"I shall go to the Continent," replied van Heerden, folding up the paper and laying it on the table. "I can conduct operations from there with greater ease. Gregory goes to Canada. Mitchell and Samps have already organized Australia, and our three men in India will have ready workers."

" What about the States ? "

" That has an organization of its own," Van Heerden said ; " it is costing me a lot of money. All the men except you are at their stations waiting for the word ' Go.' You will take the Canadian supplies with you."

" Do I take Bridgers ? "

Van Heerden shook his head.

" I can't trust that fool. Otherwise he would be an ideal assistant for you. Your work is simple. Before you leave I will give you a sealed envelope containing a list of all our Canadian agents. You will also find two code sentences, one of which means ' Commence operations,' and the other, ' Cancel all instructions and destroy apparatus.' "

" Will the latter be necessary ? " asked Milsom.

" It may be, though it is very unlikely. But I must provide against all contingencies. I have made the organization as simple as possible. I have a chief agent in every country, and on receipt of my message by the chief of the organization, it will be repeated to the agents, who also have a copy of the code."

" It seems too easy," said Milsom. " What chance is there of detection ? "

" None whatever," said the doctor promptly. " Our only danger for the moment is this man Beale, but he knows nothing, and so long as we only have him guessing there is no great harm done—and, anyway, he hasn't much longer to guess."

" It seems much too simple," said Milsom, shaking his head.

Van Heerden had heard a footfall in the hall, stepped quickly to the door and opened it.

" Well, Gregory ? " he said.

" He is here," replied the other, and waved his hand to a figure who stood behind him. " Also, the parson is coming down the road."

" Good, let us have our friend in."

The pink-faced foreigner with his stiff little moustache

and his yellow boots stepped into the room, clicked his heels and bowed.

" Have I the honour of addressing Doctor von Heerden ? "

" Van Heerden," corrected the doctor with a smile, " that is my name."

Both men spoke in German.

" I have a letter for your excellency," said the messenger. " I have been seeking you for many days and I wish to report that unauthorized persons have attempted to take this from me."

Van Heerden nodded, tore open the envelope and read the half a dozen lines.

" The test-word is ' Breslau,' " he said in a low voice, and the messenger beamed.

" I have the honour to convey to you the word." He whispered something in van Heerden's ear and Milsom, who did not understand German very well and had been trying to pick up a word or two, saw the look of exultation that came to the doctor's face.

He leapt back and threw out his arms, and his strong voice rang with the words which the German hymnal has made famous :

" Gott sei Dank durch alle Welt, Gott sei Dank durch alle Welt ! "

" What are you thanking God about ? " asked Milsom.

" It's come, it's come ! " cried van Heerden, his eyes ablaze. " The Government is with me ; behind me, my beautiful country. Oh, Gott sei Dank ! "

" The parson," warned Milsom.

A young man stood looking through the open door.

" The parson, yes," said van Heerden, " there's no need for it, but we'll have this wedding. Yes, we'll have it ! Come in, sir."

He was almost boyishly jovial. Milsom had never seen him like that before.

" Come in, sir."

" I am sorry to hear your fiancée is ill," said the curate.

" Yes, yes, but that will not hinder the ceremony. I'll go myself and prepare her."

Milsom had walked round the table to the window, and it was he who checked the doctor as he was leaving the room.

" Doctor," he said, " come here."

Van Heerden detected a strain of anxiety in the other's voice.

" What is it ? " he said.

" Do you hear somebody speaking ? "

They stood by the window and listened intently.

" Come with me," said the doctor, and he walked noise-lessly and ascended the stairs, followed more slowly by his heavier companion.

CHAPTER XX

THE MARRIAGE

A QUARTER of a mile from Deans Folly a motor-car was halted on the side of a hill overlooking the valley in which van Heerden's house was set.

" That's the house," said Beale, consulting the map, " and that wall that runs along the road is the wall the tramp described."

" You seem to put a lot of faith in the statement of a man suffering from delirium tremens," said Parson Homo dryly.

" He was not suffering from delirium tremens this morn-ing. You didn't see him ? "

Homo shook his head.

" I was in London fixing the preliminaries of your nup-tials," he said sarcastically. " It may be the house," he admitted ; " where is the entrance ? "

" There's a road midway between here and the river and a private road leading off," said Beale ; " the gate, I presume, is hidden somewhere in those bushes."

He raised a pair of field-glasses and focused them.

" Yes, the gate's there," he said. " Do you see that man ? "

Homo took the glasses and looked.

" Looks like a watcher," he said, " and if it is your friend's place the gate will be locked and barred. Why don't you get a warrant ? "

Beale shook his head.

" He'd get wind of it and be gone. No, our way in is over the wall. The ' hobo ' said there's a garden door somewhere."

They left the car and walked down the hill and presently came to a corner of the high wall which surrounded Deans Folly.

Beale passed on ahead.

" Here's the door," he said.

He tried it gingerly and it gave a little.

" It's clogged, and you won't get it open," said Homo ; " it's the wall or nothing."

Beale looked up and down the road. There was nobody in sight and he made a leap, caught the top of the wall and drew himself up. Luckily the usual *chevaux de frise* was absent. Beneath him and a little to the right was a shed built against the wall, the door of which was closed.

He signalled Homo to follow and dropped to the ground. In a minute both men were sheltering in the clump of bushes where on the previous day Oliva had waited before making a dart for the garden door.

" There's been a fire here," said Homo in a low voice, and pointed to a big ugly patch of black amidst the green.

Beale surveyed it carefully, then wormed his way through the bushes until he was within reach of the ruined plot. He stretched out his hand and pulled in a handful of the debris, examined it carefully and stuffed it into his pocket.

" You are greatly interested in a grass fire," said Homo curiously.

" Yes, aren't I ? " replied Beale.

They spent the next hour reconnoitring the ground. Once the door of the wall-shed opened, two men came out and walked to the house, and they had to lie motionless until after a seemingly interminable interval they returned again, stopping in the middle of the black patch to talk. Beale saw one pointing to the ruin and the other shook his head and they both returned to the shed and the door closed behind them.

"There's somebody coming down the main drive," whispered Homo.

They were now near the house and from where they lay had a clear view of fifty yards of the drive.

"It's a brother brush!" said Homo, in a chuckling whisper.

"A what?" asked Beale.

"A parson."

"A parson?"

He focused his glasses. Some one in clerical attire accompanied by the man whom Beale recognized as the guard of the gate, was walking quickly down the drive. There was no time to be lost. But now for the first time doubts assailed him. His great scheme seemed more fantastic and its difficulties more real. What could be easier than to spring out and intercept the clergyman, but would that save the girl? What force did the house hold? He had to deal with men who would stop short at nothing to achieve their purpose and in particular one man who had not hesitated at murder.

He felt his heart thumping, not at the thought of danger, though danger he knew was all round, but from sheer panic that he himself was about to play an unworthy part. Whatever fears or doubts he may have had suddenly fell away from him and he rose to his knees, for not twenty yards away at a window, her hands grasping the bars, her apathetic eyes looking listlessly toward where he crouched, was Oliva Cresswell.

Regardless of danger, he broke cover and ran toward her.

"Miss Cresswell," he called.

She looked at him across the concrete well without astonishment and without interest.

"It is you," she said, with extraordinary calm.

He stood on the brink of the well hesitating. It was too far to leap and he remembered that behind the lilac bush he had seen a builder's plank. This he dragged out and passed it across the chasm, leaning the other end upon a ledge of brickwork which butted from the house.

He stepped quickly across, gripped the bars and found a foothold on the ledge, the girl standing watching him without any sign of interest. He knew something was wrong. He could not even guess what that something was. This was not the girl he knew, but an Oliva Cresswell from whom all vitality and life had been sapped.

" You know me ? " he said. " I am Mr. Beale."

" I know you are Mr. Beale," she replied evenly.

" I have come to save you," he said rapidly. " Will you trust me ? I want you to trust me," he said earnestly. " I want you to summon every atom of faith you have in human nature and invest it in me. Will you do this for me ? "

" I will do this for you," she said, like a child repeating a lesson.

" I—I want you to marry me." He realized as he said these words in what his fear was founded. He knew now that it was her refusal even to go through the form of marriage which he dared not face.

The truth leapt up to him and sent the blood pulsing through his head, that behind and beyond his professional care for her he loved her. He waited with bated breath, expecting her amazement, her indignation, her distress. But she was serene and untroubled, did not so much as raise her eyelids by the fraction of an inch as she answered :

" I will marry you."

He tried to speak but could only mutter a hoarse, " Thank you."

He turned his head. Homo stood at the end of the plank and he beckoned him.

Parson Homo came to the centre of the frail bridge, slipped a Prayer Book from his tail pocket and opened it.

" Dearly beloved, we are come together here in the sight of God to join together this Man and this Woman in Holy Matrimony. . . .

" I require and charge you both as ye will answer at the

dreadful Day of Judgment when the secret of all hearts shall be disclosed that if either of you know any impediment why ye may not be joined together in Matrimony ye do now confess it."

Beale's lips were tight pressed. The girl was looking serenely upward to a white cloud that sailed across the western skies.

Homo read quickly, his enunciation beautifully clear, and Beale found himself wondering when last this man had performed so sacred an office. He asked the inevitable question and Beale answered. Homo hesitated, then turned to the girl.

"Wilt thou have this man to be thy wedded husband to live together after God's ordinance in the holy estate of Matrimony ? Wilt thou obey him and serve him, love, honour and keep him in sickness and in health ; and forsaking all others keep thee only unto him, so long as ye both shall live ? "

The girl did not immediately answer, and the pause was painful to the two men, but for different reasons. Then she suddenly withdrew her gaze from the sky and looked Homo straight in the face.

"I will," she said.

The next question in the service he dispensed with. He placed their hands together, and together repeating his words, they plighted their troth. Homo leant forward and again joined their hands and a note of unexpected solemnity vibrated in his voice when he spoke.

"Those whom God hath joined together let no man put asunder."

Beale drew a deep breath then :

"Very pretty indeed," said a voice.

The detective swung across the window to bring the speaker into a line of fire.

"Put down your gun, admirable Mr. Beale." Van Heerden stood in the centre of the room and the bulky figure of Milsom filled the doorway.

"Very pretty indeed, and most picturesque," said van Heerden. "I didn't like to interrupt the ceremony. Perhaps you will now come into the house, Mr. Beale, and

I will explain a few things to you. You need not trouble about your—wife. She will not be harmed."

Beale, revolver still in hand, made his way to the door and was admitted.

" You had better come along, Homo," he said, " we may have to bluff this out."

Van Heerden was waiting for him in the hall and invited him no farther.

" You are perfectly at liberty to take away your wife," said van Heerden ; " she will probably explain to you that I have treated her with every consideration. Here she is."

Oliva was descending the stairs with slow, deliberate steps.

" I might have been very angry with you," van Heerden went on, with that insolent drawl of his ; " happily I do not find it any longer necessary to marry Miss Cresswell. I was just explaining to this gentleman "—he pointed to the pallid young curate in the background—" when your voices reached me. Nevertheless, I think it only right to tell you that your marriage is not a legal one, though I presume you are provided with a special licence."

" Why is it illegal ? " asked Beale.

He wondered if Parson Homo had been recognized.

" In the first place because it was not conducted in the presence of witnesses," said van Heerden.

It was Homo who laughed.

" I am afraid that would make it illegal but for the fact that you witnessed the ceremony by your own confession, and so presumably did your fat friend behind you."

Mr. Milsom scowled.

" You were always a bitter dog to me, Parson," he said, " but I can give you a reason why it's illegal," he said triumphantly. " That man is Parson Homo, a well-known crook who was kicked out of the Church fifteen years ago. I worked alongside him in Portland."

Homo smiled crookedly.

" You are right up to a certain point, Milsom," he said, " but you are wrong in one essential. By a curious oversight I was never unfrocked, and I am still legally a priest of the Church of England."

"Heavens!" gasped Beale, "then this marriage is legal!"

"It's as legal as it can possibly be," said Parson Homo complacently.

CHAPTER XXI

BEALE SEES WHITE

" IN a sense," said Lawyer Kitson, "it is a tragedy. In a sense it is a comedy. The most fatal comedy of errors that could be imagined."

Stanford Beale sat on a low chair, his head in his hands, the picture of dejection.

" I don't mind your kicks," he said, without looking up; "you can't say anything worse about me than I am saying about myself. Oh, I've been a fool, an arrogant mad fool."

Kitson, his hands clasped behind his back under his tail coat, his gold-rimmed pince-nez perched on his nose, looked down at the young man.

" I am not going to tell you that I was against the idea from the beginning, because that is unnecessary. I ought to have put my foot down and stopped it. I heard you were pretty clever with a gun, Stanford. Why didn't you sail in and rescue the girl as soon as you found where she was?"

" I don't think there would have been a ghost of a chance," said the other, looking up. " I am not finding excuses, but I am telling you what I know. There were four or five men in the house and they were all pretty tough citizens—I doubt if I would have made it that way."

" You think he would have married her?"

"He admitted as much," said Stanford Beale, "the parson was already there when I butted in."

"What steps are you taking to deal with this man van Heerden?"

Beale laughed helplessly.

"I cannot take any until Miss Cresswell recovers."

"Mrs. Beale," murmured Kitson, and the other went red.

"I guess we'll call her Miss Cresswell, if you don't mind," he said sharply, "see here, Mr. Kitson, you needn't make things worse than they are. I can do nothing until she recovers and can give us a statement as to what happened. McNorton will execute the warrant just as soon as we can formulate a charge. In fact, he is waiting downstairs in the hope of seeing——" he paused, "Miss Cresswell. What does the doctor say?"

"She's sleeping now."

"It's maddening, maddening," groaned Beale, "and yet if it weren't so horrible I could laugh. Yesterday I was waiting for a 'hobo' to come out of delirium tremens. To-day I am waiting for Miss Cresswell to recover from some devilish drug. I've made a failure of it, Mr. Kitson."

"I'm afraid you have," said the other dryly; "what do you intend doing?"

"But does it occur to you," asked Kitson slowly, "that this lady is not aware that she has married you and that we've got to break the news to her? That's the part I don't like."

"And you can bet it doesn't fill me with rollicking high spirits," snapped Beale; "it's a most awful situation."

"What are you going to do?" asked the other again.

"What are you going to do?" replied the exasperated Beale, "after all, you're her lawyer."

"And you're her husband," said Kitson grimly, "which reminds me." He walked to his desk and took up a slip of paper. "I drew this out against your coming. This is a certified cheque for £400,000, that is nearly two million dollars, which I am authorized to hand to Oliva's husband on the day of her wedding."

Beale took it from the other's fingers, read it carefully

and tore it into little pieces, after which conversation flagged. After awhile Beale asked :

" What do I have to do to get a divorce ? "

" Well," said the lawyer, " by the English law if you leave your wife and go away, and refuse to return to her she can apply to a judge of the High Court, who will order you to return within fourteen days."

" I'd come back in fourteen seconds if she wanted me," said Beale fervently.

" You're hopeless," said Kitson, " you asked how you could get a divorce. I presume you want one."

" Of course I do. I want to undo the whole of this horrible tangle. It's absurd and undignified. Can nothing be done without Miss Cresswell knowing ? "

" Nothing can be done without your wife's knowledge," said Kitson.

He seemed to take a fiendish pleasure in reminding the unhappy young man of his misfortune.

" I am not blaming you," he said more soberly, " I blame myself. When I took this trust from poor John Millinborn I never realized all that it meant or all the responsibility it entailed. How could I imagine that the detective I employed to protect the girl from fortune hunters would marry her ? I am not complaining," he said hastily, seeing the wrath rise in Beale's face, " it is very unfortunate, and you are as much the victim of circumstances as I. But unhappily we have not been the real victims."

" I suppose," said Beale, looking up at the ceiling, " if I were one of those grand little mediæval knights or one of those gallant gentlemen one reads about I should blow my brains out."

" That would be a solution," said Mr. Kitson, " but we should still have to explain to your wife that she was a widow."

" Then what am I to do ? "

" Have a cigar," said Kitson.

He took two from his vest pocket and handed one to his companion, and his shrewd old eyes twinkled.

" It's years and years since I read a romantic story,"

he said, "and I haven't followed the trend of modern literature very closely, but I think that your job is to sail in and make the lady love you."

Beale jumped to his feet.

"Do you mean that? Pshaw! It's absurd! It's ridiculous! She would never love me."

"I don't see why anybody should, least of all your wife," said Kitson, "but it would certainly simplify matters."

"And then?"

"Marry her all over again," said Kitson, sending a big ring of smoke into the air, "there's no law against it. You can marry as many times as you like, providing you marry the same woman."

"But, suppose—suppose she loves somebody else?" asked Beale hoarsely.

"Why then it will be tough on you," said Kitson, "but tougher on her. Your business is to see that she doesn't love somebody else."

"But how?"

A look of infinite weariness passed across Kitson's face. He removed his glasses and put them carefully into their case.

"Really, as a detective," he said, "you may be a prize exhibit, but as an ordinary human being you wouldn't even get a consolation prize. You have got me into a mess and you have got to get me out. John Millinborn was concerned only with one thing—the happiness of his niece. If you can make your wife, Mrs. Stanford Beale" (Beale groaned), "if you can make your good lady happy," said the remorseless lawyer, "my trust is fulfilled. I believe you are a white man, Beale," he said with a change in his tone, "and that her money means nothing to you. I may not be able to give a young man advice as to the best method of courting his wife, but I know something about human nature, and if you are not straight, I have made one of my biggest mistakes. My advice to you is to leave her alone for a day or two until she's quite recovered. You have plenty to occupy your mind. Go out and fix van Heerden, but not for his treatment of the girl—she mustn't figure in a case of that kind, for all the facts will come out. You think you have another charge against him; well, prove it. That man killed John Millinborn and I believe you can put him behind bars. As the guardian angel of Oliva Cresswell you have shown certain lamentable deficiencies "—the smile in his eyes was infectious; and Stanford Beale smiled in sympathy. " In that capacity I have no further use for your services and you are fired, but you can consider yourself re-engaged on the spot to settle with van Heerden. I will pay all the expenses of the chase—but get him."

He put out his hand and Stanford gripped it.

" You're a great man, sir," he breathed.

The old man chuckled.

" And you may even be a great detective," he said. " In five minutes your Mr. Lassimus White will be here. You suggested I should send for him—who is he, by the way ? "

" The managing director of Punsonby's. A friend of van Heerden's and a shareholder in his Great Adventure."

" But he knows nothing ? "

There was a tap at the door and a page-boy came into the sitting-room with a card.

" Show the gentleman up," said Kitson; " it is our friend," he explained.

" And he may know a great deal," said Beale.

Mr. White stalked into the room dangling his glasses with the one hand and holding his shiny silk hat with the other. He invariably carried his hat as though it were a rifle he were shouldering.

He bowed ceremoniously and closed the door behind him.

" Mr.—ah—Kitson ? " he said, and advanced a big hand. " I received your note and am, as you will observe, punctual. I may say that my favourite motto is ' Punctuality is the politeness of princes.' "

" You know Mr. Beale ? "

Mr. White bowed stiffly.

" I have—ah—met Mr. Beale."

"In my unregenerate days," said Beale cheerfully, "but I am quite sober now."

"I am delighted to learn this," said Mr. White. "I am extremely glad to learn this."

"Mr. Kitson asked you to come, Mr. White, but really it is I who want to see you," said Beale. "To be perfectly frank, I learnt that you were in some slight difficulty."

"Difficulty?" Mr. White bristled. "Me, sir, in difficulty? The head of the firm of Punsonby's, whose credit stands, sir, as a model of sound industrial finance? Oh no, sir."

Beale was taken aback. He had depended upon information which came from unimpeachable sources to secure the co-operation of this pompous windbag.

"I'm sorry," he said. "I understood that you had called a meeting of creditors and had offered to sell certain shares in a syndicate which I had hoped to take off your hands."

Mr. White inclined his head graciously.

"It is true, sir," he said, "that I asked a few—ah—wholesale firms to meet me and to talk over things. It is also true that I—ah—had shares which had ceased to interest me, but those shares are sold."

"Sold! Has van Heerden bought them in?" asked Beale eagerly; and Mr. White nodded.

"Doctor van Heerden, a remarkable man, a truly remarkable man." He shook his head as if he could not bring himself and never would bring himself to understand how remarkable a man the doctor was. "Doctor van Heerden has repurchased my shares and they have made me a very handsome profit."

"When was this?" asked Beale.

"I really cannot allow myself to be cross-examined, young man," he said severely, "by your accent I perceive that you are of trans-Atlantic origin, but I cannot allow you to hustle me—hustle I believe is the word. The firm of Punsonby's——"

"Forget 'em," said Beale tersely. "Punsonby's has been on the verge of collapse for eight years. Let's get square, Mr. White. Punsonby's is a one man company and you're that man. Its balance sheets are faked, its reserves are non-existent. Its sinking fund is *spurlos versenkt.*"

" Sir ! "

" I tell you I know Punsonby's—I've had the best accountants in London working out your position, and I know you live from hand to mouth and that the margin between your business and bankruptcy is as near as the margin between you and prison."

Mr. White was very pale.

" But that isn't my business and I dare say that the money van Heerden paid you this morning will stave off your creditors. Anyway, I'm not running a Pure Business Campaign. I'm running a campaign against your German friend van Heerden."

" A German ? " said the virtuous Mr. White in loud astonishment. " Surely not—a Holland gentleman——"

" He's a German and you know it. You've been financing him in a scheme to ruin the greater part of Europe and the United States, to say nothing of Canada, South America, India and Australia."

" I protest against such an inhuman charge," said Mr. White solemnly, and he rose. " I cannot stay here any longer——"

" If you go I'll lay information against you," said Beale. " I'm in dead earnest, so you can go or stay. First of all, I want to know in what form you received the money ? "

" By cheque," replied White in a flurry.

" On what bank ? "

" The London branch of the Swedland National Bank."

" A secret branch of the Dresdner Bank," said Beale. " That's promising. Has Doctor Van Heerden ever paid you money before ? "

By now Mr. White was the most tractable of witnesses. All his old assurance had vanished, and his answers were almost apologetic in tone.

" Yes, Mr. Beale, small sums."

" On what bank ? "

" On my own bank."

" Good again. Have you ever known that he had an

account elsewhere—for example, you advanced him a very considerable sum of money ; was your cheque cleared through the Swedland National Bank ? "

" No, sir—through my own bank."

Beale fingered his chin.

" Money this morning and he took his loss in good part—that can only mean one thing." He nodded. " Mr. White, you have supplied me with valuable information."

" I trust I have said nothing which may—ah—incriminate one who has invariably treated me with the highest respect," Mr. White hastened to say.

" Not more than he is incriminated," smiled Stanford. " One more question. You know that van Heerden is engaged in some sort of business—the business in which you invested your money. Where are his factories ? "

But here Mr. White protested he could offer no information. He recalled, not without a sinking of heart, a similar cross-examination on the previous day at the hands of McNorton. There were factories—van Heerden had hinted as much—but as to where they were located—well, confessed Mr. White, he hadn't the slightest idea.

" That's rubbish," said Beale roughly, " you know. Where did you communicate with van Heerden ? He wasn't always at his flat and you only came there twice."

" I assure you——" began Mr. White, alarmed by the other's vehemence.

" Assure nothing," thundered Beale, " your policies won't sell—where did you see him ? "

" On my honour——"

" Let's keep jokes outside of the argument," said Beale truculently, " where did you see him ? "

" Believe me, I never saw him—if I had a message to send, my cashier—ah—Miss Glaum, an admirable young lady—carried it for me."

" Hilda Glaum ! "

Beale struck his palm. Why had he not thought of Hilda Glaum before?

" That's about all I want to ask you, Mr. White," he said mildly ; " you're a lucky man."

" Lucky, sir ! " Mr. White recovered his hauteur as

quickly as Beale's aggressiveness passed. " I fail to perceive my fortune. I fail to see, sir, where luck comes in."

" You have your money back," said Beale significantly,
" if you hadn't been pressed for money and had not pressed
van Heerden you would have whistled for it."

" Do you suggest," demanded White, in his best judicial
manner, " do you suggest in the presence of a witness
with a due appreciation of the actionable character of your
words that Doctor van Heerden is a common swindler ? "

" Not common," replied Beale, " thank goodness ! "

CHAPTER XXII

HILDA GLAUM LEADS THE WAY

BEALE had a long consultation with McNorton at
Scotland Yard, and on his return to the hotel, had
his dinner sent up to Kitson's private room and dined
amidst a litter of open newspapers. They were representative journals of the past week, and he scanned their columns
carefully. Now and again he would cut out a paragraph
and in one case half a column.

Kitson, who was dining with a friend in the restaurant
of the hotel, came up toward nine o'clock and stood looking
with amusement at the detective's silent labours.

" You're making a deplorable litter in my room," he
said, " but I suppose there is something very mysterious
and terrible behind it all. Do you mind my reading your
cuttings ? "

" Go ahead," said Beale, without raising his eyes from
his newspaper.

Kitson took up a slip and read aloud :

" The reserves of the Land Bank of the Ukraine
have been increased by ten million roubles. This
increase has very considerably eased the situation

in Southern Ukraine and in Galicia, where there has been considerable unrest amongst the peasants due to the high cost of textiles."

"That is fascinating news," said Kitson sardonically. "Are you running a scrap-book on high finance ? "

"No," said the other shortly, "the Land Bank is a Loan Bank. It finances peasant proprietors."

"You a shareholder ? " asked Mr. Kitson wonderingly. "No."

Kitson picked up another cutting. It was a telegraphic dispatch dated from Berlin :

"As evidence of the healthy industrial tone which prevails in Germany and the rapidity with which the Government is recovering from the effects of the war, I may instance the fact that an order has been placed with the Leipzieger Spoorwagen Gesselshaft for 60,000 box cars. The order has been placed by the L.S.G. with thirty firms, and the first delivery is due in six weeks."

"That's exciting," said Kitson, "but why cut it out ? "

The next cutting was also dated "Berlin" and announced the revival of the "War Purchase Council" of the old belligerent days as "a temporary measure."

"It is not intended," said the dispatch, "to invest the committee with all its old functions, and the step has been taken in view of the bad potato crop to organize distribution."

"What's the joke about that ? " asked Kitson, now puzzled.

"The joke is that there is no potato shortage—there never was such a good harvest," said Beale. "I keep tag of these things and I know. The *Western Mail* had an article from its Berlin correspondent last week saying that potatoes were so plentiful that they were a drug on the market."

" H'm ! "

" Did you read about the Zeppelin sheds ? " asked
Beale. " You will find it amongst the others. All the
old Zepp. hangars throughout Germany are to be put in
a state of repair and turned into skating-rinks for the
physical development of young Germany. Wonderful
concrete floors are to be laid down, all the dilapidations
are to be made good, and the bands will play daily, wet or
fine."

" What does it all mean ? " asked the bewildered lawyer.

" That The Day—the real Day is near at hand," said
Beale soberly.

" War ? "

" Against the world, but without the flash of a bayonet
or the boom of a cannon. A war fought by men sitting
in their little offices and pulling the strings that will choke
you and me, Mr. Kitson. To-night I am going after van
Heerden. I may catch him and yet fail to arrest his evil
work—that's a funny word, ' evil,' for everyday people to
use, but there's no other like it. To-morrow, whether
I catch him or not, I will tell you the story of the plot
I accidentally discovered. The British Government thinks
that I have got on the track of a big thing—so does Wash-
ington, and I'm having all the help I want."

" It's a queer world," said Kitson.

" It may be queerer," responded Beale, then boldly :
" How is my wife ? "

" Your—well, I like your nerve ! " gasped Kitson.

" I thought you preferred it that way—how is Miss
Cresswell ? "

" The nurse says she is doing famously. She is sleeping
now; but she woke up for food and is nearly normal. She
did not ask for you," he added pointedly.

Beale flushed and laughed.

" My last attempt to be merry," he said. " I suppose
that to-morrow she will be well."

" But not receiving visitors," Kitson was careful to
warn him. " You will keep your mind off Oliva and keep
your eye fixed on van Heerden if you are wise. No man
can serve two masters."

Stanford Beale looked at his watch.

" It is the hour," he said oracularly, and got up.

" I'll leave this untidiness for your man to clear," said Kitson. " Where do you go now ? "

" To see Hilda Glaum—if the fates are kind," said Beale. " I'm going to put up a bluff, believing that in her panic she will lead me into the lion's den with the idea of van Heerden making one mouthful of me. I've got to take that risk. If she is what I think she is, she'll lay a trap for me—I'll fall for it, but I'm going to get next to van Heerden to-night."

Kitson accompanied him to the door of the hotel.

" Take no unnecessary risks," he said at parting, " don't forget that you're a married man."

" That's one of the things I want to forget if you'll let me," said the exasperated young man.

Outside the hotel he hailed a passing taxi and was soon speeding through Piccadilly westward. He turned by Hyde Park Corner, skirted the grounds of Buckingham Palace and plunged into the maze of Pimlico. He pulled up before a dreary-looking house in a blank and dreary street, and telling the cabman to wait, mounted the steps and rang the bell.

A diminutive maid opened the door.

" Is Miss Glaum in ? " he demanded.

" Yes, sir. Will you step into the drawing-room. All the other boarders are out. What name shall I say ? "

" Tell her a gentleman from Krooman Mansions," he answered diplomatically.

He walked into the tawdry parlour and put down his hat and stick, and waited. Presently the door opened and the girl came in. She stopped open-mouthed with sur- prise at the sight of him, and her surprise deepened to suspicion.

" I thought——" she began, and checked herself.

" You thought I was Doctor van Heerden ? Well, I am not."

" You're the man I saw at Heyler's," she said, glowering at him.

" Yes, my name is Beale."

"Oh, I've heard about you. You'll get nothing by prying here," she cried.

"I shall get a great deal by prying here, I think," he said calmly. "Sit down, Miss Hilda Glaum, and let us understand one another. You are a friend of Doctor van Heerden's?"

"I shall answer no questions," she snapped.

"Perhaps you will answer this question," he said, "why did Doctor van Heerden secure an appointment for you at Punsonby's, and why, when you were there, did you steal three registered envelopes which you conveyed to the doctor?"

Her face went red and white.

"That's a lie!" she gasped.

"You might tell a judge and jury that and then they wouldn't believe you," he smiled. "Come, Miss Glaum, let us be absolutely frank with one another. I am telling you that I don't intend bringing your action to the notice of the police, and you can give me a little information which will be very useful to me."

"It's a lie," she repeated, visibly agitated, "I did not steal anything. If Miss Cresswell says so——"

"Miss Cresswell is quite ignorant of your treachery," said the other quietly; "but as you are determined to deny that much, perhaps you will tell me this, what business brings you to Doctor van Heerden's flat in the small hours of the morning?"

"Do you insinuate——?"

"I insinuate nothing. And least of all do I insinuate that you have any love affair with the doctor, who does not strike me as that kind of person."

Her eyes narrowed and for a moment it seemed that her natural vanity would overcome her discretion.

"Who says I go to Doctor van Heerden's?"

"I say so, because I have seen you. Surely you don't forget that I live opposite the amiable doctor?"

"I am not going to discuss my business or his," she said, "and I don't care what you threaten me with or what you do."

"I will do something more than threaten you," he said

ominously, "you will not fool me, Miss Glaum, and the sooner you realize the fact the better. I am going all the way with you if you give me any trouble, and if you don't answer my questions. I might tell you that unless this interview is a very satisfactory one to me I shall not only arrest Doctor van Heerden to-night but I shall take you as an accomplice."

"You can't, you can't." She almost screamed the words.

All the sullen restraint fell away from her and she was electric in the violence of her protest.

"Arrest him! That wonderful man! Arrest me? You dare not! You dare not!"

"I shall dare do lots of things unless you tell me what I want to know."

"What do you want to know?" she demanded defiantly.

"I want to know the most likely address at which your friend the doctor can be found—the fact is, Miss Glaum, the game is up—we know all about the Green Rust."

She stepped back, her hand raised to her mouth.

"The—the Green Rust!" she gasped. "What do you mean?"

"I mean that I have every reason to believe that Doctor van Heerden is engaged in a conspiracy against this State. He has disappeared, but is still in London. I want to take him quietly—without fuss."

Her eyes were fixed on his. He saw doubt, rage, a hint of fear and finally a steady light of resolution shining. When she spoke her voice was calm.

"Very good. I will take you to the place," she said.

She went out of the room and came back five minutes later with her hat and coat on.

"It's a long way," she began.

"I have a taxi at the door."

"We cannot go all the way by taxi. Tell the man to drive to Baker Street," she said.

She spoke no word during the journey, nor was Beale inclined for conversation. At Baker Street Station they stopped and the cab was dismissed. Together they walked in silence, turning from the main road, passing the Central Station and plunging into a labyrinth of streets which was foreign territory to the American.

It seemed that he had passed in one step from one of the best-class quarters of the town to one of the worst. One minute he was passing through a sedate square, lined with the houses of the well-to-do, another minute he was in a slum.

"The place is at the end of this street," she said.

They came to what seemed to be a stable-yard. There was a blank wall with one door and a pair of gates. The girl took a key from her bag, opened the small door and stepped in, and Beale followed.

They were in a yard littered with casks. On two sides of the yard ran low-roofed buildings which had apparently been used as stables. She locked the door behind her, walked across the yard to the corner and opened another door.

"There are fourteen steps down," she said, "have you a light of any kind?"

He took his electric torch from his pocket.

"Give it to me," she said, "I will lead the way."

"What is this place?" he asked, after she had locked the door.

"It used to be a wine merchant's," she said shortly, "we have the cellars."

"We?" he repeated.

She made no reply. At the bottom of the steps was a short passage and another door which was opened, and apparently the same key fitted them all, or else as Beale suspected she carried a pass key.

They walked through, and again she closed the door behind them.

"Another?" he said, as her light flashed upon a steel door a dozen paces ahead.

"It is the last one," she said, and went on.

Suddenly the light was extinguished.

"Your lamp's gone wrong," he heard her say, "but I can find the lock."

He heard a click, but did not see the door open and did

not realize what had happened until he heard a click
again. The light was suddenly flashed on him, level with his
eyes.

" You can't see me," said a mocking voice, " I'm looking
at you through the little spy-hole. Did you see the spy-
hole, clever Mr. Beale ? And I am on the other side of
the door." He heard her laugh. " Are you going to arrest
the doctor to-night ? " she mocked. " Are you going
to discover the secret of the Green Rust—ah ! That is
what you want, isn't it ? "

" My dear little friend," said Beale smoothly, " you will
be very sensible and open that door. You don't suppose
that I came here alone. I was shadowed all the way."

" You lie," she said coolly, " why did I dismiss the cab
and make you walk ? Oh, clever Mr. Beale ! "

He chuckled, though he was in no chuckling mood.

" What a sense of humour ! " he said admiringly, " now
just listen to me ! "

He made one stride to the door, his revolver had flicked
out of his hip-pocket, when he heard the snap of a shutter,
and the barrel that he thrust between the bars met steel.
Then came the grind of bolts and he pocketed his gun.

" So that's that," he said.

Then he walked back to the other door, struck a match
and examined it. It was sheathed with iron. He tapped
the walls with his stick, but found nothing to encourage
him. The floor was solidly flagged, the low roof of the
passage was vaulted and cased with stone.

He stopped in his search suddenly and listened. Above
his head he heard a light patter of feet, and smiled. It
was his boast that he never forgot a voice or a footfall.

" That's my little friend on her way back, running like
the deuce, to tell the doctor," he said. " I have something
under an hour before the shooting starts ! "

CHAPTER XXIII

AT THE DOCTOR'S FLAT

D R. VAN HEERDEN did not hurry his departure from his Staines house. He spent the morning following Oliva's marriage in town, transacting certain important business and making no attempt to conceal his comings and goings, though he knew that he was shadowed. Yet he was well aware that every hour that passed brought danger nearer. He judged (and rightly) that his peril was not to be found in the consequences to his detention of Oliva Cresswell.

" I may have a week's grace," he said to Milsom, " and in the space of a week I can do all that I want."

He spent the evening superintending the dismantling of apparatus in the shed, and it was past ten o'clock on Tuesday before he finished.

It was not until he was seated by Milsom's side in the big limousine and the car was running smoothly through Kingston that he made any further reference to the previous afternoon.

" Is Beale content ? " he asked.

" Eh ? "

Milsom, dozing in the corner of the car, awoke with a start.

" Is Beale content with his prize—and his predicament ? " asked van Heerden.

" Well, I guess he should be. That little job brings him a million. He shouldn't worry about anything further."

But van Heerden shook his head.

" I don't think you have things quite right, Milsom," he said. " Beale is a better man than I thought, and knows my mind a little too well. He was astounded when Homo claimed to be a priest—I never saw a man more stunned in my life. He intended the marriage as a bluff to keep me away from the girl. He analysed the situation exactly, for he knew I was after her money, and that she

as a woman had no attraction for me. He believed—
and there he was justified—that if I could not marry her
I had no interest in detaining her, and engaged Homo
to follow him around with a special licence. He timed
everything too well for my comfort."

Milsom shifted round and peered anxiously at his
companion.

"How do you mean?" he asked. "It was only by
a fluke that he made it in time."

"That isn't what I mean. It is the fact that he knew
that every second was vital, that he guessed I was keen
on a quick marriage and that to forestall me he carried
his (as he thought) pseudo-clergyman with him so that he
need not lose a minute : these are the disturbing factors."

"I don't see it," said Milsom, "the fellow's a crook,
all these Yankee detectives are grafters. He saw a chance
of a big rake off and took it, fifty-fifty of a million fortune
is fine commission ! "

"You're wrong. I'd like to think as you do. Man !
Can't you see that his every action proves that he knows
all about the Green Rust ? "

" Eh ? "

Milsom sat up.

"How—what makes you say that ? "

"It's clear enough. He has already some idea of the
scheme. He has been pumping old Heyler; he even
secured a sample of the stuff—it was a faulty cultivation,
but it might have been enough for him. He surmised
that I had a special use for old Millinborn's money and
why I was in a hurry to get it."

The silence which followed lasted several minutes.

"Does anybody except Beale know? If you settled
him . . . ? "

"We should have to finish him to-night" said van
Heerden, "that is what I have been thinking about all
day."

Another silence.

"Well, why not ? " asked Milsom, "it is all one to
me. The stake is worth a little extra risk."

" It must be done before he finds the Paddington place;

that is the danger which haunts me." Van Heerden was uneasy, and he had lost the note of calm assurance which ordinarily characterized his speech. "There is sufficient evidence there to spoil everything."

"There is that," breathed Milsom, "it was madness to go on. You have all the stuff you want, you could have closed down the factory a week ago."

"I must have a margin of safety—besides, how could I do anything else? I was nearly broke and any sign of closing down would have brought my hungry workers to Krooman Mansions."

"That's true," agreed the other, "I've had to stall 'em off, but I didn't know that it was because you were broke. It seemed to me just a natural reluctance to part with good money."

Further conversation was arrested by the sudden stoppage of the car. Van Heerden peered through the window ahead and caught a glimpse of a red lamp.

"It is all right," he said, "this must be Putney Common, and I told Gregory to meet me with any news."

A man came into the rays of the head-lamp and passed to the door.

"Well," asked the doctor, "is there any trouble?"

"I saw the green lamp on the bonnet," said Gregory (Milsom no longer wondered how the man had recognized the car from the score of others which pass over the common), "there is no news of importance."

"Where is Beale?"

"At the old man's hotel. He has been there all day."

"Has he made any further visits to the police?"

"He was at Scotland Yard this afternoon."

"And the young lady?"

"One of the waiters at the hotel, a friend of mine, told me that she is much better. She has had two doctors."

"And still lives?" said the cynical Milsom. "That makes four doctors she has seen in two days."

Van Heerden leant out of the car window and lowered his voice.

"The Fräulein Glaum, you saw her?"

"Yes, I told her that she must not come to your laboratory again until you sent for her. She asked when you leave."

"That she must not know, Gregory—please remember."

He withdrew his head, tapped at the window and the car moved on.

"There's another problem for you, van Heerden," said Milsom with a chuckle.

"What?" demanded the other sharply.

"Hilda Glaum. I've only seen the girl twice or so, but she adores you. What are you going to do with her?"

Van Heerden lit a cigarette, and in the play of the flame Milsom saw him smiling.

"She comes on after me," he said, "by which I mean that I have a place for her in my country, but not——"

"Not the sort of place she expects," finished Milsom bluntly. "You may have trouble there."

"Bah!"

"That's foolish," said Milsom, "the convict establishments of England are filled with men who said 'Bah' when they were warned against jealous women. If," he went on, "if you could eliminate jealousy from the human outfit, you'd have half the prison warders of England unemployed."

"Hilda is a good girl," said the other complacently, "she is also a good German girl, and in Germany women know their place in the system. She will be satisfied with what I give her."

"There aren't any women like that," said Milsom with decision, and the subject dropped.

The car stopped near the Marble Arch to put down Milsom, and van Heerden continued his journey alone, reaching his apartments a little before midnight. As he stepped out of the car a man strolled across the street. It was Beale's watcher. Van Heerden looked round with a smile, realizing the significance of this nonchalant figure, and passed through the lobby and up the stairs.

He had left his lights full on for the benefit of watchers, and the hall-lamp glowed convincingly through the fan-light. Beale's flat was in darkness, and a slip of paper fastened to the door gave his address.

The doctor let himself into his own rooms, closed the door, switched out the light and stepped into his bureau.

" Hello," he said angrily, " what are you doing here ?— I told you not to come."

The girl who was sitting at the table and who now rose to meet him was breathless, and he read trouble in her face. He could have read pride there, too, that she had so well served the man whom she idolized as a god.

" I've got him, I've got him, Julius ! "

" Got him ! Got whom ? " he asked, with a frown.

" Beale ! " she said eagerly, " the great Beale ! "

She gurgled with hysterical laughter.

" He came to me, he was going to arrest me to-night, but I got him."

" Sit down," he said firmly, " and try to be coherent, Hilda. Who came to you ? "

" Beale. He came to my boarding-house and wanted to know where you had taken Oliva Cresswell. Have you taken her ? " she asked earnestly.

" Go on," he said.

" He came to me full of arrogance and threats. He was going to have me arrested, Julius, because of those letters which I gave you. But I didn't worry about myself, Julius. It was all for you that I thought. The thought that you, my dear, great man, should be put in one of these horrible English prisons—oh, Julius ! "

She rose, her eyes filled with tears, but he stood over her, laid his hands on her shoulders and pressed her back.

" Now, now. You must tell me everything. This is very serious. What happened then ? "

" He wanted me to take him to one of the places."

" One of what places ? " he asked quickly.

" I don't know. He only said that he knew that you had other houses—I don't even know that he said that, but that was the impression that he gave me, that he knew you were to be found somewhere."

" Go on," said the doctor.

" And so I thought and I thought," said the girl, her hands clasped in front of her, her eyes looking up into his,

" and I prayed God would give me some idea to help you.
And then the scheme came to me, Julius. I said I would
lead him to you."

" You said you would lead him to me ? " he said steadily,
" and where did you lead him ? "

" To the factory in Paddington," she said.

" There ! " he stared at her.

" Wait, wait, wait ! " she said, " oh, please don't blame
me ! I took him into the passage with the doors. I
borrowed his light, and after we had passed and locked
the second door I slipped through the third and slammed
it in his face."

" Then——"

" He is there ! Caught ! Oh, Julius, did I do well ?
Please don't be angry with me ! I was so afraid for you ! "

" How long have you been here ? " he asked.

" Not ten minutes, perhaps five minutes, I don't know.
I have no knowledge of time. I came straight back to
see you."

He stood by the table, gnawing his finger, his head bowed
in concentrated thought.

" There, of all places ! " he muttered ; " there, of all
places ! "

" Oh, Julius, I did my best," she said tearfully.

He looked down at her with a little sneer.

" Of course you did your best. You're a woman and
you haven't brains."

" I thought——"

" You thought ! " he sneered. " Who told you you
could think ? You fool ! Don't you know it was a bluff,
that he could no more arrest me than I could arrest him ?
Don't you realize—did he know you were in the habit of
coming here ? "

She nodded.

" I thought so," said van Heerden with a bitter laugh.
" He knows you are in love with me and he played upon
your fears. You poor little fool ! Don't cry or I shall
do something unpleasant. There, there. Help yourself
to some wine, you'll find it in the tantalus."

He strode up and down the room.

" There's nothing to be done but to settle accounts with Mr. Beale," he said grimly. " Do you think he was watched ? "

" Oh no, no, Julius "—she checked her sobs—" I was so careful."

She gave him a description of the journey and the precautions she had taken.

" Well, perhaps you're not such a fool after all."

He unlocked a drawer in his desk and took out a long-barrelled Browning pistol, withdrew the magazine from the butt, examined and replaced it, and slipped back the cover.

" Yes, I think I must settle accounts with this gentleman, but I don't want to use this," he added thoughtfully, as he pushed up the safety-catch and dropped the weapon in his pocket ; " we might be able to gas him. Anyway, you can do no more good or harm," he said cynically.

She was speechless, her hands, clasped tightly at her breast, covered a damp ball of handkerchief, and her tear-stained face was upturned to his.

" Now, dry your face." He stooped and kissed her lightly on the cheek. " Perhaps what you have done is the best after all. Who knows ? Anyway," he said, speaking his thoughts aloud, " Beale knows about the Green Rust and it can't be very long before I have to go to earth, but only for a little time, my Hilda." He smiled, showing his white teeth, but it was not a pleasant smile, " only for a little time, and then," he threw up his arms, " we shall be rich beyond the dreams of Frankfurt."

" You will succeed, I know you will succeed, Julius," she breathed, " if I could only help you ! If you would only tell me what you are doing ! What is the Green Rust ? Is it some wonderful new explosive ? "

" Dry your face and go home," he said shortly, " you will find a detective outside the door watching you, but I do not think he will follow you."

He dismissed the girl and followed her after an interval of time, striding boldly past the shadow and gaining the cab-stand in Shaftesbury Avenue without, so far as he could see, being followed. But he dismissed the cab in the neighbourhood of Baker Street and continued his journey on foot. He opened the little door leading into the yard but did not follow the same direction as the girl had led Stanford Beale. It was through another door that he entered the vault, which at one time had been the innocent repository of bubbling life and was now the factory where men worked diligently for the destruction of their fellows.

CHAPTER XXIV

THE GREEN RUST FACTORY

STANFORD BEALE spent a thoughtful three minutes in the darkness of the cellar passage to which Hilda Glaum had led him and then he began a careful search of his pockets. He carried a little silver cigar-lighter, which had fortunately been charged with petrol that afternoon, and this afforded him a beam of adequate means to take note of his surroundings.

The space between the two locked doors was ten feet, the width of the passage three, the height about seven feet. The roof, as he had already noted, was vaulted. Now he saw that along the centre ran a strip of beading. There had evidently been an electric light installation here, probably before the new owners took possession, for at intervals was a socket for an electric bulb. The new occupants had covered these and the rest of the wall with whitewash, and yet the beading and the electric fittings looked comparatively new. One wall, that on his left as he had come in, revealed nothing under his close inspection, but on the right wall, midway between the two doors, there had been a notice painted in white letters on a black background, and this showed faintly through the thick coating of distemper which had been applied. He damped a handkerchief with his tongue and rubbed away some of the whitewash where the letters were least legible and read :

AID
LTER.

ULANCE &
T   AID.

This was evidently half an inscription which had been cut off exactly in the middle. To the left there was no sign of lettering. He puzzled the letters for a few moments before he came to an understanding.

"Air-raid shelter. Ambulance and first aid!" he read.

So that explained the new electric fittings. It was one of those underground cellars which had been ferreted out by the Municipality or the Government for the shelter of the people in the neighbourhood during air-raids in the Great War. Evidently there was extensive accommodation here, since this was also an ambulance post. Faintly discernible beneath the letters was a painted white hand which pointed downward. What had happened to the other half of the inscription? Obviously it had been painted on the door leading into the first-aid room and as obviously that door had been removed and had been bricked up. In the light of this discovery he made a more careful inspection of the wall to the left. For the space of four feet the brickwork was new. He tapped it. It sounded hollow. Pressing his back against the opposite wall to give him leverage he put his foot against the new brickwork and pushed.

He knew that the class of workmanship which was put into this kind of job was not of the best, that only one layer of brick was applied, and it was a mechanical fact that pressure applied to the centre of new work would produce a collapse.

At the first push he felt the wall sag. Releasing his pressure it came back. This time he put both feet against the wall and bracing his shoulders he put every ounce of strength in his body into a mighty heave. The next second he was lying on his back. The greater part of the wall had collapsed. He was curious enough to examine the work he had demolished. It had evidently been done by amateurs, and the whitewash which had been thickly applied to the passage was explained.

A current of fresh air came to meet him as he stepped gingerly across the debris. A flight of six stone steps led down to a small room containing a sink and a water supply, two camp beds which had evidently been part of the ambulance equipment and which the new owners had not thought necessary to remove, and a broken chair. The room was still littered with the paraphernalia of first-aid. He found odd ends of bandages, empty medicine bottles and a broken glass measure on the shelf above the sink.

What interested him more was a door which he had not dared to hope he would find. It was bolted on his side, and when he had slid this back he discovered to his relief that it was not locked. He opened it carefully, first extinguishing his light. Beyond the door was darkness and he snapped back the light again. The room led to another, likewise empty. There were a number of shelves, a few old wine-bins, a score of empty bottles, but nothing else. At the far corner was yet another door, also bolted on the inside. Evidently van Heerden did not intend this part of the vault to be used.

He looked at the lock and found it was broken. He must be approaching the main workroom in this new factory, and it was necessary to proceed with caution. He took out his revolver, spun the cylinder and thrust it under his waistcoat, the butt ready to his hand. The drawing of the bolts was a long business. He could not afford to risk detection at this hour, and could only move them by a fraction of an inch at a time. Presently his work was done and he pulled the door cautiously.

Instantly there appeared between door and jamb a bright green line of light. He dare not move it any farther, for he heard now the shuffle of feet, and occasionally the sound of hollow voices, muffled and indistinguishable. In that light the opening of the door would be seen, perhaps by a dozen pair of eyes. For all he knew every man in that room might be facing his way. He had expected to hear the noise of machinery, but beyond the strangled voices, occasionally the click of glass against glass and the shuff-shuff-shuff of slippered feet crossing the floor, he heard nothing.

He pulled the door another quarter of an inch and glued his eye to the crack. At this angle he could only see one of the walls of the big vault and the end of a long vapour-lamp which stood in one of the cornices and which supplied the ghastly light. But presently he saw something which filled him with hope. Against the wall was a high shadow which even the overhead lamp did not wholly neutralize. It was an irregular shadow such as a stack of boxes might make, and it occurred to him that perhaps beyond his range of vision there was a barricade of empty cases which hid the door from the rest of the room.

He spent nearly three-quarters of an hour taking a bearing based upon the problematical position of the lights, the height and density of the box screen and then boldly and rapidly opened the door, stepped through and closed it behind him. His calculations had been accurate. He found himself in a room, the extent of which he could only conjecture. What, however, interested him mostly was the accuracy of his calculation that the door was hidden. An " L "-shaped stack of crates was piled within two feet of the ceiling, and formed a little lobby to anybody entering the vault the way Beale had come. They were stacked neatly and methodically, and with the exception of two larger packing-cases which formed the " corner stone " the barrier was made of a large number of small boxes about ten inches square.

There was a small step-ladder, evidently used by the person whose business it was to keep this stack in order. Beale lifted it noiselessly, planted it against the corner and mounted cautiously.

He saw a large, broad chamber, its groined roof supported by six squat stone pillars. Light came not only from mercurial lamps affixed to the ceiling, but from others suspended above the three rows of benches which ran the length of the room.

Mercurial lamps do not give a green light, as he knew, but a violet light, and the green effect was produced by shades of something which Beale thought was yellow silk, but which he afterwards discovered was tinted mica.

At intervals along the benches sat white-clad figures, their faces hidden behind rubber masks, their hands covered with gloves. In front of each man was a small microscope under a glass shade, a pair of balances and a rack filled with shallow porcelain trays. Evidently the work on which they were engaged did not endanger their eyesight, for the eye-pieces in the masks were innocent of protective covering, a circumstance which added to the hideous animal-like appearance of the men. They all looked alike in their uniform garb, but one figure alone Beale recognized. There was no mistaking the stumpy form and the big head of the Herr Professor, whose appearance in Oliva Cresswell's room had so terrified that young lady.

He had expected to see him, for he knew that this old German, poverty-stricken and ill-favoured, had been roped in by van Heerden, and Beale, who pitied the old man, had been engaged for a fortnight in trying to worm from the ex-professor of chemistry at the University of Heidelberg the location of van Heerden's secret laboratory. His efforts had been unsuccessful. There was a streak of loyalty in the old man, which had excited an irritable admiration in the detective but had produced nothing more.

Beale's eyes followed the benches and took in every detail. Some of the men were evidently engaged in tests, and remained all the time with their eyes glued to their microscopes. Others were looking into their porcelain trays and stirring the contents with glass rods, now and again transferring something to a glass slide which was placed on the microscope and earnestly examined.

Beale was conscious of a faint musty odour permeating the air, an indescribable earthy smell with a tang to it which made the delicate membrane of the nostrils smart and ache. He tied his handkerchief over his nose and mouth before he took another peep. Only part of the room was visible from his post of observation. What was going on immediately beneath the far side of the screen he could only conjecture. But he saw enough to convince him that this was the principal factory, from whence van Heerden was distilling the poison with which he planned humanity's death.

Some of the workers were filling and sealing small test-tubes with the contents of dishes. These tubes were extraordinarily delicate of structure, and Beale saw at least three crumble and shiver in the hands of the fillers.

Every bench held a hundred or so of these tubes and a covered gas-jet for heating the wax. The work went on methodically, with very little conversation between the masked figures (he saw that the masks covered the heads of the chemists so that not a vestige of hair showed), and only occasionally did one of them leave his seat and disappear through a door at the far end of the room, which apparently led to a canteen.

Evidently the fumes against which they were protected were not virulent, for some of the men stripped their masks as soon as they left their benches.

For half an hour he watched, and in the course of that time saw the process of filling the small boxes which formed his barrier and hiding-place with the sealed tubes. He observed the care with which the fragile tubes were placed in their beds of cotton wool, and had a glimpse of the lined interior of one of the boxes. He was on the point of lifting down a box to make a more thorough examination when he heard a quavering voice beneath him.

" What you do here—eh ? "

Under the step-ladder was one of the workers who had slipped noiselessly round the corner of the pile and now stood, grotesque and menacing, his uncovered eyes glowering at the intruder, the black barrel of his Browning pistol covering the detective's heart.

" Don't shoot, colonel," said Beale softly. " I'll come down."

CHAPTER XXV

THE LAST MAN AT THE BENCH

AFTER all, it was for the best—van Heerden could almost see the hand of Providence in this deliverance of his enemy into his power. There must be a settlement with Beale, that play-acting drunkard, who had so deceived him at first.

Dr. van Heerden could admire the ingenuity of his enemy and could kill him. He was a man whose mental poise permitted the paradox of detached attachments. At first he had regarded Stanford Beale as a smart police officer, the sort of man whom Pinkerton and Burns turn out by the score. Shrewd, assertive, indefatigable, such men piece together the scattered mosaics of humdrum crimes, and by their mechanical patience produce for the satisfaction of courts sufficient of the piece to reveal the design. They figure in divorce suits, in financial swindles and occasionally in more serious cases.

Van Heerden knew instinctively their limitations and had too hastily placed Beale in a lower category than he deserved. Van Heerden came to his workroom by way of the buffet which he had established for the use of his employees. As he shut the steel door behind him he saw Milsom standing at the rough wooden sideboard which served as bar and table for the workers.

" This is an unexpected pleasure," said Milsom, and then quickly, as he read the other's face : " Anything wrong ? "

" If the fact that the cleverest policeman in America or England is at present on the premises can be so described, then everything is wrong," said van Heerden, and helped himself to a drink.

" Here—in the laboratory ? " demanded Milsom, fear in his eyes. " What do you mean ? "

" I'll tell you," said the other, and gave the story as he had heard it from Hilda Glaum.

" He's in the old passage, eh ? " said Milsom, thought-

fully, " well there's no reason why he should get out—
alive."

" He won't," said the other.

" Was he followed—you saw nobody outside ? "

" We have nothing to fear on that score. He's working
on his own."

Milsom grunted.

" What are we going to do with him ? "

" Gas him," said van Heerden, " he is certain to have
a gun."

Milsom nodded.

" Wait until the men have gone. I let them go at three
—a few at a time, and it wants half an hour to that. He
can wait. He's safe where he is. Why didn't Hilda tell
me ? I never even saw her."

" She went straight up from the old passage—through
the men's door—she didn't trust you probably."

Milsom smiled wryly. Though he controlled these
works and knew half the doctor's secrets, he suspected
that the quantity of van Heerden's trust was not greatly
in excess of his girl's.

" We'll wait," he said again, " there's no hurry and,
anyway, I want to see you about old man Heyler."

" Von Heyler ? I thought you were rid of him ? "
said van Heerden in surprise, " that is the old fool that
Beale has been after. He has been trying to suck him
dry, and has had two interviews with him. I told you to
send him to Deans Folly. Bridgers would have taken
care of him."

" Bridgers can look after nothing," said Milsom.

His eyes roved along the benches and stopped at a worker
at the farther end of the room.

" He's quiet to-night," he said, " that fellow is too full
of himself for my liking. Earlier in the evening before
I arrived he pulled a gun on Schultz. He's too full of gun-
play that fellow—excuse the idiom, but I was in the same
tailor's shop at Portland Gaol as Ned Garrand, the Yankee
bank-smasher."

Van Heerden made a gesture of impatience.

" About old Heyler," Milsom went on, " I know you

think he's dangerous, so I've kept him here. There's a
room where he can sleep, and he can take all the exercise
he wants at night. But the old fool is restless—he's been
asking me what is the object of his work."

"He's difficult. Twice he has nearly betrayed me.
As I told you in the car, I gave him some experimental
work to do and he brought the result to me—that was
the sample which fell into Beale's hands."

"Mr. Beale is certainly a danger," said Milsom thoughtfully.

Van Heerden made a move toward the laboratory, but
Milsom's big hand detained him.

"One minute, van Heerden," he said, "whilst you're
here you'd better decide—when do we start dismantling?
I've got to find some excuse to send these fellows away."

Van Heerden thought.

"In two days," he said, "that will give you time to
clear. You can send the men—well, send them to Scotland,
some out-of-the-way place where news doesn't travel.
Tell them we're opening a new factory, and put them up
at the local hotel."

Milsom inclined his head.

"That sounds easy," he said, "I could take charge
of them until the time came to skip. One can get a boat
at Greenock."

"I shall miss you," said van Heerden frankly, "you
were necessary to me, Milsom. You're the driving force
I wanted, and the only man of my class and calibre I can
ever expect to meet, one who would go into this business
with me."

They had reached the big vault and van Heerden stood
regarding the scene of mental activity with something
approaching complacency.

"There is a billion in process of creation," he said.

"I could never think in more than six figures," said
Milsom, "and it is only under your cheering influence
that I can stretch to seven. I am going to live in the
Argentine, van Heerden. A house on a hill——"

The other shivered, but Milsom went on.

"A gorgeous palace of a house, alive with servants.

A string band, a perfectly equipped laboratory where I can indulge my passion for research, a high-powered auto, wine of the rarest—ah ! "

Van Heerden looked at his companion curiously.

"That appeals to you, does it ? For me, the control of finance. Endless schemes of fortune ; endless smashings of rivals, railways, ships, great industries juggled and shuffled—that is the life I plan."

"Fine ! " said the other laconically.

They walked to a bench and the worker looked up and took off his mask.

He was an old man, and grinned toothlessly at van Heerden.

"Good evening, Signor Doctor," he said in Italian. " Science is long and life is short, signor."

He chuckled and, resuming his mask, returned to his work, ignoring the two men as though they had no existence.

"A little mad, old Castelli," said Milsom, " that's his one little piece—what crooked thing has he done ? "

"None that I know," said the other carelessly; " he lost his wife and two daughters in the Messina earthquake. I picked him up cheap. He's a useful chemist."

They walked from bench to bench, but van Heerden's eyes continuously strayed to the door, behind which he pictured a caged Stanford Beale, awaiting his doom. The men were beginning to depart now. One by one they covered their instruments and their trays, slipped off their masks and overalls and disappeared through the door, upon which van Heerden's gaze was so often fixed. Their exit, however, would not take them near Beale's prison. A few paces along the corridor was another passage leading to the yard above, and it was by this way that Hilda Glaum had sped to the doctor's room.

Presently all were gone save one industrious worker, who sat peering through the eye-piece of his microscope, immovable.

"That's our friend Bridgers," said Milsom, " he's all lit up with the alkaloid of *Enythroxylon Coca*—— Well, Bridgers, nearly finished ? "

"Huh ! " grunted the man without turning.

Milsom shrugged his shoulders.

"We must let him finish what he's doing. He is quite oblivious to the presence of anybody when he has these fits of industry. By the way, the passing of our dear enemy"—he jerked his head to the passage door—"will make no change in your plans?"

"How?"

"You have no great anxiety to marry the widow?"

"None," said the ·doctor.

"And she isn't a widow yet."

It was not Milsom who spoke, but the man at the bench, the industrious worker whose eye was still at the microscope.

"Keep your comments to yourself," said van Heerden angrily, "finish your work and get out."

"I've finished."

The worker rose slowly and loosening the tapes of his mask pulled it off.

"My name is Beale," he said calmly, "I think we've met before. Don't move, Milsom, unless you want to save living-expenses—I'm a fairly quick shot when I'm annoyed."

Stanford Beale pushed back the microscope and seated himself on the edge of the bench.

"You addressed me as Bridgers," he said, "you will find Mr. Bridgers in a room behind that stack of boxes. The fact is he surprised me spying and was all for shooting me up, but I induced him to come into my private office, so to speak, and the rest was easy—he dopes, doesn't he? He hadn't the strength of a rat. However, that is all beside the point; Dr. van Heerden, what have you to say against my arresting you out of hand on a conspiracy charge?"

Van Heerden smiled contemptuously.

"There are many things I can say," he said. "In the first place, you have no authority to arrest anybody. You're not a police officer but only an American amateur."

"American, yes; but amateur, no," said Beale gently. "As to the authority, why I guess I can arrest you first and get the authority after."

"On what charge?" demanded Milsom, "there is nothing secret about this place, except Doctor van Heerden's association with it—a professional man is debarred from mixing in commercial affairs. Is it a crime to run a——" He looked to van Heerden.

"A germicide factory," said van Heerden promptly.

"Suppose I know the character of this laboratory?" asked Beale quietly.

"Carry that kind of story to the police and see what steps they will take," said van Heerden scornfully. "My dear Mr. Beale, as I have told you once before, you have been reading too much exciting detective fiction."

"Very likely," he said, "but anyhow the little story that enthralls me just now is called the Green Terror, and I'm looking to you to supply a few of the missing pages. And I think you'll do it."

The doctor was lighting a cigarette, and he looked at the other over the flaring match with a gleam of malicious amusement in his eyes.

"Your romantic fancies would exasperate me, but for your evident sincerity. Having stolen my bride you seem anxious to steal my reputation," he said mockingly.

"That," said Beale, slipping off the bench and standing, hands on hips, before the doctor, "would take a bit of finding. I tell you, van Heerden, that I'm going to call your bluff. I shall place this factory in the hands of the police, and I am going to call in the greatest scientists in England, France and America, to prove the charge I shall make against you on the strength of this!"

He held up between his forefinger and thumb a crystal tube, filled to its seal with something that looked like green sawdust.

"The world, the sceptical world, shall know the hell you are preparing for them." Stanford Beale's voice trembled with passion and his face was dark with the thought of a crime so monstrous that even the outrageous treatment of a woman who was more to him than all the world was for the moment obliterated from his mind in the contemplation of the danger which threatened humanity.

"You say that the police and even the government of this country will dismiss my charge as being too fantastic for belief. You shall have the satisfaction of knowing that you are right. They think I am mad—but I will convince them! In this tube lies the destruction of all your fondest dreams, van Heerden. To realize those dreams you have murdered two men. For these you killed John Millinborn and the man Prédeaux. But you shall not——"

" Bang ! "

The explosion roared thunderously in the confined space of the vault. Beale felt the wind of the bullet and turned, pistol upraised.

CHAPTER XXVI

THE SECRET OF THE GREEN RUST

A DISHEVELLED figure stood by the boxes, revolver in hand—it was Bridgers, the man he had left strapped and bound in the " ambulance-room," and Beale cursed the folly which had induced him to leave the revolver behind.

"I'll fix you—you brute!" screamed Bridgers, "get away from him—ah!"

Beale's hand flew up, a pencil of flame quivered and again the vault trembled to the deafening report.

But Bridgers had dropped to cover. Again he shot, this time with unexpected effect. The bullet struck the fuse-box on the opposite wall and all the lights went out.

Beale was still holding the glass tube, and this Milsom had seen. Quick as thought he hurled himself upon the detective, his big, powerful hands gripped the other's wrist and wrenched it round.

Beale set his teeth and manœuvred for a lock grip, but he was badly placed, pressed as he was against the edge of the bench. He felt van Heerden's fingers clawing at his hand and the tube was torn away.

Then somebody pulled the revolver from the other hand and there was a scamper of feet. He groped his way through the blackness and ran into the pile of boxes. A bullet whizzed past him from the half-crazy Bridgers, but that was a risk he had to take. He heard the squeak of an opening door and stumbled blindly in its direction. Presently he found it. He had watched the other men go out and discovered the steps—two minutes later he was in the street.

There was no sign of either of the two men. He found a policeman after he had walked half a mile, but that intelligent officer could not leave his beat and advised him to go to the police station. It was an excellent suggestion, for although the sergeant on duty was wholly unresponsive there was a telephone, and at the end of the telephone in his little Haymarket flat, a Superintendent McNorton, the mention of whose very name galvanized the police office to activity.

"I have found the factory I've been looking for, Mc-Norton," said Beale. "I'll explain the whole thing to you in the morning. What I want now is a search made of the premises."

"We can't do that without a magistrate's warrant,' said McNorton's voice, " but what we can do is to guard the premises until the warrant is obtained. Ask the station sergeant to speak on the 'phone—by the way, how is Miss Cresswell, better, I hope ? "

"Much better," said the young man shortly.

It was unbelievable that she could ever fill his heart with the ache which came at the mention of her name.

He made way for the station sergeant and later accompanied four men back to the laboratory. They found all the doors closed. Beale scaled the wall but failed to find a way in. He rejoined the sergeant on the other side of the wall.

"What is the name of this street ? " he asked.

"Playbury Street, sir—this used to be Henderson's Wine Vaults in my younger days."

Beale jotted down the address and finding a taxi drove back to the police station, wearied and sick at heart.

He arrived in time to be a witness to a curious scene. In the centre of the charge-room and facing the sergeant's desk was a man of middle age, shabbily dressed, but bearing the indefinable air of one who had seen better days. The grey hair was carefully brushed from the familiar face and gave him that venerable appearance which pale eyes and a pair of thin straight lips (curled now in an amused smile) did their best to discount.

By his side stood his captor, a station detective, a bored and apathetic man.

"It seems," the prisoner was saying, as Stanford Beale came noiselessly into the room, "it seems that under this detestable system of police espionage, a fellow may not even take a walk in the cool of the morning."

His voice was that of an educated man, his drawling address spoke of his confidence.

"Now look here, Parson," said the station sergeant, in that friendly tone which the police adopt when dealing with their pet criminals, "you know as well as I do that under the Prevention of Crimes Act you, an old lag, are liable to be arrested if you are seen in any suspicious circumstances—you oughtn't to be wandering about the streets in the middle of the night, and if you do, why you mustn't kick because you're pinched—anything found on him, Smith?"

"No, sergeant—he was just mouching round, so I pulled him in."

"Where are you living now, Parson?"

The man with extravagant care searched his pockets.

"I have inadvertently left my card-case with my coiner's outfit," he said gravely, "but a wire addressed to the Doss House, Mine Street, Paddington, will find me—but I don't think I should try. At this moment I enjoy the protection of the law. In four days' time I shall be on the ocean —why, Mr. Beale?"

Mr. Beale smiled.

"Hullo, Parson—I thought you had sailed to-day."

"The first-class berths are all taken and I will not travel to Australia with the common herd."

He turned to the astonished sergeant.

" Can I go—Mr. Beale will vouch for me ? "

As he left the charge-room he beckoned the detective, and when they were together in the street Beale found that all the Parson's flippancy had departed.

" I'm sorry I got you into that scrape," he said seriously. " I ought to have been unfrocked, but I was sentenced for my first crime under an assumed name. I was not attached to any church at the time and my identity has never been discovered. Mr. Beale," he went on with a quizzical smile, " I have yet to commit my ideal crime—the murder of a bishop who allows a curate to marry a wife on sixty pounds a year." His face darkened, and Beale found himself wondering at the contents of the tragic years behind the man. Where was the wife . . . ?

"But my private grievances against the world will not interest you," Parson Homo resumed, " I only called you out to—well, to ask your pardon."

" It was my own fault, Homo," said Beale quietly, and held out his hand. " Good luck—there may be a life for you in the new land."

He stood till the figure passed out of sight, then turned wearily toward his own rooms. He went to his room and lay down on his bed fully dressed. He was aroused from a troubled sleep by the jangle of the 'phone. It was McNorton.

" Come down to Scotland House and see the Assistant-Commissioner," he said, " he is very anxious to hear more about this factory. He tells me that you have already given him an outline of the plot."

" Yes—I'll give you details—I'll be with you in half an hour."

He had a bath and changed his clothes, and breakfastless, for the woman who waited on him and kept his flat and who evidently thought his absence was likely to be a long one, had not arrived. He drove to the grim grey building on the Thames Embankment.

Assistant-Commissioner O'Donnel, a white-haired police veteran, was waiting for him, and McNorton was in the office.

" You look fagged," said the commissioner, " take that

chair—and you look hungry, too. Have you break-
fasted ? ''

Beale shook his head with a smile.

'' Get him something, McNorton—ring that bell. Don't
protest, my good fellow—I've had exactly the same kind
of nights as you've had, and I know that it is grub that
counts more than sleep.''

He gave an order to an attendant and not until twenty
minutes later, when Beale had finished a surprisingly good
meal in the superintendent's room, did the commissioner
allow the story to be told.

'' Now I'm ready,'' he said.

'' I'll begin at the beginning,'' said Stanford Beale.
'' I was a member of the United States Secret Service until
after the war when, at the request of Mr. Kitson, who is
known to you, I came to Europe to devote all my time to
watching Miss Cresswell and Doctor van Heerden. All that
you know.

'' One day when searching the doctor's rooms in his
absence, my object being to discover some evidence in
relation to the Millinborn murder, I found this.''

He took a newspaper cutting from his pocket-book and
laid it on the table.

'' It is from *El Imparcial*, a Spanish newspaper, and I
will translate it for you.

'' 'Thanks to the discretion and eminent genius
of Dr. Alphonso Romanos, the Chief Medical Officer
of Vigo, the farmers of the district have been spared
a catastrophe much lamentable ' (I am translating
literally). ' On Monday last, Señor Don Marin
Fernardey, of La Linea, discovered one of his fields
of corn had died in the night and was already in a
condition of rot. In alarm, he notified the Chief of
Medicines at Vigo, and Dr. Alphonso Romanos, with
that zeal and alacrity which has marked his acts,
was quickly on the spot, accompanied by a foreign
scientist. Happily the learned and gentle doctor
is a bacteriologist superb. An examination of the
dead corn, which already emitted unpleasant odours,

revealed the presence of a new disease, the verde orin (green rust). By his orders the field was burnt. Fortunately, the area was small and dissociated from the other fields of Señor Fernardey by wide *zanzas*. With the exception of two small pieces of the infected corn, carried away by Dr. Romanos and the foreign medical-cavalier, the pest was incinerated.' "

" The Foreign Medical-Cavalier," said Beale, " was Doctor van Heerden. The date was 1915, when the doctor was taking his summer holiday, and I have had no difficulty in tracing him. I sent one of my men to Vigo to interview Doctor Romanos, who remembers the circumstances perfectly. He himself had thought it wisest to destroy the germ after carefully noting their characteristics, and he expressed the anxious hope that his whilom friend, van Heerden, had done the same. Van Heerden, of course, did nothing of the sort. He has been assiduously cultivating the germs in his laboratory. So far as I can ascertain from Professor Heyler, an old German who was in van Heerden's service and who seems a fairly honest man, the doctor nearly lost the culture, and it was only by sending out small quantities to various seedy scientists and getting them to experiment in the cultivation of the germ under various conditions that he found the medium in which they best flourish. It is, I believe, fermented rye-flour, but I am not quite sure."

" To what purpose do you suggest van Heerden will put his cultivations ? " asked the commissioner.

" I am coming to that. In the course of my inquiries and searchings I found that he was collecting very accurate data concerning the great wheatfields of the world. From the particulars he was preparing I formed the idea that he intended, and intends, sending an army of agents all over the world who, at a given signal, will release the germs in the growing wheat."

" But surely a few germs sprinkled on a great wheat-field such as you find in America would do no more than local damage ? "

Beale shook his head.

"Mr. O'Donnel," he said soberly, "if I broke a tube of that stuff in the corner of a ten-thousand-acre field the whole field would be rotten in twenty-four hours! It spreads from stalk to stalk with a rapidity that is amazing. One germ multiplies itself in a living cornfield a billion times in twelve hours. It would not only be possible, but certain that twenty of van Heerden's agents in America could destroy the harvests of the United States in a week."

"But why should he do this—he is a German, you say —and Germans do not engage in frightfulness unless they see a dividend at the end of it."

"There is a dividend—a dividend of millions at the end of it," said Beale, graver, "that much I know. I cannot tell you any more yet. But I can say this: that up till yesterday van Heerden was carrying on the work without the aid of his Government. That is no longer the case. There is now a big syndicate in existence to finance him, and the principal shareholder is the German Government. He has already spent thousands, money he has borrowed and money he has stolen. As a side-line and sheerly to secure her money he carried off John Millinborn's heiress with the object of forcing her into a marriage."

The commissioner chewed the end of his cigar.

"This is a State matter and one on which I must consult the Home Office. You tell me that the Foreign Office believe your story—of course I do, too," he added quickly, "though it sounds wildly improbable. Wait here."

He took up his hat and went out.

"It is going to be a difficult business to convict van Heerden," said the superintendent when his chief had gone, "you see, in the English courts, motive must be proved to convict before a jury, and there seems no motive except revenge. A jury would take a lot of convincing that a man spent thousands of pounds to avenge a wrong done to his country."

Beale had no answer to this. At the back of his mind he had a dim idea of the sheer money value of the scheme, but he needed other evidence than he possessed. The commissioner returned soon after.

"I have been on the 'phone to the Under-Secretary, and we will take action against van Heerden on the evidence the factory offers. I'll put you in charge of the case, McNorton, you have the search-warrant already ? Good ! "

He shook hands with Beale.

" You will make a European name over this, Mr. Beale," he said.

" I hope Europe will have nothing more to talk about," said Beale.

They passed back to McNorton's office.

" I'll come right along," said the superintendent. He was taking his hat from a peg when he saw a closed envelope lying on his desk.

" From the local police station," he said. " How long has this been here ? "

His clerk shook his head.

" I can't tell you, sir—it has been there since I came in."

" H'm—I must have overlooked it. Perhaps it is news from your factory."

He tore it open, scanned the contents and swore.

" There goes your evidence, Beale," he said.

" What is it ? " asked Beale quickly.

" The factory was burned to the ground in the early hours of the morning," he said. " The fire started in the old wine vault and the whole building has collapsed."

The detective stared out of the window.

" Can we arrest van Heerden on the evidence of Professor Heyler ? "

For answer McNorton handed him the letter. It ran :

" From Inspector-in-charge, S. Paddington, to Supt. McNorton. Factory in Playbury St. under P.O. (Police Observation) completely destroyed by fire, which broke out in basement at 5.20 this morning. One body found, believed to be a man named Heyler."

CHAPTER XXVII

A SCHEME TO STARVE THE WORLD

THERE is a menace about Monday morning which few have escaped. It is a menace which in one guise or another clouds hundreds of millions of pillows, gives to the golden sunlight which filters through a billion panes the very hues and character of jaundice. It is the menace of factory and workshop, harsh prisons which shut men and women from the green fields and the pleasant by-ways ; the menace of new responsibilities to be faced and new difficulties to be overcome. Into the space of Monday morning drain the dregs of last week's commitments to gather into stagnant pools upon the desks and benches of toiling and scheming humanity. It is the end of the holiday, the foot of the new hill whose crest is Saturday night and whose most pleasant outlook is the Sunday to come.

Men go to their work reluctant and resentful and reach out for the support which the lunch-hour brings. One o'clock in London is about six o'clock in Chicago. Therefore the significance of shoals of cablegrams which lay on the desks of certain brokers was not wholly apparent until late in the evening, and was not thoroughly understood until late on Tuesday morning, when to other and greater shoals of cables came the terse price-lists from the Board of Trade in Chicago, and on top of all the wirelessed Press accounts for the sensational jump in wheat.

" Wheat soaring," said one headline. " Frantic scenes in the Pit," said another. " Wheat reaches famine price," blared a third.

Beale passing through to Whitehall heard the shrill call of the newsboys and caught the word " wheat." He snatched a paper from the hands of a boy and read.

Every corn-market in the Northern Hemisphere was in a condition of chaos. Prices were jumping to a figure beyond any which the most stringent days of the war had produced.

He slipped into a telephone booth, gave a Treasury number and McNorton answered.

"Have you seen the papers?" he asked.

"No, but I've heard. You mean about the wheat boom?"

"Yes—the game has started."

"Where are you—wait for me, I'll join you."

Three minutes later McNorton appeared from the White-hall end of Scotland Yard. Beale hailed a cab and they drove to the hotel together.

"Warrants have been issued for van Heerden and Milsom and the girl Glaum," he said. "I expect we shall find the nest empty, but I have sent men to all the railway stations—do you think we've moved too late?"

"Everything depends on the system that van Heerden has adopted," replied Beale, "he is the sort of man who would keep everything in his own hands. If he has done that, and we catch him, we may prevent a world catastrophe."

At the hotel they found Kitson waiting in the vestibule.

"Well?" he asked, "I gather that you've lost van Heerden, but if the newspapers mean anything, his hand is down on the table. Everybody is crazy here," he said, as he led the way to the elevator, "I've just been speaking to the Under-Minister for Agriculture—all Europe is scared. Now what is the story?" he asked, when they were in his room.

He listened attentively and did not interrupt until Stanford Beale had finished.

"That's big enough," he said. "I owe you an apology —much as I was interested in Miss Cresswell, I realize that her fate was as nothing beside the greater issue."

"What does it mean?" asked McNorton.

"The Wheat Panic? God knows. It may mean bread at a guinea a pound—it is too early to judge."

The door was opened unceremoniously and a man strode in. McNorton was the first to recognize the intruder and rose to his feet.

"I'm sorry to interrupt you," said Lord Sevington

—it was the Foreign Secretary of Great Britain himself.
" Well, Beale, the fantastic story you told me seems in
a fair way to being realized."

" This is Mr. Kitson," introduced Stanford, and the
grey-haired statesman bowed.

" I sent for you, but decided I couldn't wait—so I came
myself. Ah, McNorton, what are the chances of catching
van Heerden ? "

" No man has ever escaped from this country once his
identity was established," said the police chief hope-
fully.

" If we had taken Beale's advice we should have the
gentleman under lock and key," said the Foreign Minister,
shaking his head. " You probably know that Mr. Beale
has been in communication with the Foreign Office for some
time ? " he said, addressing Kitson.

" I did not know," admitted the lawyer.

" We thought it was one of those brilliant stories which
the American newspaper reporter loves," smiled the
minister.

" I don't quite get the commercial end of it," said Kitson.
" How does van Heerden benefit by destroying the crops
of the world ? "

" He doesn't benefit, because the crops won't be
destroyed," said the minister. " The South Russian crops
are all right, the German crops are intact—but are practically all mortgaged to the German Government."

" The Government ? "

" This morning the German Government have made
two announcements. The first is the commandeering of
all the standing crops, and at the same time the taking over
of all options on the sale of wheat. Great granaries are
being established all over Germany. The old Zeppelin
sheds——"

" Great heavens ! " cried Kitson, and stared at Stanford
Beale. " That was the reason they took over the sheds ? "

" A pretty good reason, too," said Beale, " storage is
everything in a crisis like this. What is the second
announcement, sir ? "

" They prohibit the export of grain," said Lord Sevington, " the whole of Germany is to be rationed for a year, bread is to be supplied by the Government free of all cost to the people ; in this way Germany handles the surpluses for us to buy."

" What will she charge ? "

" What she wishes. If van Heerden's scheme goes through, if throughout the world the crops are destroyed and only that which lies under Germany's hand is spared, what must we pay ? Every penny we have taken from Germany ; every cent of her war costs must be returned to her in exchange for wheat."

" Impossible ! "

" Why impossible ? There is no limit to the price of rarities. What is rarer than gold is more costly than gold. You who are in the room are the only people in the world who know the secret of the Green Rust, and I can speak frankly to you. I tell you that we must either buy from Germany or make war on Germany, and the latter course is impossible, and if it were possible would give us no certainty of relief. We shall have to pay, Britain, France, America, Italy—we shall have to pay. We shall pay in gold, we may have to pay in battleships and material. Our stocks of corn have been allowed to fall and to-day we have less than a month's supply in England. Every producing country in the world will stop exporting instantly, and they, too, with the harvest nearly due, will be near the end of their stocks. Now tell me, Mr. Beale, in your judgment, is it possible to save the crops by local action ? "

Beale shook his head.

" I doubt it," he said ; " it would mean the mobilisation of millions of men, the surrounding of all corn-tracts— and even then I doubt if your protection would be efficacious. You could send the stuff into the fields by a hundred methods. The only thing to do is to catch van Heerden and stifle the scheme at its fountain-head."

The Chief of the Foreign Ministry strode up and down the room, his hands thrust into his pockets, his head upon his breast.

" It means our holding out for twelve months," he said. " Can we do it ? "

"It means more than that, sir," said Beale quietly.

Lord Sevington stopped and faced him.

"More than that? What do you mean?"

"It may mean a cornless world for a generation," said Beale. "I have consulted the best authorities, and they agree that the soil will be infected for ten years."

The four men looked at one another helplessly.

"Why," said Sevington, in awe, "the whole social and industrial fabric of the world would crumble into dust. America would be ruined for a hundred years, there would be deaths by the million. It means the very end of civilization!"

Beale glanced from one to the other of the little group.

Sevington, with his hard old face set in harsh lines, a stony sphinx of a man showing no other sign of his emotions than a mop of ruffled hair.

Kitson, an old man and almost as hard of feature, yet of the two more human, stood with pursed lip, his eyes fixed on the floor, as if he were studying the geometrical pattern of the parquet for future reference.

McNorton, big, red-faced and expressionless, save that his mouth dropped and that his arms were tightly folded as if he were hugging himself in a sheer ecstasy of pain. From the street outside came the roar and rumble of London's traffic, the dull murmur of countless voices and the shrill high-pitched whine of a newsboy.

Men and women were buying newspapers and seeing no more in the scare headlines than a newspaper sensation.

To-morrow they might read further and grow a little uncomfortable, but for the moment they were only mildly interested, and the majority would turn to the back page for the list of "arrivals" at Lingfield.

"It is unbelievable," said Kitson. "I have exactly the same feeling I had on August 1, 1914—that sensation of unreality."

His voice seemed to arouse the Foreign Minister from the meditation into which he had fallen, and he started.

"Beale," he said, "you have unlimited authority to

act—Mr. McNorton, you will go back to Scotland Yard and ask the Chief Commissioner to attend at the office of the Privy Seal. Mr. Beale will keep in touch with me all the time."

Without any formal leave-taking he made his exit, followed by Superintendent McNorton.

"That's a badly rattled man," said Kitson shrewdly, "the Government may fall on this news. What will you do ? "

"Get van Heerden," said the other.

"It is the job of your life," said Kitson quietly, and Beale knew within a quarter of an hour that the lawyer did not exaggerate.

Van Heerden had disappeared with dramatic suddenness. Detectives who visited his flat discovered that his personal belongings had been removed in the early hours of the morning. He had left with two trunks (which were afterwards found in a cloak-room of a London railway terminus) and a companion who was identified as Milsom. Whether the car had gone east or north, south or west, nobody knew.

In the early editions of the evening newspapers, side by side with the account of the panic scenes on 'Change was the notice :

"The Air Ministry announce the suspension of Order 63 of Trans-Marine Flight Regulations. No aeroplane will be allowed to cross the coastline by day or night without first descending at a coast control station. Aerial patrols have orders to force down any machine which does not obey the 'Descend' signal. This signal is now displayed at all coast stations."

Every railway station in England, every port of embarkation, were watched by police. The one photograph of van Heerden in existence, thousands of copies of an excellent snapshot taken by one of Beale's assistants, were distributed by aeroplane to every district centre. At two o'clock Hilda Glaum was arrested and conveyed to Bow Street. She

showed neither surprise nor resentment and offered no
information as to van Heerden's whereabouts.

Throughout the afternoon there were the usual crops of
false arrest and detention of perfectly innocent people,
and at five o'clock it was announced that all telegraphic
communication with the Continent and with the Western
Hemisphere was suspended until further notice.

Beale came back from Barking, whither he had gone to
interview a choleric commercial traveller who bore some
facial resemblance to van Heerden, and had been arrested
in consequence, and discovered that something like a Council
of War was being held in Kitson's private room.

McNorton and two of his assistants were present. There
was an Under-Secretary from the Foreign Office, a great
scientist whose services had been called upon, and a man
whom he recognized as a member of the Committee of the
Corn Exchange. He shook his head in answer to
McNorton's inquiring glance, and would have taken his
seat at the table, but Kitson, who had risen on his entrance,
beckoned him to the window.

"We can do without you for a little while, Beale,"
he said, lowering his voice. "There's somebody there,"
he jerked his head to a door which led to another room
of his suite, "who requires an explanation, and I think
your time will be so fully occupied in the next few days
that you had better seize this opportunity whilst you
have it."

"Miss Cresswell!" said Beale, in despair.

The old man nodded slowly.

"What does she know?"

"That is for you to discover," said Kitson gently, and
pushed him toward the door.

With a quaking heart he turned the knob and stepped
guiltily into the presence of the girl who in the eyes of the
law was his wife.

CHAPTER XXVIII

THE COMING OF DR. MILSOM

SHE rose to meet him, and he stood spellbound, still holding the handle of the door. It seemed that she had taken on new qualities, a new and an ethereal grace. At the very thought even of his technical possession of this smiling girl who came forward to greet him, his heart thumped so loudly that he felt she must hear it. She was pale, and there were dark shadows under her eyes, but the hand that gripped his was firm and warm and living.

"I have to thank you for much, Mr. Beale," she said. "Mr. Kitson has told me that I owe my rescue to you."

"Did he?" he asked awkwardly, and wondered what else Kitson had told her.

"I am trying to be very sensible, and I want you to help me, because you are the most sensible man I know."

She went back to the lounge-chair where she had been sitting, and pointed to another.

"It was horribly melodramatic, wasn't it? but I suppose the life of a detective is full of melodrama."

"Oh, brimming over," he said. "If you keep very quiet I will give you a résumé of my most interesting cases," he said, making a pathetic attempt to be flippant, and the girl detected something of his insincerity.

"You have had a trying day," she said, with quick sympathy, "have you arrested Doctor van Heerden?"

He shook his head.

"I am glad," she said.

"Glad?"

She nodded.

"Before he is arrested," she spoke with some hesitation, "I want one little matter cleared up. I asked Mr. Kitson, but he put me off and said you would tell me everything."

"What is it?" he asked steadily.

She got up and went to her bag which stood upon a side-table, opened it and took out something which she laid on the palm of her hand. She came back with hand extended, and Beale looked at the glittering object on her palm and was speechless.

" Do you see that ? " she asked.

He nodded, having no words for the moment, for " that " was a thin gold ring.

" It is a wedding ring," she said, " and I found it on my finger when I recovered."

" Oh ! " said Beale blankly.

" Was I married ? " she asked.

He made two or three ineffectual attempts to speak and ended by nodding.

" I feared so," she said quietly, " you see I recollect nothing of what happened. The last thing I remembered was Doctor van Heerden sitting beside me and putting something into my arm. It hurt a little, but not very much, and I remember I spoke to him. I think it was about you," a little colour came to her face, " or perhaps he was speaking about you, I am not sure," she said hurriedly; " I know that you came into it somehow, and that is all I can recall."

" Nothing else ? " he asked dismally.

" Nothing," she said.

" Try, try, try to remember," he urged her.

He realized he was being a pitiable coward and that he wanted to shift the responsibility for the revelation upon her. She smiled, and shook her head.

" I am sorry but I can't remember anything. Now you are going to tell me."

He discovered that he was sitting on the edge of the chair and that he was more nervous than he had ever been in his life.

" So I am going to tell you," he said, in a hollow voice, " of course I'll tell you. It is rather difficult, you understand."

She looked at him kindly.

" I know it must be difficult for a man like you to speak of your own achievements. But for once you are going to be immodest," she laughed.

" Well, you see," he began, " I knew van Heerden wanted to marry you. I knew that all along. I guessed he wanted to marry you for your money, because in the circumstances there was nothing else he could want to marry you for," he added. " I mean," he corrected himself hastily, " that money was the most attractive thing to him."

" This doesn't sound very flattering," she smiled.

" I know I am being crude, but you will forgive me when you learn what I have to say," he said huskily. " Van Heerden wanted to marry you——"

" And he married me," she said, " and I am going to break that marriage as soon as I possibly can."

" I know, I hope so," said Stanford Beale. " I believe it is difficult, but I will do all I possibly can. Believe me, Miss Cresswell——"

" I am not Miss Cresswell any longer," she said with a wry little face, " but please don't call me by my real name."

" I won't," he said fervently.

" You knew he wanted to marry me for my money and not for my beauty or my accomplishments," she said, " and so you followed me down to Deans Folly."

" Yes, yes, but I must explain. I know it will sound horrible to you and you may have the lowest opinion of me, but I have got to tell you."

He saw the look of alarm gather in her eyes and plunged into his story.

" I thought that if you were already married van Heerden would be satisfied and take no further steps against you."

" But I wasn't already married," she said, puzzled.

" Wait, wait, please," he begged, " keep that in your mind, that I was satisfied van Heerden wanted you for your money, and that if you were already married or even if you weren't and he thought you were I could save you from dangers, the extent of which even I do not know. And there was a man named Homo, a crook. He had been a parson and had all the manner and style of his profession. So I got a special licence in my own name."

" You ? " she said breathlessly. " A marriage licence ? To marry me ? "

He nodded.

"And I took Homo with me in my search for you. I knew that I should have a very small margin of time, and I thought if Homo performed the ceremony and I could confront van Heerden with the accomplished deed——"

She sprang to her feet with a laugh.

"Oh, I see, I see," she said. "Oh, how splendid! And you went through this mock ceremony! Where was I?"

"You were at the window," he said miserably.

"But how lovely! And you were outside and your parson with the funny name—but that's delicious! So I wasn't married at all and this is your ring." She picked it up with a mocking light in her eyes, and held it out to him, but he shook his head.

"You were married," he said, in a voice which was hardly audible.

"Married? How?"

"Homo was not a fake! He was a real clergyman! And the marriage was legal!"

They looked at one another without speaking. On the girl's part there was nothing but pure amazement; but Stanford Beale read horror, loathing, consternation and unforgiving wrath, and waited, as the criminal waits for his sentence, upon her next words.

"So I am really married—to you," she said wonderingly.

"You will never forgive me, I know." He did not look at her now. "My own excuse is that I did what I did because I—wanted to save you. I might have sailed in with a gun and shot them up. I might have waited my chance and broken into the house. I might have taken a risk and surrounded the place with police, but that would have meant delay. I didn't do the normal things or take the normal view—I couldn't with you."

He did not see the momentary tenderness in her eyes, because he was not looking at her, and went on:

"That's the whole of the grisly story. Mr. Kitson will advise you as to what steps you may take to free yourself. It was a most horrible blunder, and it was all the more tragic because you were the victim, you of all the persons in the world!"

She had put the ring down, and now she took it up again and examined it curiously.

"It is rather—quaint, isn't it?" she asked.

"Oh, very."

He thought he heard a sob and looked up. She was laughing, at first silently, then, as the humour of the thing seized her, her laugh rang clear and he caught its infection.

"It's funny," she said at last, wiping her eyes, "there is a humorous side to it. Poor Mr. Beale!"

"I deserve a little pity," he said ruefully.

"Why?" she asked quickly. "Have you committed bigamy?"

"Not noticeably so," he answered, with a smile.

"Well, what are you going to do about it? It's rather serious when one thinks of it—seriously. So I am Mrs. Stanford Beale—poor Mr. Beale, and poor Mrs. Beale-to-be. I do hope," she said, and this time her seriousness was genuine, "that I have not upset any of your plans—too much. Oh," she sat down suddenly, staring at him, "it would be awful," she said in a hushed voice, "and I would never forgive myself. Is there—forgive my asking the question, but I suppose," with a flashing smile, "as your wife I am entitled to your confidence—is there somebody you are going to marry?"

"I have neither committed bigamy nor do I contemplate it," said Beale, who was gradually recovering his grip of the situation, "if you mean am I engaged to somebody—in fact, to a girl," he said recklessly, "the answer is in the negative. There will be no broken hearts on my side of the family. I have no desire to probe your wounded heart——"

"Don't be flippant," she stopped him sternly; "it is a very terrible situation, Mr. Beale, and I hardly dare to think of it."

"I realize how terrible it is," he said, suddenly bold, ' and as I tell you, I will do everything I can to correct my blunder."

"Does Mr. Kitson know?" she asked.

He nodded.

"What did Mr. Kitson say? Surely he gave you some advice."

"He said——" began Stanford, and went red.

The girl did not pursue the subject.

"Come, let us talk about the matter like rational beings," she said cheerfully. "I have got over my first inclination to swoon. You must curb your very natural desire to be haughty."

"I cannot tell you what we can do yet. I don't want to discuss the unpleasant details of a divorce," he said, "and perhaps you will let me have a few days before we decide on any line of action. Van Heerden is still at large, and until he is under lock and key and this immense danger which threatens the world is removed, I can hardly think straight."

"Mr. Kitson has told me about van Heerden," she said quietly. "Isn't it rather a matter for the English police to deal with? As I have reason to know," she shivered slightly, "Doctor van Heerden is a man without any fear or scruple."

"My scruples hardly keep me awake at night," he said, "and I guess I'm not going to let up on van Heerden. I look upon it as my particular job."

"Isn't it"—she hesitated—"isn't it rather dangerous?"

"For me?" he laughed, "no, I don't think so. And even if it were in the most tragic sense of the word dangerous, why, that would save you a great deal of unpleasantness."

"I think you are being horrid," she said.

"I am sorry," he responded quickly, "I was fishing for a little pity, and it was rather cheap and theatrical. No, I do not think there is very much danger. Van Heerden is going to keep under cover, and he is after something bigger than my young life."

"Is Milsom with him?"

"He is the weak link in van Heerden's scheme," Beale said. "Somehow van Heerden doesn't strike me as a

good team leader, and what little I have seen of Milsom
leads me to the belief that he is hardly the man to follow
the doctor's lead blindly. Besides, it is always easier to
catch two men than one," he laughed. " That is an old
detective's axiom and it works out."

She put out her hand.

" It's a tangled business, isn't it ? " she said. " I
mean us. Don't let it add to your other worries. Forget
our unfortunate relationship until we can smooth things
out."

He shook her hand in silence.

" And now I am coming out to hear all that you clever
people suggest," she said. " Please don't look alarmed.
I have been talking all the afternoon and have been narrat-
ing my sad experience—such as I remember—to the most
important people. Cabinet Ministers and police commis-
sioners and doctors and things."

" One moment," he said.

He took from his pocket a stout book.

" I was wondering what that was," she laughed. " You
haven't been buying me reading-matter ? "

He nodded, and held the volume so that she could read
the title.

" 'A Friend in Need,' by S. Beale. I didn't know
you wrote ! " she said in surprise.

" I am literary and even worse," he said flippantly.
" I see you have a shelf of books here. If you will allow
me I will put it with the others."

" But mayn't I see it ? "

He shook his head.

" I just want to tell you all you have said about van
Heerden is true. He is a most dangerous man. He may
yet be dangerous to you. I don't want you to touch that
little book unless you are in really serious trouble. Will
you promise me ? "

She opened her eyes wide.

" But, Mr. Beale—— ? "

" Will you promise me ? " he said again.

" Of course I'll promise you, but I don't quite understand."

" You will understand," he said.

He opened the door for her and she passed out ahead of him. Kitson came to meet them.

" I suppose there is no news ? " asked Stanford.

" None," said the other, " except high political news. There has been an exchange of notes between the Triple Alliance and the German Government. All communication with the Ukraine is cut off, and three ships have been sunk in the Bosphorus so cleverly that our grain ships in the Black Sea are isolated."

" That's bad," said Beale.

He walked to the table. It was littered with maps and charts and printed tabulations. McNorton got up and joined them.

" I have just had a 'phone message through from the Yard," he said. " Carter, my assistant, says that he's certain van Heerden has not left London."

" Has the girl spoken ? "

" Glaum ? No, she's as dumb as an oyster. I doubt if you would get her to speak even if you put her through the third degree, and we don't allow that."

" So I am told," said Beale dryly.

There was a knock at the door.

" Unlock it somebody," said Kitson. " I turned the key."

The nearest person was the member of the Corn Exchange Committee, and he clicked back the lock and the door opened to admit a waiter.

" There's a man here——" he said ; but before he could say more he was pushed aside and a dusty, dishevelled figure stepped into the room and glanced round.

" My name is Milsom," he said. " I have come to give King's Evidence ! "

CHAPTER XXIX

THE LOST CODE

' I 'M Milsom," said the man in the doorway again.

His clothes were grimed and dusty, his collar limp and soiled. There were two days' growth of red-grey stubble on his big jaw, and he bore himself like a man who was faint from lack of sleep.

He walked unsteadily to the table and fell into a chair.

" Where is van Heerden ? " asked Beale, but Milsom shook his head.

" I left him two hours ago, after a long and unprofitable talk on patriotism," he said, and laughed shortly. " At that time he was making his way back to his house in Southwark."

" Then he is in London—here in London ! "

Milsom nodded.

" You won't find him," he said brusquely. " I tell you I've left him after a talk about certain patriotic misgivings on my part—look ! "

He lifted his right hand, which hitherto he had kept concealed by his side, and Oliva shut her eyes and felt deathly sick.

" Right index digit and part of the phalanges shot away," said Milsom philosophically. " That was my trigger-finger—but he shot first. Give me a drink ! "

They brought him a bottle of wine, and he drank it from a long tumbler in two great breathless gulps.

" You've closed the coast to him," he said, " you shut down your wires and cables, you're watching the roads, but he'll get his message through, if——"

" Then he hasn't cabled ? " said Beale eagerly. " Milsom, this means liberty for you—liberty and comfort. Tell us the truth, man, help us hold off this horror that van Heerden is loosing on the world and there's no reward too great for you."

Milsom's eyes narrowed.

" It wasn't the hope of reward or hope of pardon that made me break with van Heerden," he said in his slow way. " You'd laugh yourself sick if I told you. It was—it was the knowledge that this country would be down and out ; that the people who spoke my tongue and thought more or less as I thought should be under the foot of the Beast —fevered sentimentality ! You don't believe that ? "

" I believe it."

It was Oliva who spoke, and it appeared that this was the first time that Milsom had noticed her presence, for his eyes opened wider.

" You—oh, you believe it, do you ? " and he nodded.

" But why is van Heerden waiting ? " asked McNorton. " What is he waiting for ? "

The big man rolled his head helplessly from side to side, and the hard cackle of his laughter was very trying to men whose nerves were raw and on edge.

" That's the fatal lunacy of it ! I think it must be a national characteristic. You saw it in the war again and again—a wonderful plan brought to naught by some piece of over-cleverness on the part of the super-man."

A wild hope leapt to Beale's heart.

" Then it has failed ! The rust has not answered—— ? "

But Milsom shook his head wearily.

" The rust is all that he thinks—and then some," he said. " No, it isn't that. It is in the work of organization where the hitch has occurred. You know something of the story. Van Heerden has agents in every country in the world. He has spent nearly a hundred thousand pounds in perfecting his working plans, and I'm willing to admit that they are wellnigh perfect. Such slight mistakes as sending men to South Africa and Australia where the crops are six months later than the European and American harvests may be forgiven, because the German thinks longitudinally, and north and south are the two points of the compass which he never bothers his head about. If the Germans had been a seafaring people they'd have discovered America before Columbus, but they would never have found the North Pole or rounded the Cape in a million years."

He paused, and they saw the flicker of a smile in his weary eyes.

"The whole scheme is under van Heerden's hand. At the word ' Go ' thousands of his agents begin their work of destruction—but the word must come from him. He has so centralized his scheme that if he died suddenly without that word being uttered, the work of years would come to naught. I guess he is suspicious of everybody, including his new Government. For the best part of a year he has been arranging and planning. With the assistance of a girl, a compatriot of his, he has reduced all things to order. In every country is a principal agent who possesses a copy of a simple code. At the proper moment van Heerden would cable a word which meant ' Get busy ' or ' Hold off until you hear from me,' or ' Abandon scheme for this year and collect cultures.' I happen to be word-perfect in the meanings of the code words because van Heerden has so often drummed them into me."

"What are the code words ? "

"I'm coming to that," nodded Milsom. "Van Heerden is the type of scientist that never trusts his memory. You find that kind in all the school—they usually spend their time making the most complete and detailed notes, and their studies are packed with memoranda. Yet he had a wonderful memory for the commonplace things— for example, in the plain English of his three messages he was word perfect. He could tell you off-hand the names and addresses of all his agents. But when it came to scientific data his mind was a blank until he consulted his authorities. It seemed that once he made a note his mind was incapable of retaining the information he had committed to paper. That, as I say, is a phenomenon which is not infrequently met with amongst men of science."

"And he had committed the code to paper ? " asked Kitson.

"I am coming to that. After the fire at the Paddington works, van Heerden said the time had come to make a get away. He was going to the Continent, I was to sail for Canada. ' Before you go,' he said, ' I will give you the code—but I am afraid that I cannot do that until after ten o'clock.'"

McNorton was scribbling notes in shorthand and carefully circled the hour.

"We went back to his flat and had breakfast together —it was then about five o'clock. He packed a few things and I particularly noticed that he looked very carefully at the interior of a little grip which he had brought the previous night from Staines. He was so furtive, carrying the bag to the light of the window, that I supposed he was consulting his code, and I wondered why he should defer giving me the information until ten o'clock. Anyway, I could swear he took something from the bag and slipped it into his pocket. We left the flat soon after and drove to a railway station where the baggage was left. Van Heerden had given me bank-notes for a thousand pounds in case we should be separated, and I went on to the house in South London. You needn't ask me where it is because van Heerden is not there."

He gulped again at the wine.

"At eleven o'clock van Heerden came back," resumed Milsom, "and if ever a man was panic-stricken it was he —the long and the short of it is that the code was mislaid."

"Mislaid!" Beale was staggered.

Here was farce interpolated into tragedy—the most grotesque, the most unbelievable farce.

"Mislaid," said Milsom. "He did not say as much, but I gathered from the few disjointed words he flung at me that the code was not irredeemably lost; in fact, I have reason to believe that he knows where it is. It was after that that van Heerden started in to do some tall cursing of me, my country, my decadent race and the like. Things have been strained all the afternoon. To-night they reached a climax. He wanted me to help him in a burglary—and burglary is not my forte."

"What did he want to burgle?" asked McNorton, with professional interest.

"Ah! There you have me! It was the question I asked and he refused to answer. I was to put myself in his hands and there was to be some shooting if, as he thought likely, a caretaker was left on the premises to be entered. I told him flat—we were sitting on Wandsworth Common at the time—that he could leave me out, and that is where we became mutually offensive."

He looked at his maimed hand.

" I dressed it roughly at a chemist's. The iodine open dressing isn't beautiful, but it is antiseptic. He shot to kill, too, there's no doubt about that. A very perfect little gentleman ! "

" He's in London ? " said McNorton. " That simplifies matters."

" To my mind it complicates rather than simplifies," said Beale. " London is a vast proposition. Can you give us any idea as to the hour the burglary was planned for ? "

" Eleven," said Milsom promptly, " that is to say, in a little over an hour's time."

" And you have no idea of the locality ? "

" Somewhere in the East of London. We were to have met at Aldgate."

" I don't understand it," said McNorton. " Do you suggest that the code is in the hands of somebody who is not willing to part with it ? And now that he no longer needs it for you, is there any reason why he should wait ? "

" Every reason," replied Milsom, and Stanford Beale nodded in agreement. " It was not only for me he wanted it. He as good as told me that unless he recovered it he would be unable to communicate with his men."

" What do you think he'll do ? "

" He'll get Bridgers to assist him. Bridgers is a pretty sore man, and the doctor knows just where he can find him."

As Oliva listened an idea slowly dawned in her mind that she might supply a solution to the mystery of the missing code. It was a wildly improbable theory she held, but even so slender a possibility was not to be discarded. She slipped from the group and went back to her room. For the accommodation of his ward, James Kitson had taken the adjoining suite to his own and had secured a lady's maid from an agency for the girl's service. She passed through the sitting-room to her own bedroom, and found the maid putting the room ready for the night.

"Minnie," she said, throwing a quick glance about the apartment, "where did you put the clothes I took off when I came?"

"Here, miss."

The girl opened the wardrobe and Oliva made a hurried search.

"Did you find—anything, a little ticket?"

The girl smiled.

"Oh yes, miss. It was in your stocking."

Oliva laughed.

"I suppose you thought it was rather queer, finding that sort of thing in a girl's stocking," she asked, but the maid was busily opening the drawers of the dressing-table in search of something.

"Here it is, miss."

She held a small square ticket in her hand and held it with such disapproving primness that Oliva nearly laughed.

"I found it in your stocking, miss," she said again.

"Quite right," said Oliva coolly, "that's where I put it. I always carry my pawn tickets in my stocking."

The admirable Minnie sniffed.

"I suppose you have never seen such a thing," smiled Oliva, "and you hardly knew what it was."

The lady's maid turned very red. She had unfortunately seen many such certificates of penury, but all that was part of her private life, and she had been shocked beyond measure to be confronted with this too-familiar evidence of impecuniosity in the home of a lady who represented to her an assured income and comfortable pickings.

Oliva went back to her sitting-room and debated the matter. It was a sense of diffidence, the fear of making herself ridiculous, which arrested her. Otherwise she might have flown into the room, declaimed her preposterous theories and leave these clever men to work out the details. She opened the door and with the ticket clenched in her hand stepped into the room.

If they had missed her after she had left nobody saw her return. They were sitting in a group about the table, firing questions at the big unshaven man who had made such a dramatic entrance to the conference and who, with a long cigar in the corner of his mouth, was answering readily and fluently.

But faced with the tangible workings of criminal investigation her resolution and her theories shrank to vanishing-point. She clasped the ticket in her hand and felt for a pocket, but the dressmaker had not provided her with that useful appendage.

So she turned and went softly back to her room, praying that she would not be noticed. She closed the door gently behind her and turned to meet a well-valeted man in evening-dress who was standing in the middle of the room, a light overcoat thrown over his arm, his silk hat tilted back from his forehead, a picture of calm assurance.

" Don't move," said van Heerden, " and don't scream. And be good enough to hand over the pawn ticket you are holding in your hand."

Silently she obeyed, and as she handed the little paste-board across the table which separated them she looked past him to the bookshelf behind his head, and particularly to a new volume which bore the name of Stanford Beale.

CHAPTER XXX

THE WATCH

" THANKS," said van Heerden, pocketing the ticket, " it is of no use to me now, for I cannot wait. I gather that you have not disclosed the fact that this ticket is in your possession."

" I don't know how you gather that," she said.

" Lower your voice ! " he hissed menacingly. " I gather as much because Beale knew the ticket would not be in my possession now. If he only knew, if he only had a hint of its existence, I fear my scheme would fail. As it is, it will succeed. And now," he said with a smile, " time is short and your preparations must be of the briefest. I will save you the trouble of asking questions by telling you that I am going to take you along with me. I certainly cannot afford to leave you. Get your coat."

With a shrug she walked past him to the bedroom and he followed.

" Are we going far ? " she asked.

There was no tremor in her voice and she felt remarkably self-possessed.

" That you will discover," said he.

" I am not asking out of idle curiosity, but I want to know whether I ought to take a bag."

" Perhaps it would be better," he said.

She carried the little attaché case back to the sitting-room.

" You have no objection to my taking a little light reading-matter ? " she asked contemptuously. " I am afraid you are not a very entertaining companion, Dr. van Heerden."

" Excellent girl," said van Heerden cheerfully. " Take anything you like."

She slipped a book from the shelf and nearly betrayed herself by an involuntary exclamation as she felt its weight.

" You are not very original in your methods," she said, " this is the second time you have spirited me off."

" The gaols of England, as your new-found friend Milsom will tell you, are filled with criminals who departed from the beaten tracks," said van Heerden. " Walk out into the corridor and turn to the right. I will be close behind you. A little way along you will discover a narrow passage which leads to the service staircase. Go down that. I am sure you believe me when I say that I will kill you if you attempt to make any signal or scream or appeal for help."

She did not answer. It was because of this knowledge and this fear, which was part of her youthful equipment —for violent death is a very terrible prospect to the young and the healthy—that she obeyed him at all.

They walked down the stone stairs, through an untidy,

low-roofed lobby, redolent of cooking food, into the street, without challenge and without attracting undue notice.

Van Heerden's car was waiting at the end of the street, and she thought she recognized the chauffeur as Bridgers.

"Once more we ride together," said van Heerden gaily, "and what will be the end of this adventure for you depends entirely upon your loyalty—what are you opening your bag for?" he asked, peering in the dark.

"I am looking for a handkerchief," said Oliva. "I am afraid I am going to cry!"

He settled himself back in the corner of the car with a sigh of resignation, accepting her explanation—sarcasm was wholly wasted on van Heerden.

* * * * *

"Well, gentlemen," said Milsom, "I don't think there's anything more I can tell you. What are you going to do with me?"

"I'll take the responsibility of not executing the warrant," said McNorton. "You will accompany one of my men to his home to-night and you will be under police supervision."

"That's no new experience," said Milsom, "there's only one piece of advice I want to give you."

"And that is?" asked Beale.

"Don't underrate van Heerden. You have no conception of his nerve. There isn't a man of us here," he said, "whose insurance rate wouldn't go up to ninety per cent. if van Heerden decided to get him. I don't profess that I can help you to explain his strange conduct to-day. I can only outline the psychology of it, but how and where he has hidden his code and what circumstances prevent its recovery, is known only to van Heerden."

He nodded to the little group, and accompanied by McNorton left the room.

"There goes a pretty bad man," said Kitson, "or I am no judge of character. He's an old lag, isn't he?"

Beale nodded.

"Murder," he said laconically. "He lived after his time. He should have been a contemporary of the Borgias."

"A poisoner!" shuddered one of the under-secretaries. "I remember the case. He killed his nephew and defended himself on the plea that the youth was a degenerate, as he undoubtedly was."

"He might have got that defence past in America or France," said Beale, "but unfortunately there was a business end to the matter. He was the sole heir of his nephew's considerable fortune, and a jury from the Society of Eugenics would have convicted him on that."

He looked at his watch and turned his eyes to Kitson.

"I presume Miss Cresswell is bored and has retired for the night," he said.

"I'll find out in a moment," said Kitson. "Did you speak to her?"

Beale nodded, and his eyes twinkled.

"Did you make any progress?"

"I broke the sad news to her, if that's what you mean."

"You told her she was married to you? Good heavens! What did she say?"

"Well, she didn't faint, I don't think she's the fainting kind. She is cursed with a sense of humour, and refused even to take a tragic view."

"That's bad," said Kitson, shaking his head. "A sense of humour is out of place in a divorce court, and that is where your little romance is going to end, my friend."

"I am not so sure," said Beale calmly, and the other stared at him.

"You have promised me," he began, with a note of acerbity in his voice.

"And you have advised me," said Beale.

Kitson choked down something which he was going to say, but which he evidently thought was better left unsaid.

"Wait," he commanded, "I will find out whether Miss Cresswell," he emphasized the words, "has gone to bed."

He passed through the door to Oliva's sitting-room and was gone a few minutes. When he came back Beale saw his troubled face, and ran forward to meet him.

"She's not there," said Kitson.

" Not in her room ? "

" Neither in the sitting-room nor the bedroom. I have rung for her maid. Oh, here you are."

Prim Minnie came through the bedroom door.

" Where is your mistress ? "

" I thought she was with you, sir."

" What is this ? " said Beale, stooped and picked up a white kid glove. " She surely hasn't gone out," he said in consternation.

" That's not a lady's glove, sir," said the girl, " that is a gentleman's."

It was a new glove, and turning it over he saw stamped inside the words : " Glebler, Rotterdam."

" Has anybody been here ? " he asked.

" Not to my knowledge, sir. The young lady told me she did not want me any more to-night." The girl hesitated. It seemed a veritable betrayal of her mistress to disclose such a sordid matter as the search for a pawn ticket.

Beale noticed the hesitation.

" You must tell me everything, and tell me quickly," he said.

" Well, sir," said the maid, " the lady came in to look for something she brought with her when she came here."

" I remember ! " cried Kitson, " she told me she had brought away something very curious from van Heerden's house and made me guess what it was. Something interrupted our talk—what was it ? "

" Well, sir," said the maid, resigned, " I won't tell you a lie, sir. It was a pawn ticket."

" A pawn ticket ! " cried Kitson and Beale in unison.

" Are you sure ? " asked the latter.

" Absolutely sure, sir."

" But she couldn't have brought a pawn ticket from van Heerden's house. What was it for ? "

" I beg your pardon, sir."

" What was on the pawn ticket ? " said Kitson impatiently. " What article had been pledged ? "

Again the girl hesitated. To betray her mistress was

unpleasant. To betray herself—as she would if she confessed that she had most carefully and thoroughly read the voucher—was unthinkable.

"You know what was on it," said Beale, in his best third degree manner, "now don't keep us waiting. What was it?"

"A watch, sir."

"How much was it pledged for?"

"Ten shillings, sir."

"Do you remember the name."

"In a foreign name, sir—van Horden."

"Van Heerden," said Beale quickly, "and at what pawnbrokers?"

"Well, sir," said the girl, making a fight for her reputation, "I only glanced at the ticket and I only noticed——"

"Yes, you did," interrupted Beale sharply, "you read every line of it. Where was it?"

"Rosenblaum Bros., of Commercial Road," blurted the girl.

"Any number?"

"I didn't see the number."

"You will find them in the telephone book," said Kitson. "What does it mean?"

But Beale was half-way to Kitson's sitting-room, arriving there in time to meet McNorton who had handed over his charge to his subordinate.

"I've found it!" cried Beale.

"Found what?" asked Kitson.

"The code!"

"Where? How?" asked McNorton.

"Unless I am altogether wrong the code is contained, either engraved on the case or written on a slip of paper enclosed within the case of a watch. Can't you see it all plainly now? Van Heerden neither trusted his memory nor his subordinates. He had his simple code written, as we shall find, upon thin paper enclosed in the case of a hunter watch, and this he pledged. A pawnbroker's is the safest of safe deposits. Searching for clues, suppose the police had detected his preparations, the pledged ticket might have been easily overlooked."

Kitson was looking at him with an expression of amazed indignation. Here was a man who had lost his wife, and Kitson believed that this young detective loved the girl as few women are loved; but in the passion of the chase, in the production of a new problem, he was absorbed to the exclusion of all other considerations in the greater game.

Yet he did Beale an injustice if he only knew, for the thought of Oliva's new peril ran through all his speculations, his rapid deductions, his lightning plans.

" Miss Cresswell found the ticket and probably extracted it as a curiosity. These things are kept in little envelopes, aren't they, McNorton ? "

The police chief nodded.

" That was it, then. She took it out and left the envelope behind, and van Heerden did not discover his loss until he went to find the voucher to give Milsom the code. Don't you remember ? In the first place he said he couldn't give him the code until after ten o'clock, which is probably the hour the pawnbrokers open for business."

McNorton nodded again.

" Then do you remember that Milsom said that the code was not irredeemably lost and that van Heerden knew where it was. In default of finding the ticket he decided to burgle the pawnbroker's, and that burglary is going through to-night."

" But he could have obtained a duplicate of the ticket," said McNorton.

" How ? " asked Beale quickly.

" By going before a magistrate and swearing an affidavit."

" In his own name," said Beale, " you see, he couldn't do that. It would mean walking into the lion's den. No, burglary was his only chance."

" But what of Oliva ? " said Kitson impatiently, " I tell you, Beale, I am not big enough or stoical enough to think outside of that girl's safety."

Beale swung round at him.

" You don't think I've forgotten that, do you ? " he said in a low voice. " You don't think that has been out of my mind ? " His face was tense and drawn. " I think,

I believe that Oliva is safe," he said quietly. "I believe that Oliva and not any of us here will deliver van Heerden to justice."

"Are you mad?" asked Kitson in astonishment.

"I am very sane. Come here!"

He gripped the old lawyer by the arm and led him back to the girl's room.

"Look," he said, and pointed.

"What do you mean, the bookshelf?"

Beale nodded.

"Half an hour ago I gave Oliva a book," he said, "that book is no longer there."

"But in the name of Heaven how can a book save her?" demanded the exasperated Kitson.

Stanford Beale did not answer.

"Yes, yes, she's safe. I know she's safe," he said. "If Oliva is the girl I think she is then I see van Heerden's finish."

CHAPTER XXXI

A CORN CHANDLER'S BILL

THE church bells were chiming eleven o'clock when a car drew up before a gloomy corner shop, bearing the dingy sign of the pawnbroker's calling, and Beale and McNorton alighted.

It was a main street and was almost deserted. Beale looked up at the windows. They were dark. He knocked at the side-entrance of the shop, and presently the two men were joined by a policeman.

"Nobody lives here, sir," explained the officer, when McNorton had made himself known. "Old Rosenblaum runs the business, and lives at Highgate."

He flashed his lamp upon the door and tried it, but it did not yield. A nightfarer who had been in the shade on the opposite side of the street came across and volunteered information.

He had seen another car drive up and a gentleman had alighted. He had opened the door with a key and gone in. There was nothing suspicious about him. He was "quite a gentleman, and was in evening-dress." The constable thought it was one of the partners of Rosenblaum in convivial and resplendent garb. He had been in the house ten minutes then had come out again, locking the door behind him, and had driven off just before Beale's car had arrived.

It was not until half an hour later that an agitated little man brought by the police from Highgate admitted the two men.

There was no need to make a long search. The moment the light was switched on in the shop Beale made his discovery. On the broad counter lay a sheet of paper and a little heap of silver coins. He swept the money aside and read:

"For the redemption of one silver hunter, 10s. 6d."

It was signed in the characteristic handwriting that Beale knew so well "Van Heerden, M.D."

The two men looked at one another.

"What do you make of that ? " asked McNorton.

Beale carried the paper to the light and examined it, and McNorton went on :

"He's a pretty cool fellow. I suppose he had the money and the message all ready for our benefit."

Beale shook his head.

"On the contrary," he said, "this was done on the spur of the moment. A piece of bravado which occurred to him when he had the watch. Look at this paper. You can imagine him searching his pocket for a piece of waste paper and taking the first that came to his hand. It is written in ink with the pawnbroker's own pen. The inkwell is open," he lifted up the pen, "the nib is still wet," he said.

McNorton took the paper from his hands.

It was a bill from a corn-chandler's at Horsham, the type of bill that was sent in days of war economy which folded over and constituted its own envelope. It was addressed to "J. B. Harden, Esq." ("That was the *alias* he used when he took the wine vaults at Paddington," explained McNorton) and had been posted about a week before. Attached to the bottom of the account, which was for £3 10s., was a little slip calling attention to the fact that "this account had probably been overlooked."

Beale's finger traced the item for which the bill was rendered, and McNorton uttered an exclamation of surprise.

"Curious, isn't it ? " said Beale, as he folded the paper and put it away in his pocket, " how these very clever men always make some trifling error which brings them to justice. I don't know how many great schemes I have seen brought to nothing through some such act of folly as this, some piece of theatrical bravado which benefited the criminal nothing at all."

"Good gracious," said McNorton wonderingly, " of course, that's what he is going to do. I never thought of that. It is in the neighbourhood of Horsham we must look for him, and I think if we can get one of the Messrs. Billingham out of bed in a couple of hours' time we shall do a good night's work."

They went outside and again questioned the policeman. He remembered the car turning round and going back the way it had come. It had probably taken one of the innumerable side-roads which lead from the main thoroughfare, and in this way they had missed it.

"I want to go to the '*Megaphone*' office first," said Beale. "I have some good friends on that paper and I am curious to know how bad the markets are. The night cables from New York should be coming in by now."

In his heart was a sickening fear which he dared not express. What would the morrow bring forth ? If this one man's cupidity and hate should succeed in releasing the terror upon the world, what sort of a world would it leave ? Through the windows of the car he could see the placid policemen patrolling the streets, caught a glimpse of other cars brilliantly illuminated bearing their laughing men and women back to homes, who were ignorant of the monstrous danger which threatened their security and life.

He passed the façades of great commercial mansions which in a month's time might but serve to conceal the stark ruin within.

To him it was a night of tremendous tragedy, and for the second time in his life in the numbness induced by the greater peril and the greater anxiety he failed to wince at the thought of the danger in which Oliva stood.

Indeed, analysing his sensations she seemed to him on this occasion less a victim than a fellow-worker and he found a strange comfort in that thought of partnership.

The *Megaphone* buildings blazed with light when the car drew up to the door, messenger-boys were hurrying through the swing-doors, the two great elevators were running up and down without pause. The grey editor with a gruff voice threw over a bundle of flimsies.

" Here are the market reports," he growled, " they are not very encouraging."

Beale read them and whistled, and the editor eyed him keenly.

" Well, what do you make of it ? " he asked the detective. " Wheat at a shilling a pound already. God knows what it's going to be to-morrow ! "

" Any other news ? " asked Beale.

" We have asked Germany to explain why she has prohibited the export of wheat and to give us a reason for the stocks she holds and the steps she has taken during the past two months to accumulate reserves."

" An ultimatum ? "

" Not exactly an ultimatum. There's nothing to go to war about. The Government has mobilized the fleet and the French Government has partially mobilized her army. The question is," he said, " would war ease the situation ? "

Beale shook his head.

" The battle will not be fought in the field," he said, " it will be fought right here in London, in all your great towns, in Manchester, Coventry, Birmingham, Cardiff. It will be fought in New York and in a thousand townships between the Pacific and the Atlantic, and if the German scheme comes off we shall be beaten before a shot is fired."

" What does it mean ? " asked the editor, " why is every-body buying wheat so frantically ? There is no shortage. The harvests in the United States and Canada are good."

" There will be no harvests," said Beale solemnly ; and the journalist gaped at him.

CHAPTER XXXII

THE END OF VAN HEERDEN

DR. VAN HEERDEN expected many things and was prepared for contingencies beyond the imagination of the normally minded, but he was not prepared to find in Oliva Cresswell a pleasant travelling-companion. When a man takes a girl, against her will, from a pleasant suite at the best hotel in London, compels her at the peril of death to accompany him on a motor-car ride in the dead of the night, and when his offence is a duplication of one which had been committed less than a week before, he not unnaturally anticipates tears, supplications, or in the alternative a frigid and unapproachable silence.

To his amazement Oliva was extraordinarily cheerful and talkative and even amusing. He had kept Bridgers at the door of the car whilst he investigated the pawn-broking establishment of Messrs. Rosenblaum Bros., and had returned in triumph to discover that the girl who up to then had been taciturn and uncommunicative was in quite an amiable mood.

" I used to think," she said, " that motor-car abductions were the invention of sensational writers, but you seem to make a practice of it. You are not very original, Dr. van Heerden. I think I've told you that before."

He smiled in the darkness as the car sped smoothly through the deserted streets.

" I must plead guilty to being rather unoriginal," he said, " but I promise you that this little adventure shall not end as did the last."

"It can hardly do that," she laughed, "I can only be married once whilst Mr. Beale is alive."

"I forgot you were married," he said suddenly, then after a pause, "I suppose you will divorce him?"

"Why?" she asked innocently.

"But you're not fond of that fellow, are you?"

"Passionately," she said calmly, "he is my ideal."

The reply took away his breath and certainly silenced him.

"How is this adventure to end?" she demanded. "Are you going to maroon me on a desert island, or are you taking me to Germany?"

"How did you know I am trying to get to Germany?" he asked sharply.

"Oh, Mr. Beale thought so," she replied, in a tone of indifference, "he reckoned that he would catch you somewhere near the coast."

"He did, did he?" said the other calmly. "I shall deny him that pleasure. I don't intend taking you to Germany. Indeed, it is not my intention to detain you any longer than is necessary."

"For which I am truly grateful," she smiled, "but why detain me at all?"

"That is a stupid question to ask when I am sure you have no doubt in your mind as to why it is necessary to keep you close to me until I have finished my work. I think I told you some time ago," he went on, "that I had a great scheme The other day you called me a Hun, by which I suppose you meant that I was a German. It is perfectly true that I am a German and I am a patriotic German. To me even in these days of his degradation the Kaiser is still little less than a god."

His voice quivered a little, and the girl was struck dumb with wonder that a man of such intelligence, of such a wide outlook, of such modernity, should hold to views so archaic.

"Your country ruined Germany. You have sucked us dry. To say that I hate England and hate America —for you Anglo-Saxons are one in your soulless covetousness—is to express my feelings mildly."

"But what is your scheme?" she asked.

"Briefly I will tell you, Miss Cresswell, that you may understand that to-night you accompany history and are a participant in world politics. America and England are going to pay. They are going to buy corn from my country at the price that Germany can fix. It will be a price," he cried, and did not attempt to conceal his joy, "which will ruin the Anglo-Saxon people more effectively than they ruined Germany."

"But how?" she asked, bewildered.

"They are going to buy corn," he repeated, "at our price, corn which is stored in Germany."

"But what nonsense!" she said scornfully, "I don't know very much about harvests and things of that kind, but I know that most of the world's wheat comes from America and from Russia."

"The Russian wheat will be in German granaries," he said softly, "the American wheat—there will be no American wheat."

And then his calmness deserted him. The story of the Green Rust burst out in a wild flood of language which was half-German and half-English. The man was beside himself, almost mad, and before his gesticulating hands she shrank back into the corner of the car. She saw his silhouette against the window, heard the roar and scream of his voice as he babbled incoherently of his wonderful scheme and had to piece together as best she could his disconnected narrative. And then she remembered her work in Beale's office, the careful tabulation of American farms, the names of the sheriffs, the hotels where conveyances might be secured.

So that was it! Beale had discovered the plot, and had already moved to counter this devilish plan. And she remembered the man who had come to her room in mistake for van Heerden's and the phial of green sawdust he carried and Beale's look of horror when he examined it. And suddenly she cried with such vehemence that his flood of talk was stopped:

"Thank God! Oh, thank God!"

"What—what do you mean?" he demanded suspiciously. "What are you thanking God about?"

" Oh, nothing, nothing." She was her eager, animated self. " Tell me some more. It is a wonderful story. It is true, is it not ? "

" True ? " he laughed harshly, " you shall see how true it is. You shall see the world lie at the feet of German science. To-morrow the word will go forth. Look ! " He clicked on a little electric light and held out his hand. In his palm lay a silver watch.

" I told you there was a code " (she was dimly conscious that he had spoken of a code but she had been so occupied by her own thoughts that she had not caught all that he had said). " That code was in this watch. Look ! "

He pressed a knob and the case flew open. Pasted to the inside of the case was a circular piece of paper covered with fine writing.

" When you found that ticket you had the code in your hands," he chuckled ; " if you or your friends had the sense to redeem that watch I could not have sent to-morrow the message of German liberation ! See, it is very simple ! " He pointed with his finger and held the watch half-way to the roof that the light might better reveal the wording. " This word means ' Proceed.' It will go to all my chief agents. They will transmit it by telegram to hundreds of centres. By Thursday morning great stretches of territory where the golden corn was waving so proudly to-day will be blackened wastes. By Saturday the world will confront its sublime catastrophe."

" But why have you three words ? " she asked huskily.

" We Germans provide against all contingencies," he said, " we leave nothing to chance. We are not gamblers. We work on lines of scientific accuracy. The second word is to tell my agents to suspend operations until they hear from me. The third word means ' Abandon the scheme for this year ' ! We must work with the markets. A more favourable opportunity might occur —with so grand a conception it is necessary that we should obtain the maximum results for our labours."

He snapped the case of the watch and put it back in his pocket, turned out the light and settled himself back with a sigh of content.

"You see you are unimportant," he said, "you are a beautiful woman and to many men you would be most desirable. To me, you are just a woman, an ordinary fellow-creature, amusing, beautiful, possessed of an agile mind, though somewhat frivolous by our standards. Many of my fellow-countrymen who do not think like I do would take you. It is my intention to leave you just as soon as it is safe to do so unless——" A thought struck him, and he frowned.

"Unless —— ?" she repeated with a sinking heart in spite of her assurance.

"Bridgers was speaking to me of you. He who is driving." He nodded to the dimly outlined shoulders of the chauffeur. "He has been a faithful fellow——"

"You wouldn't ?" she gasped.

"Why not ?" he said coolly. "I don't want you. Bridgers thinks that you are beautiful."

"Is he a Hun, too ?" she asked, and he jerked round toward her.

"If Bridgers wants you he shall have you," he said harshly.

She knew she had made a mistake. There was no sense in antagonizing him, the more especially so since she had not yet learnt all that she wanted to know.

"I think your scheme is horrible," she said after awhile, "the wheat destruction scheme, I mean, not Bridgers. But it is a very great one."

The man was susceptible to flattery, for he became genial again.

"It is the greatest scheme that has ever been known to science. It is the most colossal crime—I suppose they will call it a crime—that has ever been committed."

"But how are you going to get your code word away ? The telegraphs are in the hands of the Government and I think you will find it difficult even if you have a secret wireless."

"Wireless, bah ! " he said scornfully. "I never expected to send it by telegraph with or without wires. I have a much surer way, fräulein, as you will see."

"But how will you escape ?" she asked.

" I shall leave England to-morrow, soon after day-break," he replied, with assurance, " by aeroplane, a long-distance flying-machine will land on my Sussex farm which will have British markings—indeed, it is already in England, and I and my good Bridgers will pass your coast without trouble."

He peered out of the window.

" This is Horsham, I think," he said, as they swept through what appeared to the girl to be a square. " That little building on the left is the railway station. You will see the signal lamps in a moment. My farm is about five miles down the Shoreham Road."

He was in an excellent temper as they passed through the old town and mounted the hill which leads to Shore-ham, was politeness itself when the car had turned off the main road and had bumped over cart tracks to the door of a large building.

" This is your last escapade, Miss Cresswell, or Mrs. Beale I suppose I should call you," he said jovially, as he pushed her before him into a room where supper had been laid for two. " You see, you were not expected, but you shall have Bridgers'. It will be daylight in two hours," he said inconsequently, " you must have some wine."

She shook her head with a smile, and he laughed as if the implied suspicion of her refusal was the best joke in the world.

" Nein, nein, little friend," he said, " I shall not doctor you again. My days of doctoring have passed."

She had expected to find the farm in occupation, but apparently they were the only people there. The doctor had opened the door himself with a key, and no servant had appeared, nor apparently did he expect them to appear. She learnt afterwards that there were two farm servants, an old man and his wife, who lived in a cottage on the estate and came in the daytime to do the house-work and prepare a cold supper against their master's coming.

Bridgers did not make his appearance. Apparently he was staying with his car. About three o'clock in the morning, when the first streaks of grey were showing in

the sky, van Heerden rose to go in search of his assistant.
Until then he had not ceased to talk of himself, of his
scheme, of his great plan, of his early struggles, of his difficulties in persuading members of his Government to afford
him the assistance he required. As he turned to the door
she checked him with a word :

" I am immensely interested," she said, " but still, you
have not told me how you intend to send your message."

" It is simple," he said, and beckoned to her.

They passed out of the house into the chill sweet dawn,
made a half-circuit of the farm and came to a courtyard
surrounded on three sides by low buildings. He opened
a door to reveal another door covered with wire netting.

" Behold ! " he laughed.

" Pigeons ! " said the girl.

The dark interior of the shed was aflicker with white
wings.

" Pigeons ! " repeated van Heerden, closing the door,
" and every one knows his way back to Germany. It has
been a labour of love collecting them. And they are all
British," he said with a laugh. " There I will give the
British credit, they know more about pigeons than we
Germans and have used them more in the war."

" But suppose your pigeon is shot down or falls by the
way ? " she asked, as they walked slowly back to the
house.

" I shall send fifty," replied van Heerden calmly; " each
will carry the same message and some at least will get
home."

Back in the dining-room he cleared the remains of the
supper from the table and went out of the room for a few
minutes, returning with a small pad of paper, and she
saw from the delicacy with which he handed each sheet
that it was of the thinnest texture. Between each page
he placed a carbon and began to write, printing the characters. There was only one word on each tiny sheet.
When this was written he detached the leaves, putting
them aside and using his watch as a paper-weight, and
wrote another batch.

She watched him, fascinated, until he showed signs that

he had completed his task. Then she lifted the little valise which she had at her side, put it on her knees, opened it and took out a book. It must have been instinct which made him raise his eyes to her.

"What have you got there ? " he asked sharply.

" Oh, a book," she said, with an attempt at carelessness.

" But why have you got it out ? You are not reading."

He leant over and snatched it from her and looked at the title.

" ' A Friend in Need,' " he read. " By Stanford Beale —by Stanford Beale," he repeated, frowning. " I didn't know your husband wrote books ? "

She made no reply. He turned back the cover and read the title page.

" But this is ' Smiles's Self Help,' " he said.

" It's the same thing," she replied.

He turned another page or two, then stopped, for he had come to a place where the centre of the book had been cut right out. The leaves had been glued together to disguise this fact, and what was apparently a book was in reality a small box.

"What was in there ? " he asked, springing to his feet.

" This," she said, " don't move, Dr. van Heerden ! "

The little hand which held the Browning was firm and did not quiver.

" I don't think you are going to send your pigeons off this morning, doctor," she said. " Stand back from the table." She leant over and seized the little heap of papers and the watch. " I am going to shoot you," she said steadily, " if you refuse to do as I tell you ; because if I don't shoot you, you will kill me."

His face had grown old and grey in the space of a few seconds. The white hands he raised were shaking. He tried to speak but only a hoarse murmur came. Then his face went blank. He stared at the pistol, then stretched out his hands slowly toward it.

" Stand back ! " she cried.

He jumped at her, and she pulled the trigger, but nothing happened, and the next minute she was struggling in his arms. The man was hysterical with fear and relief and was giggling and cursing in the same breath. He wrenched the pistol from her hand and threw it on the table.

"You fool! You fool!" he shouted, "the safety-catch! You didn't put it down!"

She could have wept with anger and mortification. Beale had put the catch of the weapon at safety, not realizing that she did not understand the mechanism of it, and van Heerden in one lightning glance had seen his advantage.

"Now you suffer!" he said, as he flung her in a chair. "You shall suffer, I tell you! I will make an example of you. I will leave your husband something which he will not touch!"

He was shaking in every limb. He dashed to the door and bellowed "Bridgers!"

Presently she heard a footstep in the hall.

"Come, my friend," van Heerden shouted, "you shall have your wish. It is——"

"How are you going, van Heerden? Quietly or rough?"

He spun round. There were two men in the doorway, and the first of these was Beale.

"It's no use your shouting for Bridgers because Bridgers is on the way to the jug," said McNorton. "I have a warrant for you, van Heerden."

The doctor turned with a howl of rage, snatched up the pistol which lay on the table, and thumbed down the safety-catch.

Beale and McNorton fired together, so that it seemed like a single shot that thundered through the room. Van Heerden slid forward, and fell sprawling across the table.

* * * * *

It was the Friday morning, and Beale stepped briskly through the vestibule of the Ritz-Carlton, and declining the elevator went up the stairs two at a time. He burst into the room where Kitson and the girl were standing by the window.

"Wheat prices are tumbling down," he said, "the message worked."

"Thank Heaven for that!" said Kitson. "Then van Heerden's code message telling his gang to stop operations reached its destination!"

"Its destinations," corrected Beale cheerfully. "I released thirty pigeons with the magic word. The agents have been arrested," he said; "we notified the Government authorities, and there was a sheriff or a policeman in every post office when the code word came through —van Heerden's agents saw some curious telegraph messengers yesterday."

Kitson nodded and turned away.

"What are you going to do now?" asked the girl, with a light in her eyes. "You must feel quite lost without this great quest of yours."

"There are others," said Stanford Beale.

"When do you return to America?" she asked.

He fenced the question, but she brought him back to it.

"I have a great deal of business to do in London before I go," he said.

"Like what?" she asked.

"Well," he hesitated, "I have some legal business."

"Are you suing somebody?" she asked, wilfully dense.

He rubbed his head in perplexity.

"To tell you the truth," he said, "I don't exactly know what I've got to do or what sort of figure I shall cut. I have never been in the Divorce Court before."

"Divorce Court?" she said, puzzled, "are you giving evidence? Of course I know detectives do that sort of thing. I have read about it in the newspapers. It must be rather horrid, but you are such a clever detective—oh, by the way you never told me how you found me."

"It was a very simple matter," he said, relieved to change the subject, "van Heerden, by one of those curious lapses which the best of criminals make, left a message at the pawnbroker's which was written on the back of an account for pigeon food, sent to him from a Horsham tradesman. I knew he would not try to dispatch his message by the ordinary courses and I suspected all along that he had established a pigeon-post. The bill gave me all the information I wanted. It took us a long time to find the tradesman, but once we had discovered him he directed us to the farm. We took along a couple of local policemen and arrested Bridgers in the garage."

She shivered.

" It was horrible, wasn't it ? " she said.

He nodded.

" It was rather dreadful, but it might have been very much worse," he added philosophically.

" But how wonderful of you to switch yourself from the crime of that enthralling character to a commonplace divorce suit."

" This isn't commonplace," he said, " it is rather a curious story."

" Do tell me." She made a place for him on the window-ledge and he sat down beside her.

" It is a story of a mistake and a blunder," he said. " The plaintiff, a very worthy young man, passably good looking, was a man of my profession, a detective engaged in protecting the interests of a young and beautiful girl."

" I suppose you have to say she's young and beautiful or the story wouldn't be interesting," she said.

" It is not necessary to lie in this case," he said, " she is certainly young and undoubtedly beautiful. She has the loveliest eyes——"

" Go on," she said hastily.

" The detective," he resumed, " hereinafter called the petitioner, desiring to protect the innocent maiden from the machinations of a fortune-hunting gentleman no longer with us, contracted as he thought a fraudulent marriage with this unfortunate girl, believing thereby he could choke off the villain who was pursuing her."

" But why did the unfortunate girl marry him, even fraudulently ? "

" Because," said Beale, " the villain of the piece had drugged her and she didn't know what she was doing. After the marriage," he went on, " he discovered that so far from being illegal it was good in law and he had bound this wretched female."

" Please don't be rude," she said.

" He had bound this wretched female to him for life. Being a perfect gentleman, born of poor but American parents, he takes the first opportunity of freeing her."

" And himself," she murmured.

"As to the poor misguided lad," he said firmly, "you need feel no sympathy. He had behaved disgracefully."

"How?" she asked.

"Well, you see, he had already fallen in love with her and that made his offence all the greater. If you go red I cannot tell you this story, because it embarrasses me."

"I haven't gone red," she denied indignantly. "So what are you—what is he going to do?"

Beale shrugged his shoulders.

"He is going to work for a divorce."

"But why?" she demanded. "What has she done?"

He looked at her in astonishment.

"What do you mean?" he stammered.

"Well"—she shrugged her shoulders slightly and smiled in his face—"it seems to me that it is nothing to do with him. It is the wretched female who should sue for a divorce, not the handsome detective—do you feel faint?"

"No," he said hoarsely.

"Don't you agree with me?"

"I agree with you," said the incoherent Beale. "But suppose her guardian takes the necessary steps?"

She shook her head.

"The guardian can do nothing unless the wretched female instructs him," she said. "Does it occur to you that even the best of drugs wear off in time and that there is a possibility that the lady was not as unconscious of the ceremony as she pretends? Of course," she said hurriedly, "she did not realize that it had actually happened, and until she was told by Apollo from the Central Office—that's what you call Scotland Yard in New York, isn't it?—that the ceremony had actually occurred she was under the impression that it was a beautiful dream—when I say beautiful," she amended, in some hurry, "I mean not unpleasant."

"Then what am I to do?" said the helpless Beale.

"Wait till I divorce you," said Oliva, and turned her head hurriedly, so that Beale only kissed the tip of her ear.

THE END

If you enjoyed this book and would like to have information sent to you about other Pulp Fictions titles, please write to the address below by completing the coupon or writing clearly on a plain piece of paper. Please enclose an SAE / IRC for response.

In addition to our catalogue you will receive information regarding our creative competition
(see below; closing date 30th June 1999), and will be automatically entitled to :

FREE ENTRY INTO THE PRIZE DRAW!

Twice a year in June and December, coupons will be drawn 'from the hat' and the winner will receive a complete set of Pulp Fictions paperbacks.

> Pulp Publications Ltd
> PO Box 144
> Polegate
> East Sussex
> BN26 6NW
> England
> UK.

Full Name ....

Address ....

.........................Postcode...............

City/State/Zip....................................

Age.........................

Creative Competition: Please send me details of the search for new writing/artistic talent for the millenium ......YES/NO

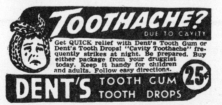

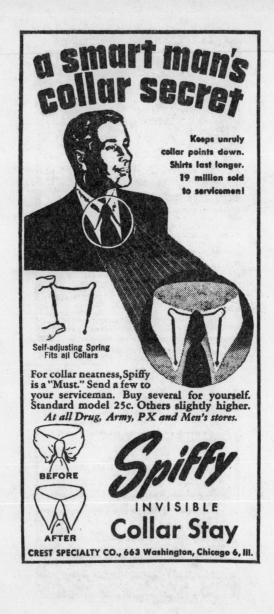